VULTURE

Phoebe Greenwood

VULTURE

Europa
editions

Europa Editions
8 Blackstock Mews
London N4 2BT
www.europaeditions.co.uk

This book is a work of fiction. Any references to historical events,
real people, or real locales are used fictitiously.

Copyright © 2025 by Phoebe Greenwood
First publication 2025 by Europa Editions

All rights reserved, including the right of reproduction
in whole or in part in any form.

The right of Phoebe Greenwood to be identified as the author of
this Work has been asserted by her in accordance with the
Copyright, Designs & Patents Act 1988

A catalogue record for this title is available from the British Library
ISBN 978-1-78770-579-1

Greenwood, Phoebe
Vulture

Cover design by Ginevra Rapisardi

Cover illustration © Leila Peacock

Prepress by Grafica Punto Print – Rome

The authorized representative in the EEA
is Edizioni e/o, via Gabriele Camozzi 1, 00192 Rome, Italy.

Printed and bound in Great Britain by Clays Ltd, Elcograf S.p.A

CONTENTS

1. 14 November 2012 - 13
2. Sad Mohammed - 17
3. Nasser's Problem - 24
4. Peter Jones - 29
5. Fadi - 37
6. Little Jihad - 44
7. Where the Wild Beasts Are - 54
8. Deadline - 59
9. Dad - 66
10. Unbelievable News - 74
11. Child Monsters - 80
12. Jiminy Cricket - 90
13. Cancer Cathy - 97
14. The Bold and the Beautiful - 103
15. Understanden - 110
16. Kids Are Annoying - 124
17. The Gatekeepers - 128
18. In the Manner of an Animal - 137
19. Spies Get Executed - 143

20. Do You Know Birds? - 148
21. The Commander - 153
22. Grave Concerns - 158
23. Love - 168
24. Always Say Yes - 173
25. A Big Yellow Eye - 181
26. Mad or Not Mad - 187
27. To Live Is to Fight - 194
28. Hunting Birds - 200
29. The Truce - 208
30. The Cradle of Civilisation - 217
31. Blood - 225
32. Sad Psychopath - 231
33. Something Light - 235
34. Michael - 241
35. Do Not Enter! - 248
36. Checking Out - 253
37. Little Jihad's Mother - 257
38. Pigeons - 267
39. Into the Firmament - 273
40. Back to Work - 277

About the Author - 283

God sent a crow to scratch the ground to show him how to cover his brother's body. He cried out, 'How awful! Am I so helpless that I cannot do what this crow has done?' He then buried his brother and was filled with sorrow.
—Al Maidah-5:31

For the Al Deira Hotel, which no longer exists

1
14 November 2012

The first time I heard about The Beach Hotel was at a tiki bar in Jerusalem. I was there alone, sipping at a $20 glass of wine, breakfasting on complimentary nuts and eavesdropping.

'The Beach is an oasis of humanity in that blighted bloody desert,' the old correspondent next to me told a younger correspondent next to him.

The younger one, whose name was Henry, looked impressed by this, so the older one went on, saying that if you stand at Gaza City port at sunset and look back at the hotel across the Mediterranean Sea, its red domes rise from the sand like a Bedouin fortress. Which it is, he said. It's the *media's* stronghold. Their shrimps in a clay pot aren't bad either, he added, and ordered himself another beer.

When I first went to Gaza and saw The Beach for myself, I thought that if it looked like anything it was a tiramisu. Mo, the owner, was bored after months with only the United Nations for company and told me the hotel's life story as I sat waiting for Nasser. Two waiters, one fat, one skinny, loitered on the periphery, pointless sentries at Mo's deserted, seafront colosseum. His German was better than his English, so he used both and compensated for any gaps in vocabulary with mime.

Spring 2000! The Beach Hotel's grand opening! Raise a golden curtain on the glory days of Arafat and behold Gaza in those few weeks when she had her own airport! The good old days of alcohol, money, bikinis, hopes. Hopes high enough for Mo to open his Bedouinish-Ottomanish palace on the shores of the Palestinian Mediterranean to accommodate all the rich Turks with their bum-bags full of dollars.

'Have you seen beaches like ours anywhere else in the world, Sara? An empty, *klaaarer* stretch of the Mediterranean? No! Nowhere else! Now see these beaches with cocktails and girls in bikinis. *Paradies*! No?'

No. Because within a month, the Second Intifada had broken out. Mo made his fist explode, splaying his neat fingers in a starburst. Then Arafat died, boom, his other fist exploded, and Israel dragged its settlers out.

'*Wallah* Sara, say what you like about the Jews but when they left Gaza, it was bad for business.'

Mo shook his head, I drank my tea, the sentries watched.

'Then the civil war'—many hand explosions—'brothers killing brothers. *Chaos*. Zero tourists.'

Mo formed a zero between a plump finger and thumb. Fatah runs away to the West Bank and leaves us with Hamas! Lifting his right index finger in the air, he held it there. With Hamas comes the siege, the borders are sealed, and Gaza is a prison in non-stop war. *A hell*! He brought both palms down flat on the top of his smooth, brown head with a shower of cigarette ash, a man trapped in a glassless snow dome.

'*Wallahi* Sara, a siege? For five years not so much as a bread stick without Israeli permission! And thanks Hamas, I haven't seen a drop of whiskey in a year! Since the day we opened our doors, everyone has been fucking us! Fucking Gaza. E-ver-y-one!'

Mo's story stopped here, face framed by his hands, his mouth agape as if words had found their limit and he could only bulge his eyes in mystification at this extraordinary fucking of him by Fate.

The Beach had been fed an exclusive diet of middle-aged foreign correspondents, UN officials and aid agency bosses. Its VIPs were diplomats, at best Scandinavian. You could tell because disappointment dripped from its faded lime green curtains. The glossy green paint of its grand front doors had been allowed to chip and flake. Its ochre façade was dusty and pock-marked with shrapnel scars.

But it was still Gaza's nice hotel and much like rich Turks, American network news crews like nice hotels. They like airy, sea-fronting suites and restaurants with uniformed waiters where they can eat french fries and safely watch the war raging in the streets and skies outside on big TV screens.

And even better for Mo was that by the time I arrived, most warring factions had agreed that harming foreign journalists was best avoided owing to the influence injured media might have on their various international sympathisers. And so neither the Israelis nor the Islamists, the Salafists nor the communist Palestinian nationalists, not even the super fucking crazy militant Zionists, had they still been around, so much as looked at The Beach in a violent way because all the journalists stayed there. Even when the fancier Qatari hotels began to open along the coastline, the correspondents all stayed put at The Beach because everyone knew no one was ever going to bomb it. It was, as the man said, an oasis of humanity in an otherwise blighted desert.

I was not a correspondent. I was at best a stringer and should not have been enjoying expenses-paid wars at four-star hotels. But on 14 November 2012, when the Hamas man Ahmed Al Jabari was *liquidated* by an Israeli predator drone on his way home for supper with his wife, *The Tribune*'s multiple award-winning Middle East Correspondent Anthony Harper was not on his usual perch in Jerusalem, little legs dangling from his tiki bar stool. Anthony was 600km away, embedded with Syrian government forces somewhere near Idlib because that's where the story was, until Al Jabari.

And so it was me, the freelancer Sara Byrne, who was dispatched by *The Tribune*'s deputy foreign editor Neil Devereaux from my dirt-yellowed basement in West Jerusalem to Room 22 at The Beach Hotel, with its uninterrupted sea views and unusable walk-in bath. The Beach became my hotel—*Your Home in Gaza*, as the stationary read. And this would be my war.

Michael would see me every day of it, my picture byline staring up at him from a new front page: a brilliant, young woman, conquering the bloody cradle of civilisation with her understanding. The only problem was that by day four, it looked like my war wasn't going to get off the ground.

2
SAD MOHAMMED

The old man's face and hair were coated in a mask of bomb ash with snaking lines down his cheeks left by the tears he had been crying earlier. His huge, dusty hands clutched the back of a white plastic chair, which was the last in a long line of plastic chairs that ran around the ruins of his home and out into the sandy street. The chairs were waiting for the mourners who were coming to pay their respects to his dead wife, dead kids, dead grandkids and dead neighbour. The old man was waiting for me to ask whatever it was I had come to ask him and Nasser was agitating with a hostile silence for me to get the fuck on with it. But after four days of me and Nasser interviewing anyone bombed in Gaza about their bombed homes, I already knew the answer to anything I could think to ask.

Who do you blame for your house being destroyed and all your family being killed? *It was God's will, alhamdulillah.* But it was Israel really, that bombed it, and Israel says your son/ father/ uncle/ brother was Hamas. *No, none of us is Hamas.* Okay, none of you is Hamas. Do you blame Hamas then, for firing their shitty rockets into Israel when this is what Israel does back? Look at your house!

The bomb had split the old man's building neatly in two so that one half of it was now a steaming rubble hell tower and the other half a charred, five-story doll house. On the second floor, a bathroom with a dusty pink bathtub and a bright pink shagpile carpet had lost two of its walls. It looked indecent, exposed like that. Below the bathroom, a mattress balanced uncomfortably on pointy shards of wall and a child's tracksuit bottoms had wrapped themselves around a thick electrical cable. I stared hard at a navy blue flip-flop that was sitting on top of a broken wardrobe.

I was really very hot standing in the sun in my huge man's flak jacket with PRES taped in red letters across the front and the too tight helmet Nasser had found for me. I have a big head and to be fair to Nasser, it's hard to find hats that fit it, but next to the little kids with their bare chests and bare feet scrambling around after each other in the bomb rubble, I felt ridiculous. My face burned and a stream of sweat crawled down my back to pool around my coccyx. The old man squinted at me.

'Do you blame anyone? For this tragedy?' I asked him.

Nasser exhaled wearily and translated what I'd said into Arabic. The man looked at his dusty black shoes as he listened, paused for a bit then directed his answer to Nasser. He took his time speaking, with several deep, raspy pauses. Then he stopped talking, his eyes fell back to the ground and Nasser translated.

'It's God's will,' Nasser said.

'Is that it?'

'Yes.'

'I'm pretty sure he said more than that Nasser.'

Nasser gave me a look that said I've translated about as much as your capacity for the profound can grasp, move on. Irritated, I moved on.

'How many people were killed?' I asked.

The man squinted again with incomprehension at me then at Nasser. This was apparently a difficult thing to work out. After some discussion, Nasser spoke.

'My whole family. My sister is gone, my wife is gone. All my children are dead, except one son.'

'How many children do you have?'

'He *had* six.'

I wrote in my notebook: *Six children, five dead. Wife and sister dead.*

'Israel says it targeted your home because your son is a senior figure in the Hamas movement. Was that son at home at the time of the airstrike?'

Nasser asked my question and the old man looked up sharply. This time he spoke rapidly and without stopping or any need for prompting. Nasser started to translate as he spoke.

'I was at work before dawn, at the shop. My wife, my daughters and their children were at home. The airstrike hit the roof with fire, the cement fell on everyone. My cousin called me and said your home is bombed and your son is killed.'

Nasser listened for a bit to catch up, then resumed his translating.

'I came straight back home and asked my neighbours where my wife was. They told me my son was okay but my wife was dead. Some of their bodies were already outside on the street or gone in the ambulances. My son was traffic police, not Hamas. My youngest son is in the hospital with his four-year-old, he has wounds in his head. My daughter is still inside, they can't find her.'

He pointed towards the collapsed building, which had no search team looking through it, paused to study his dirty shoes, then started talking again.

'No Hamas have come here. No Islamic Jihad. There is no training ground near here. No one in this neighbourhood is resistance. There is no reason for this.'

He stopped again and looked at his dusty hands, as if he were talking only to them.

'What can you do?' he asked them. 'Everyone burned.'

It was past 10.30am and the mourners were starting to arrive. More old men, heads wrapped in red and white keffiyehs, and a few younger men in jeans, crisp shirts, hair gel and fur-lined bomber jackets. They moved as a flock with a collective funeral brain, circling the grieving man briefly before making their way to the plastic chairs. The old men sat down heavily.

Our old man was now swaying like sea grass with an absent sort of expression as the pool of people swirled around him and I saw that any further interviewing was going to be impossible. Nasser took down his details from a mourner: *Abdullah Al Muzaner, aged around 60*. I told Nasser that if we wanted to get to the morgue to check the bodies before they were taken away to be buried, we needed to get a move on. He nodded and flipped his tiny notebook shut.

Any bodies hoping to be buried that day needed to be collected by their families before the end of midday prayers. Twenty people had been killed overnight and the relatives gathered outside the Shifa Hospital morgue were angry that the morgue officials hadn't yet let them in to collect their dead. We had to push through the outraged crowd and squeeze through the heavy door to get inside. I'd been in that room at least once a day for the past four days and every time was surprised by how small it was. More like a narrow, cold corridor than a room, with a wet floor like a fishmonger's.

Two morgue men in clear plastic smocks led us to rows of metal drawers that held members of the Al Muzaner family. One of them pulled out the drawers while the other read the names and ages of the bodies. Nasser wrote down in his neat English script:

Yousef Mohamed, five.
Ibrahim Mohammed, 11 months.
Jamal, seven.
Amena Matar, four.

The small bodies were covered in dust and their faces had streaks and blotches of congealed blood. One of the little boy's blue Spiderman pyjama pants was torn. They didn't look crushed or burned like I expected. They looked like normal sleeping kids just very pale and dusted in sand and blood. The morgue men stood watching us, wiping their foreheads with the backs of their hands and talking in a low mumble to Nasser.

'Some were brought in an ambulance, some by their uncle. The girl was wrapped in a pink blanket,' Nasser translated.

The drawers holding the children were closed and the row above was opened:

Souhella Mahmoud, 45.

Sara, 26.

I couldn't look long at the women. Their faces were more dead looking and their uncovered hair messy. Patches of skin on their cheeks and arms were burned.

'10 people in one family,' the morgue man said in English.

The other shook his head and slid the women back into the wall.

'A massacre,' Nasser said grimly.

Does ten make a massacre? I counted six. Who were the others? There were three more women and a man, the morgue men said. Also, two men whose names were Abdullah and Jamal Mohammed. The noise of the angry mob of relatives outside was growing louder through the metal doors and the morgue men were getting anxious. There was no time to show us the rest of the massacred family.

As we raced across town to beat the bodies back to the Al Muzaner house, I reminded Nasser that we'd had four days of Gaza being on the front page of *The Tribune*, which was great, but there were only so many bombed families that could sustain that sort of interest and the old man Al Muzaner just wasn't going to cut it. If there wasn't a full ground invasion, or if Israel didn't start dropping some of its chemical weapons, we would need to find our own news. Which in Gaza was most likely to be underground where all the men running the war were hiding with their rockets. Right?

We needed to get into those tunnels. I asked Nasser how senior a Hamas fighter he could get me. Which neighbourhoods had the most terror tunnels? How big were they? Could

I fit? Would *Paula Miranda* fit? Could Nasser imagine, *Paula,* squeezing herself into a hole in some Qassam Brigades commander's mother's kitchen?

'Oh my Gawd Ashraf I'm stuck, push! PUUUSHHH!'

I did a pretty good Paula Miranda and looked over to grin at Nasser but found that his face was all tight and the knuckles on his poet hands were white with the effort of gripping the steering wheel.

'You want me to go into Beit Lahiya and Jabalia Camp and start asking where the tunnels are?'

I shrugged that yes, that's what I'd just been saying.

'When the one thing Hamas does really well is terrify people, you want me to get these terrified people to tell you about their secret tunnels? You'd print a map maybe?'

I couldn't tell if these were rhetorical questions, so I didn't answer. By now we'd caught up with the funeral procession that was headed to the ruins of the Al Muzaner house and were driving at a steady crawl behind it.

'Is that really what you're asking me to do, Sara?' Nasser repeated, this time looking at me with his face pointing hard. 'Do you know how many people would be killed if we ran a story like that? Israel would use it to justify bombing any mosque, home, school in Gaza. And *Hamas*? After they arrest *me*?'

I cut him off here, pointing out that reporters in Afghanistan didn't seem to have any of this trouble getting to the Taliban, who were frankly way more hardcore than Hamas. Then I asked if there was any point in my even being in Gaza if the only story we could do was *sad Mohammeds* talking about their dead kids and wives and so forth?

I'd never seen Nasser so angry and was uncertain how it would play out. He parked the car on a wide, main road with a sudden jerk. We put on our flak jackets and helmets in silence and started walking behind the procession, which had broken into a light jog.

'I'm just saying we should try,' I panted, as we walk-ran behind the funeral pack.

'No, *you're* saying *I* should try.'

Well, yes. Obviously, yes.

The limp bodies of the Al Muzaner children were being carried above the crowd, going home one last time to be washed and kissed before they were buried. They were wrapped in tight cocoons of white sheets and draped with Palestinian flags, only their little grey faces left open to the air, dark red stains creeping slowly through the white.

There was the old man Al Muzaner, washed clean of ash but still grey, standing in a black suit in front of his broken home waiting to receive his grandchildren, tears now flowing freely down his face. A thick red curtain had been put up outside the still standing part of his building and anyone who wasn't family was being pushed out as the small bodies levitated their way closer on an undulating carpet of hands. Overwhelmed child relatives were rounded up and ushered inside to say goodbye to their dead cousins. A hoarse voice shouted through a megaphone into the crowd.

'Don't think that the one who is killed in the name of God is gone! He is living still!'

'*Allahu Akbar!*' the crowd called.

'To those left alive, we are okay! Don't be sad for us!' the megaphone screamed.

Nasser gestured for me to keep as far as I could to the edge of the crowd where I caught sight of a young photographer pushed up against the wall of a neighbouring building. I recognised him because he'd won a Pulitzer for his work in Iraq and was a big deal. His cameras were dangling aimlessly from his skinny shoulders and his face was in his hands. Was he sobbing? *Jesus Christ*, I thought. What good is a crying photographer to anyone?

'*Allahu Akbar!*' the crowd called again.

3
Nasser's Problem

By the time we got back to The Beach from the funeral it was dusk, and in the way too large restaurant overlooking the sea, waiters in beige uniforms moved briskly through weather systems of nicotiney smoke to keep up with the coffee orders of the world's media and a young English blogger talking self-consciously into a headpiece attached to his laptop. The blogger wore a maroon beret.

Gaza's power had been cut and the hotel's generator-powered internet was buckling. All three dynamos roared like jet engines and the instrumental jazz version of 'Lady in Red' was playing again. The tall, quiet Danish reporter had the sweat-stained shirt and hunched shoulders of a person who had been hitting send repeatedly without success. His heavy index finger pounded the keyboard like a flesh anvil.

'Fuck. FUCK!'

Steve Sweeney was draped over his notebook, dishevelled and vexed. Sat beside him were an untouched salad and Jane Sawyer, typing mechanically with her cool, impenetrable focus. At the next table was Paula Miranda and her fixer Ashraf. All of them were working on their version of the Al Muzaner airstrike story.

'Death abounded. You say that, right? Death abounded?' Paula was talking to Ashraf but he was ignoring her because he was on a call.

Ashraf was a ginger Palestinian and the perfect fixer. He not only got all the best exclusives but spoke and wrote English better than Paula, who at that moment was spooning chocolate ice-cream into her mouth, head cocked in the attitude of someone listening for divine dictation. She must have been a fat kid. She ate like a fat kid.

'The fear was palpable? Mohammed! Excuse me! Mohammed?'

Mohammed the handsome waiter stopped and smiled at Paula. He had very white teeth and an exceptionally cleanshaven face, which was sweating delicately.

'Mohammed, I asked for a black *Americah-no* not a *lah-tay?*' Paula enunciated.

Turning to still unlistening Ashraf, she explained that her digestive system just couldn't take the fake fucking milk they serve here.

'A black coffee please Mohammed. Black. *Law-sa-maaht.*' Waiter Mohammed smiled sweetly and retrieved the rejected milky coffee from beside Paula's laptop. I tried to catch his eye so we could acknowledge this moron Paula, but he didn't see me. He was back on his fast track around the restaurant, wielding an enormous silver tray piled high with coffee cups. He moved like a dancer.

Across the huge room, Mohammed's brother Jihad was mopping up an ooze that was leaking unpleasantly from one of the bathrooms. Jihad was a lot bigger and a lot less graceful than Mohammed and only had one eye, or three, depending on how you looked at it: one working one, one glass one and a permanent circular graze in the middle of his forehead.

Despite his monstrous looks, Jihad shared a conscientious delicacy with his brother. He made the beds with an elaborate twist in the top sheet so it looked something like a swan and left Egyptian chocolates on my pillow. I had thought this was something he did with all the guests until one morning when he took me by the elbow as we past in the hallway and asked if I liked the chocolates. I'd said yes, thank you, and he'd whispered that they were a special present. I didn't want a special chocolate relationship with Jihad and had resolved to stop eating them.

Nasser and I took a table in the small courtyard off the

dining room with the rustling potted palms and sat staring with fixed concentration at a giant red sun dropping quickly over a horizon dotted with Israeli warships. I was smoking. Nasser never smoked, he just sat. It was because of him that I wasn't getting anywhere with this war. Him and his prissy sanctimoniousness blocking my efforts to report anything interesting.

I sucked hard on my cigarette so that my cheeks hurt and stole a sideways glance at him. As a physical type, he tended towards the too skinny but in a strong way. The thinner he got, the more his toughness was distilled. He was a man raisin. A strip of animated man jerky. He had lost weight even in the past five days and his skin was drawn taut across his cheekbones, the dark circles under his eyes deepened to an even darker purple. But at that moment, his sharp, fine features were softened by red sunset light. He looked sulky to me but to someone else might have appeared dignified, handsome even. Monkish handsome. Totally sexless, I shivered. We had been sitting not talking to each other long enough for it to get dark and cold and for me to have lost my anger.

'I'm going to write,' I told him, stubbing out a cigarette. 'You'd better hit the road.'

Idiomatic phrases like *hit the road* were hit and miss with Nasser but if he didn't understand this one, he was too tired or sick of me to say. He sighed one of his deep long sighs and looked at me.

'What time do we meet tomorrow?'

'I guess early-ish. Eight?'

Nasser winced. He had tried to establish mornings as family time, but I suspected he liked to sleep in.

'Nine?' I offered, feeling conciliatory.

'Eight is fine,' he said.

Through the glass I could see the restaurant filling up for dinner, not just with hotel guests but overspill journalists from the lesser hotels along the beach road who had all risked the air-struck night to dine on shrimps in a clay pot at The Beach Hotel because everyone else did.

'Listen, I get that it's complicated but let's just see if it's possible to get into those terror tunnels.'

I looked at Nasser square in the face for the first time since our fight.

'It's an important story.'

He made his bird-faced grimace and got up slowly. He had no fight left in him.

'I'll call you if anything happens later. Let me know if you need anything more for the piece,' he said, tapping the table lightly with his fingertips.

I watched his slight frame disappear into the lobby before moving myself into the restaurant, choosing an empty table near the window next to a table of humourless French, confident they wouldn't attempt conversation.

I ate hummus every evening. On the second night I'd tried the shrimps but the next day Nasser and I had gone to interview fishermen in the port who told us they were forced to fish in the sewage slicks close to the shore because the Israeli naval ships were firing on boats going further than a mile out to sea. Standing there in the port, I could smell shit-covered prawns and then I could taste them, then I could feel them smearing their shitty, semi-digested bodies across the inside of my stomach and I resolved to only eat hummus for the rest of the war. And eggs. Once the short, surly waiter had taken my order, I called Doron.

'No Sara, Israel does not target women or children, we target Hamas.'

Captain Doron Weiss was from Philadelphia and pronounced my name *Surrah*.

'And we did that successfully. We liquidated Yasser Al Muzaner, a senior Hamas terrorist who was masterminding all the rocket attacks from that neighbourhood.'

I'd never met Doron, but I'd seen him on television. He had

a square jaw, close-set brown eyes, thinning brown hair and wore a plaited brown leather bracelet. He had the face of someone who had achieved some small success in the tech industry. He probably owned a Segway.

'The dad says Yasser was a traffic cop, Doron.'

I pronounced his name like moron even though I knew it was pronounced *Dorron*. Doron laughed emptily.

'That's not what our intelligence sources say.'

'What sources are those?'

'You know I can't disclose that.'

There was a pause as the line crackled and I noted down what he had said. Doron took a long slurping gulp of something. Gatorade. Or a protein shake.

'Is that everything *Surrah*? I have a press conference.'

'Yes, that's it for now, thank you Doron.'

I hung up and started to write my story.

Sara Byrne in Gaza City

Standing in the ruins of his five-story home destroyed overnight by an Israeli airstrike, Abdullah Al Muzaner denied that his son was a member of the terror group Hamas.

'We are not fighters, but everyone burned. What can you do? It is God's will,' Al Muzaner told The Tribune.

Israel maintains that Al Muzaner's eldest son Yasser was in fact a senior Hamas member and the target of the strike that killed six members of his family.

4
Peter Jones

Autumn had always been my favourite time of year. I liked the texture of it, the smell of the crunchy brown leaves in Battersea Park. I liked dressing in brown corduroy and turtlenecks and walking alongside the Thames like I was on the cover of a Simon & Garfunkel LP. But when I was last home in London, the mulchy leaves hadn't smelled like earth or riverbed or bonfire. They smelled of decay and cloying melancholia and the stink clung to my nostrils like it would smother me.

Ma had sold our home on the park and bought her poky little flat around the corner because for one woman with an adult child to rattle around a four-bedroom house alone was obscene. In her new economic flat, there was only her bedroom and a much smaller spare room, which was also her office because she had returned to full-time community activism. Into this tiny room she had ostentatiously packed my childhood in boxes stacked wall-high alongside her *No Justice, No Peace* placards. She had also managed to squeeze in a very small plastic desk and a single bed with a bedside table of books: *the Middle Passage from Misery to Meaning in Middle Life*; *the Dialectic of Sex*; *Black Skin, White Masks the Experiences of a Black Man in a White World*; *Pharmacognosy*.

In one brutal purge she had scattered what was left of Dad among various charities: his Barbour that smelled of boat tar, his brown-papered, leather-bound Lewis & Short Latin Dictionary, his knobbly wooden walking stick, his patched woollen jumpers. The little she kept from the old house was inexplicable: all of his handkerchiefs, a shoebox of old computer cables and some lidless biros bound together with an elastic band, the old sofa, even though it was badly stained and much too large for her very much smaller new living room. The desk from Dad's study was now the kitchen table. Everything looked uncomfortable in its new place. He would have hated it. Maybe that was the point.

She also had a new personality to go with her new flat. Having strode all my life with our long, heavy legs, she now moved with careful, unsteady steps, like someone had crept in and bound her feet during her brief period of mourning. She had never been a pretty woman, she was handsome. Her strength was the appeal. I'd never seen her cry, not even when he died or when he was alive and dying, it wasn't something we did in our family. Just as being ill was weak, allergies didn't exist, fat people were ridiculed and drinking water in the street was common. But suddenly, as a widow, Ma cried. Now, she could well up at anything: TV commercials for life insurance, any mention of anyone's childhood, the news. Especially the news.

We sat next to each other on the rank sofa that stank of mildew, a tall glass of gin and tonic on the small table in front of her and a bowl of crisps balanced on a cushion between us. I gripped a large glass of red wine and we watched the six o'clock news while she commentated, because she always commentated the television. A white middle-aged reporter with dark glossy hair covered loosely with a silky green headscarf walked towards the camera through an avenue of skeletal black children in a poor Somali hospital ward. I didn't need to look at Ma to know she was in tears. Her strong, crisp-salted fingers reached over the bowl to clasp my hand.

'You've been there, haven't you Bob?'

'I was in DRC, Ma. Totally different sad country.'

I had been to Africa once on a press trip with a charity and a reality TV star before Jerusalem. I had not liked it: kid mobs with access to machetes, parasites that fell from the ceiling into your eyeballs, plagues of aid workers. Meddling, smug, nymphomaniac, pedantic, incompetent, boring fucking aid workers. Ma turned from the screen to look at me, her expression already a little loose from the half glass of gin, and stared sorrowfully at my face with huge, wet, blue eyes.

'You know darling, all the pain you've seen, it's left its mark on your face.'

She squeezed my hand too tightly with her swollen-jointed hands and nodded sadly, as if her gin-heavy head couldn't help but agree with what its mouth was saying. The reporter was also nodding. A doctor was telling her that the children were famine orphans and themselves starving to death.

'What?' I said.

'The difficult things you've put yourself through, it's given your face,' she paused, readying herself for a difficult truth, 'a hardness. It's painful to see, as a mother.'

I didn't know what difficult things she was talking about but they were certainly none we had discussed because we didn't discuss any of my things. She smiled pitifully and allowed a few tears to navigate their way unimpeded down her large, flat, flushed cheeks.

'You were so smiley and happy as a child. So sweet, and fat.'

I had stopped wearing makeup at some point in Jerusalem because it just sweated straight off—I looked like Gaddafi in a sauna, there wasn't any point—but I wasn't pinched like she was. Yes, I had been cutting my own hair and my fringe was a bit acute. But hard? If anything, I'd plumped out a bit owing to all the pita bread.

'You don't need to put yourself through this you know, Bobs. You don't need...' Ma broke off mid-sentence, her train of thought derailed by unfamiliar emotion.

My parents called me Bob because when I was four, my mother insists I'd claimed I wasn't a girl named Sara but a boy called Bob. I had not. I was talking about my cat Robert, my only friend at the time, but this fictional transgender moment stuck as did the name. Ma loved to tell people about this phase almost as much as that bit between nine and 11 when she said I'd wanted to write musicals for animals, which I also never had. I wanted to perform in the musical *Cats*. I'd liked to dance before I realised how little it suited me.

'You know you can always come back and live here with me.'

Ma gripped my hand harder and her wedding ring dug into my fingers.

'Get a nice job in local government? Or the Civil Service? They have such good pensions.'

'Thank you, but I'd sooner take Somalian famine death.'

She was looking at me so hard I felt her pinning me in place. Her eyes were starving. If they could, her eyes would have crawled out of her head and eaten my flesh then gnawed on my bones and sucked the marrow for drops of love. If only she'd had a better husband or another kid, she might not have ended up so ravenous. She pursed her lips until they were bloodless and turned back towards the television.

'You'd rather get a wasting disease than live with your mother. Nice.'

She took a deep slug of gin and let go of my hand. 'Not a wasting disease, Ma. They're malnourished.'

The news had ended and a talent show was on. A flourish of swirling graphics was followed by a cluster of waxy-looking hosts laughing. Their stupid faces and weird gym bodies made me feel sad but I was inert and unable to change the channel. Even the remote felt depressed and sweaty in my hand. The red wine, the rotting sofa, the TV people and my mother had all conspired to pull me into a deep, dark lethargy. None of my old London friends had returned my calls. Michael hadn't spoken to me since the wake. So I drank more wine and listened to my mother heckle the television because I had absolutely nothing else to do.

'Just look at those teeth! They're so obviously fake! Can you see, Bob? Why do they do it to themselves? Don't they know how weird they look?'

I'd drunk too much but didn't care. I was depressed and unaccountable.

'Have any of Dad's friends been in touch since the memorial? Have you heard from Michael?' I asked, boldly. 'Or anyone?'

Ma was still in heckling mode.

'*Sleazy* Michael Frazer?' she guffawed.

'He and Dad were close, weren't they?' I shrugged, affecting disinterest. 'He might check in.'

'Close? Your father didn't *do* friends, Bobby, you know that. A bit like you in that regard. What on Earth made you think of Michael Frazer? Was it the teeth?'

She was drunk too. I sipped deeply from my glass of wine and stared dumbly at the television. No, it wasn't the fucking teeth.

Ma said there was no point in us going to Dad's grave because if his soul was anywhere, it was not going to be in an urn in the ground in Croydon. I asked her where she thought it was. In the sofa? Apparently, it was in Peter Jones. On 19 November 2011, the first anniversary of my father's death, rather than visit his grave, my mother took me to a department store in Sloane Square because this is where she had taken me to buy shoes as a child.

It was the day before I was flying back to Israel and I could feel that she very much wanted us to have a nice time, but something leaden and bitter in my stomach wouldn't allow it. The department store café was bursting with young mothers in sportswear and their crying children. The tables next to us were too close and too loud, and the room was overly bright. Wintery sun poured in through the glass ceiling, trapping heat like a hot house. I was conscious of our outsized bodies and the unappealing red flush spreading across our matching faces.

'We'll have two Earl Grey teas with extra hot water and lemon on the side, and two slices of Victoria sponge, please.'

Ma was talking to the waitress in her ordering voice. Dad called it her haberdashery voice.

'I don't want any of that. I'll have an espresso,' I snapped.

Ma raised her eyebrows and pursed her lips. The neat waitress brought her tea and my coffee and a slice of Victoria sponge. I sat eating Ma's cake while she searched for the right parting words and I thought about how to ask her for money.

'You know, I really *am* happy that you're sticking this out. I'm happy you've committed to whatever it is you feel you need to do.'

She looked off mistily in the direction of the toilets. Was she teary again? She was. Her voice wavered.

'You know Bob, I tell everyone how proud I am of you.'

Who was everyone? Cathy? Cancer Cathy? What did she say she was proud of? She didn't fucking know anything about what I was doing because she never asked. My crumb-fingering hand was shaking. Why didn't she just ask how I was like a normal mother so I could cry and tell her bad and ask her for money?

'I wasn't looking for your approval,' I said, growling lowly so the young mothers couldn't hear.

Ma's face flushed a deeper red under her dark, dishevelled bob. Our heads were too large and our hair too thick for bobs, particularly unbrushed like that. It gave her a special look.

'Clearly,' she said.

She had worn her smart white shirt and a new red beaded necklace. Under the flush, her face was ashen and old looking. I felt a rush of remorse and suddenly wanted to hug her, but the closeness of all the other tables and the clutter of all the tea things made that impossible so I just sat sullenly mopping up the jam on her plate with my finger. Ma ordered the bill from the smiling waitress who was probably an excellent daughter and forced the receipt into her chaotic broken wallet with her mannish hands that were just like mine, only old and arthritic and liver spotted.

'I don't know what I've done to upset you Sara, but it's

obviously something pretty terrible,' she said, standing and reaching awkwardly for her coat.

I also reached for my coat. Pulling it towards me, I whipped the gym mother next to us in her ponytail with its dangling belt. The mother tutted and I told her to fuck off.

The next morning, Ma woke me much earlier than was necessary with a cup of coffee and perched in her pyjamas and dressing gown on the edge of my bed: a big, heavyhearted owl, clutching a book.

'You're a very efficient packer,' she said, after a while silently observing my suitcase.

'Thanks,' I said.

'Your father was a good packer,' she added, as though he were someone I'd never met. 'Is there room for this? I thought you might want it.'

She handed me the book she had been clutching, which was Dad's missing Lewis & Short Latin Dictionary. I held it heavy in my hands and breathed it in.

'I thought you gave that away,' I said, sniffing at its brownish pages.

Ma smiled wanly at me. I looked down at my very full suitcase.

'I'll leave it here, it'll be safer. Unless you give it away. Don't give it away!'

She followed as I dragged my bags along her narrow corridor, not remarking on the long smudge the side of my black wheels were leaving on her newly painted skirting board. We reached the front door and she folded her long, heavy arms around me. I couldn't hug her back because I was holding my bags, but I leaned into her and smelt her bristly, biscuit hair. Her newly prominent collarbone poked through her flannel robe onto my cheekbone.

'I think you're very brave Bob,' Ma's big man hand patted my back lightly.

'Thank you,' I said.

I kissed her on her papery cheek and took a step back, wondering why it was that whenever someone tells you you're brave, it immediately makes you not brave. I thought it must be because of self-pity or pride or both and set my quivering jaw.

'Are you okay here, Ma? You don't get lonely?'

Ma scoffed and rearranged her tired morning face into a picture of stoic victimhood.

'If only I had the time darling. There's always so much to do. Speaking of which, you'll really have to deal with those boxes when you're back next.'

She stood in her new doorway, waving and watching as I rolled my bag through the heavy carpet of mud and twigs on the pavement along the park fence towards the bus stop. The air smelled of dead leaves, she looked very alone and I felt dizzy with relief to be leaving her.

5
Fadi

A reporter on the giant TV screen in the restaurant was standing astride a tank. The headline running along the gutter of the screen beneath him was *Middle East on Fire: Israel positions tanks on Gaza border.*

'I'm here at Israel's border with the Gaza Strip standing on one of their 63-ton Merkava battle tanks. And Sally, let me tell you, these tanks mean business.'

The American jock TV reporter was yelling through the camera at Sally, who was a blonde in a studio. He shouted that an Israeli soldier had just told him that he had been told by his commander to prepare for a ground invasion. I called Doron.

'Is there going to be a ground invasion?' I asked him.

'The Israeli Defence Force is preparing for any option, and a ground operation is still an option that is relevant. God bless Sara. Be well.'

I emailed the desk telling them that Israel may or may not be preparing a ground offensive. When the small angry waiter finally brought me my hummus and a watermelon juice, I noticed a new, young, slick face smiling a broad crooked smile over his shoulder.

Like Mo said, *war may be hell but it's one hell of an employer.* I'd laughed and agreed when he said that because wasn't it paying all of us after all? Mo knew enough about life to take his breaks where he found them, and so dinner at The Beach cost about the same as dinner at The Ritz. It's not that he wouldn't have taken peace and a piece of rich Turkish tourist over Paula Miranda any day, but Mo was a businessman and smart enough to make the most of the hand he had been dealt.

'It's the sanctions! What can we do? They're killing us! Knafeh? More ice cream?'

Other than owning The Beach Hotel, being a smuggler, or Hamas, the only real play for anyone wanting to make any sort of living in Gaza was to be a fixer for foreign journalists. As long as there was conflict, there would be a news business. Of course, international outlets couldn't let Palestinian journalists *report* the news. Even if they were fluent in English, it wouldn't look right, because of balance and impartiality. But they were essential for setting up whatever story a foreign correspondent needed to do because they knew the place, the people, the history, the complex politics and spoke the language.

The big three were Sami, Nasser and Steve Sweeney's old, lame, blind Jim. They had laid claim to Gaza back in the Second Intifada dividing the world's biggest news organisations between them. Sami had four major American newspapers and two newswire services. Nasser dominated the Brits but also had the two big German newspapers. Old Jim had Steve Sweeney and Jane Sawyer. As the only one who spoke French he also handled the French and some Italians, which was pretty good going for someone who could neither walk nor see.

For years, this power share had worked fine because no correspondent wanted to be in Gaza unless they absolutely had to. But then Al Jabari was killed and Israel did what it had never done before, which was allow foreign journalists to stay and watch it obliterate the Gaza Strip. Within 24 hours, every single major news network and newspaper had sent at least one correspondent from Jerusalem into Gaza expecting them to work with either Sami, Nasser or old blind Jim. The big three were fucked.

Me, Sweeney and the blogger were the first ones to The Beach. *The Tribune* paid Nasser the most so he was mine, no question. Steve obviously had Jim and would share him with Jane as they shared everything, even the occasional bed, so went the rumours. Sami would work with Paula Miranda, whenever she arrived.

Everyone ignored the blogger. By the time the other correspondents turned up on day two, they found themselves fixerless. Then came the reporters with the newspapers who never had a fixer in Gaza in the first place, didn't speak Arabic and didn't know anyone other than smiley front desk Mohammed.

By day four, when the Israelis finally decided to close the border to media, the Korean and Bulgarian crews had already arrived. Local journalists and journalism students had all been commandeered. Aid agency translators went next. Harassed reporters, producers and photographers stalked the lobby asking if anyone knew a taxi driver who spoke English. Then did anyone know *anyone* who spoke English? A Belgian photographer was paying $300 a day to the girl who had sold her a SIM card at the Gaza City mall. The SIM card girl sat in the corner of reception in purple trainers, skinny jeans and a purple hijab texting and looking appalled. This war was a fixing gold rush.

Fadi loomed into view between me and the television screen where the American was still straddling his Israeli tank and offered me a cigarette, which I refused because they were the shitty Egyptian kind. He extended a long, brown skinny hand for me to shake, which I couldn't because I was using both of mine to eat, then sat down without invitation and started to talk, naming things he could see in his rapid Palestinian American. I was too concerned with eating to stop him.

'Hey that's a really big TV! They saying there's going to be a ground invasion? They're always saying there's a ground invasion, there never is. The hotel is full! I've never seen this restaurant so full! Actually, no, it was this full when my cousin got married. He got married this summer. You married? Wow, you eat a lot! Hahaha! Hungry girl! How much do those big cameras cost? Are you on TV? No you're not on TV!'

He laughed again until he noticed the look on my face and stopped.

'But you're a journalist?' he asked, his big, wide eyes trying hard to look trustworthy.

I nodded.

'American?'

'English,' I answered grudgingly.

'I'm Fadi. What's your name?'

Fadi's black hair was gelled in the stiff quiff style particular to Gaza. He wore skin-tight black jeans and a black t-shirt with *I Heart Brooklyn* written on it in red, loopy letters. He stank of aftershave that could easily have been his sister's perfume and smoked cigarettes greedily, letting his hands fall between his open knees between puffs while his ankles pumped up and down like pistons. He had that agelessness particular to war-prone places and could have been anywhere between 16 and 45. I told him my name and he leaned in confidentially to tell me that his uncle was a top fighter in the resistance. Had I heard of the Al-Yasser Salah al-Deen Front? I hadn't so he spelt it out, his knee jiggling rapidly.

'They're the ones that blew up the Israeli tank on the border last week.'

I remembered the tank.

'And kidnapped that Israeli soldier.'

I thought that was Hamas, but okay. Fadi's neat face contracted in disdain at the mention of Hamas. If I wanted, he could ask his uncle to ask the leader of the Al-Yasser Front to meet me. The commander and his uncle were friends since they were kids, like brothers. Actually they sort of were brothers since his uncle was the commander's cousin and had married his sister. And they were close like brothers. If anyone could get this leader to talk to me it would be Fadi's uncle, and if anyone could convince Fadi's uncle it was Fadi. He'd make them wear the balaclavas and pose with their guns, black flags and everything. He made a pose like a martyr poster, solemn face holding an imaginary rifle, and laughed.

Fadi wasn't a fighter but his uncle didn't mind that about him. This uncle loved Fadi way more than any of his other brother's kids because he was smart, and the others were all ginger or retarded. Like actually retarded since birth. One cousin was anyway. I told Fadi he shouldn't say retarded and he sucked tightly on his cigarette, narrowing his eyes in the attitude of someone who didn't see why not.

'You don't like Hamas?' I asked.

'Fuck Hamas! Last month? They picked me up off the street, took me to prison, shaved my head, beat my feet with sticks! For what?'

He plucked at the fabric clinging to his thigh.

'They don't like my jeans. Fuck Hamas!' he hissed again, before calming himself with a deep breath. 'Anyway, politics isn't my thing.'

Of course, his family didn't think like him. His dad was with the PFLP but he died, killed in the last war. Phosphorus shell burned him up completely. His granddad was alive though, old school Fatah. Serious guy, he said, forming his face into a solemn old man mask. Fadi had a stage school way about him.

'Do you think your uncle could get me inside the terror tunnels?'

'*Terror tunnels?*'

'Not the smuggling from Egypt tunnels everyone gets into.

The ones where they hide all the rockets and fighters.'

Fadi puffed out a smoke ring of bravado and shrugged.

'Sure. Why not?'

I told him I'd pay him $1,000 if he could get me into one of those tunnels with his uncle's brigade and he flashed a wide, white grin. Both his legs began jiggling. He would talk to his uncle, he said. The fighting happened at night so now was no good but Fadi said he would find him after sunrise and see what he could do. I told him fine.

'I'll be waiting for you at this same table. Not tomorrow but the day after, at 9am.'

'Tomorrow after tomorrow?' he frowned.

'Yes, not tomorrow, but the next day.'

We exchanged numbers and I opened my laptop, signalling

that our negotiation had come to an end. Fadi leapt up and clicked his heels together in a performance of military efficiency.

'Tomorrow after tomorrow. 9am. I won't let you down English!'

He loped away grinning. The desk had wanted words on those tanks along the border and some time ago. I wrote them quickly, quoting Doron and whatever I could remember of what the guy on the tank had said, and sent the piece off, relieved that I would soon have a proper story to write rather than this monkey journalism. It was late but I sat alone in the enormous restaurant smoking and looking around at the stragglers.

Steve Sweeney, the legendary correspondent, was at his usual table in the far corner, alone, hunched over a spread of notebooks. He must be very old because he wasn't very young when he got famous reporting on that massacred bus in Beirut. And that was nineteen-seventy-something. He knew the conflict better than any other journalist at the hotel but was always the last one up, long after everyone else had filed, checking and double fact-checking. Michael knew him but I'd never spoken with him. It was probably time that I did.

'Hello!' I said cheerfully after a while standing over his chair unnoticed.

Steve Sweeney looked up with the outraged alarm of a caged hostage. His craggy, unshaven face was framed with wild white and tobacco-coloured hair gathered in unruly clumps across his scalp. His deep-set eyes, wide with worry, served as viewing tunnels into a visibly disturbed mind. He's completely mad, I thought.

'Hi!' I said and smiled broadly. 'Mind if I sit here?'

I nodded towards the empty chairs at his table. Steve took a quick shallow breath having been holding his lungs still for quite some time. When he spoke, his voice was tight and wispy.

'Of course. Yes, of course. I was just heading upstairs.'

He gathered up his books with the speed of a fleeing hawker and evacuated the room in long strides. The only others still up were some idiot American TV producers and a table of dull, self-satisfied French, so I took Mohammed's special tea with extra honey to my room wishing it was a whiskey or something proper to celebrate with. 10 minutes with a fixer not Nasser and everything had started coming together. I lay on my huge white bed to think about my interview with the commander and stared out to sea. I saw myself in a dark tunnel surrounded by grease-smeared men in balaclavas and a rocket arsenal no journalist had ever seen before.

Then a long beach at night lit in patches by bonfires is being bombed by a screaming cloud of fighter jets, which are also Nasser. Jet Nassers chase me along the sand. They don't want to kill me, but it's the right thing to do. I try to run fast but my legs sink in the sand and I keep falling over, the hot light from the fires streak through the darkness as my face hits the beach.

6
Little Jihad

On day five of the war, the story was a shortage in medical supplies. The World Health Organization had issued a press release warning that Gaza's hospitals weren't coping, which was something I had been telling the desk for days. Every time I stepped foot inside a blood-splattered hospital and saw people dying dull-eyed on stretchers in hallways, I'd told Neil Devereaux we should probably do something about the no drugs and no beds for the injured and dying situation, but he had shown not one flicker of interest until the UN issued its press release. Now *Gaza's Hospitals Suffer Critical Medical Shortages* was urgent news for Neil and his punctuation-less email ordered 800 words 'with some colour from blood-splattered emergency rooms' and quotes from 'sleep-deprived doctors about the injured dying in crowded corridors'. I shut my laptop and trudged downstairs with my flak and helmet to wait for Nasser.

The Bold and the Beautiful was on TV in the lobby again. Jihad was slotting an inexplicably large number of conference chairs into five-high stacks. His back was to me and his huge beige-shirted body was moving slowly and methodically like an old circus bear. A tiny, muscular man was working alongside him, stacking chairs with quick, deft movements. I was watching the odd pair, thinking how much they looked like side-show hands when the little man looked up sharply and I gasped. It was a child with wild eyes and a face that made no sense. The kid must have been around 10 but had the gait and expression of a middle-aged Glaswegian nightclub bouncer. Its freckled skin was dehydrated parchment and it glared at me with unblinking, bottle-green eyes, an expression more animal than human.

'Who's *that?*' I asked the waiter Mohammed who was delivering an unsolicited coffee to me with precise care.

Mohammed told me in a soft whisper as he set down the cup and saucer that this was his nephew, Jihad's son, Jihad.

'His mum doesn't want him out playing on the streets.'

'The strikes?'

Mohammed nodded, then added with a frown of delicate sympathy.

'The other kids can be a bit rough with him.'

Little Jihad had stopped stacking and was now miraculously perched on top of a chair tower, a hard-bodied Soviet gymnast child staring with cold intensity at the boldly made-up women in evening dresses arguing on the television. Someone called Steffy in green taffeta was being accused of murder.

The Italians were gearing to leave, strapping themselves with cameras and lenses, attaching gas masks to their flak jackets. They had a uniform: white linen shirts or tight black t-shirts, chunky sports watches, too many piercings, tattoos and keffiyehs worn as scarves. They talked too loudly and laughed too much as they fiddled with their batteries and tightened their packs. The tallest had a shaved head and sparkling blue eyes and was very good-looking but kept slapping the backs of all the others like a Christian youth group leader. Italians! Always touching, always photographers.

When Nasser finally arrived with some excuse about a sick kid, it was after half nine. I told him the story we were doing and that I couldn't face another day at Shifa Hospital and could he please take us to any other hospital. As was now our norm, we drove in silence with the radio turned up high and tuned to the special 24-hour war program, which was an urgent pulse of news bulletins and bass-heavy resistance songs about brave warriors and the destruction of Zion. I tapped along on the frame of the open window and Nasser drove like he was alone in the car.

'Look out for ambulances, they come in quickly,' was the first thing he said in 25 minutes as he got out of the car and slammed the door behind him.

We had arrived at Beit Hanoun Hospital, which was small and empty. I obeyed Nasser and sat alone in the car for a cautious second before following him up the empty ramp towards the hospital building. I had to break into a brisk, heavy jog to catch up and fell into a breathless amble beside him as we passed a row of unattended ambulances lining the empty entrance. We walked through the grubby swing doors into a small, green, empty reception that reeked of chlorine.

After some searching of abandoned corridors, we finally found a doctor with red eyes and a blank expression smoking a cigarette in a side alley. I asked him how he was coping. He had studied medicine in Manchester and told us in perfect Mancunian English that they didn't have any of the drugs, equipment or staff necessary to treat emergencies. All they had were pregnant women. How were the pregnant women doing? Mostly okay, quite a lot of early labours. Brought on by shock? Probably. Any deaths? One stillbirth but mostly the complicated cases were sent straight to Shifa Hospital. The doctor shrugged in spasms of resignation at the shittiness of the situation.

'Are they coping?' I asked.

'Who?'

'Shifa.'

'No. Go and see for yourself,' he said flatly and shrugged again. His cigarette was finished.

'Excuse me. I've got twins to deliver.'

We arrived at Shifa Hospital to find a thick huddle of cameras and reporters gathered in the carpark. Some sort of press conference was happening.

'That's the Hamas spokesperson,' Nasser noticed.

'We're the only ones who didn't know about this?' I accused him as we rushed towards the pack, readying our notebooks.

Nasser gave me a mystified look. Ignoring the elbow jabs, tuts and usual hissed complaints about my giant head blocking shots, I pushed past the cameras to get inside the scrum. Nestled at its heart was a tiny little man in an immaculate black suit and shiny black shoes with facial hair so precise it could have been styled with a diamond cutter. His forehead was bejewelled with huge beads of sweat and he gave off a strong perfume of cologne and acrid breath. Behind him, a phalanx of much taller, well-gunned security guards twitched.

The Hamas spokesperson cleared his throat. There was Steve Sweeney, dishevelled sandy head peering over the pack like a spooked meerkat. Paula Miranda's bored face, masticating gum, notepad and pen raised. In rapid monotone the tiny Hamas man announced that he would read a statement in English on behalf of the Hamas leadership.

Israel started this war but will never know its end. Hamas fighters will drown Tel Aviv in blood and hellfire. Everything is a target for our Qassam rockets, Tel Aviv, Ashkelon, Jerusalem. The martyrs will be avenged.

He stopped, folded his piece of paper and looked up. Journalists will be allowed one question, he said. Paula jumped first, asking whether Hamas was expecting the Israelis to launch a ground invasion. The man resumed his blank-faced talking.

'We are in front of an enemy that doesn't know the difference between militants, women and children. The plan is prepared already for a great victory. Everyone in the world will witness a victory very soon. Thank you, *assalamu alaikum*.'

Then he was gone, disappeared behind his wall of security men like an old-timey magician. I wondered if he had been chosen for the job deliberately because of his size and being so easy to conceal and read my notes back. *War without end. Rockets everywhere, Ashkelon, Jerusalem. The war will end very soon in victory.*

My phone rang.

'*Surrah?*'

I scurried away deep into the carpark until I reached a spot behind the morgue far enough away from the other media.

'*Surrah*, this is Captain Doron Weiss of the Israeli Defence Force.'

I suspected Doron announced himself so loudly and clearly with his full name and rank every time he called in the hope that some passing Palestinian would hear and think I was Mossad. Or would it be Shin Bet?

'Yes, Doron. What is it?' I whispered, crouching behind a large, solitary eucalyptus tree.

'I'm just checking in, making sure you're safe. It's part of my job, *Surrah*, to be aware of your movements and make sure we can keep you safe. Where are you now?'

'Shifa hospital.'

'Okay. And you've been there all day?'

'No. I was just at Beit Hanoun Hospital. Actually, I need to speak with someone from your side today about the UN statement saying medical supplies aren't getting through.'

The eucalyptus appeared to be peeling excessively, some expression of tree trauma maybe.

'Beit Hanoun is very close to the border. Please, you must avoid the border areas and if you absolutely have to go, inform me. Are you planning to stay at Shifa now?'

I didn't know if I was meant to be speaking with the Israeli military like this. Having had no formal journalistic training some things were still woolly, like what was normal cooperation with state actors and what was providing intelligence to state actors.

'Maybe. Yes.'

'Good,' he said.

'What about the medical supplies, Doron?' I whispered, wandering away from a grieving man sat on the low wall outside the morgue smoking and giving me sly, side-long looks.

'I'll see if someone is available to speak with you this afternoon.'

He paused and I considered the solitary, terrified tree.

'I read your article on the Al Muzaner family this morning,' Doron said. 'It was not accurate. You failed to mention that civilians inside the building were warned to evacuate with a knock on the roof.'

Doron was a great champion of this knocking on roofs. He had argued across every English-speaking media outlet for days that Israel's *knock on the roof* policy made their airstrikes in civilian areas the most humane airstrikes in civilian areas ever. He had explained patiently to almost every breakfast host across the white world that bombing a residential building with a low-load missile one minute before the real strike arrived to pulverise it and anyone still inside allowed those people an extraordinarily humane amount of time to wake up and evacuate their children, pets, crippled parents and so forth.

'As we've already discussed Sara, civilian casualties are always regrettable but not always avoidable when Hamas terrorists surround themselves with women and children. This one was a real bad guy and we got him.'

I told him I'd look into it.

'Okay. Be well,' he said, as if my wellness depended on his specific instruction.

Tutting, I hung up and stood for a while in the shady part of the carpark disliking Doron. My tired eyes rested on a hospital security guard, who was sitting on the steps of his port-a-cabin. He had a full, black beard missing its moustache, a closely shaved head and wore a fur-collared bomber jacket and flip-flops. He was teasing a small grey kitten with a blade of dried grass. The cat had seized the grass and was chewing at it maniacally in the corner of its tiny sharp-toothed mouth. The guard scooped the animal up to stroke its head with his huge hand, forcing its eyes back into smiling slants. He caught sight of me looking and his hand recoiled from the cat's head. He shot me a yellow-toothed, coy smile and I smiled back.

Scanning the media smeared across the hospital grounds for Nasser, I finally spotted him with a group of medics smoking outside the emergency room. He was chatting to them engagingly, running prayer beads through his fingers behind his back, his face energised by some sort of success.

'Sara! There you are!' he exclaimed as I approached. 'This is Jamal Abdullah, director of the emergency unit. He has agreed to let one of his doctors show us the emergency ward.'

Jamal Abdullah smiled weakly through his cigarette smoke.

'Thank you, doctor. Nice work, Nasser!' I delivered an encouraging back slap.

Nasser winced. He hated to be touched.

Dr Osama Al Shanti was 27, had just graduated from a medical college in Egypt and was very high, either on adrenaline and lack of sleep or actual amphetamines. His eyes bulged and he spoke in machine-gun-fire English, a ball of white spit gathering mass in the corner of his mouth. He wore green scrubs, mint green Crocs and a face mask pulled beneath his chin. Moving in quick strides, he led us through an emergency room reception lined with bodies on trolley beds and moaning in stretchers on the ground.

'Most of the wounds we get are major trauma, caused by shrapnel or falling masonry.'

He threw open the doors to the emergency ward. Even if you've never smelt human guts before, it's impossible not to recognise them when you do. An animal instinct lets you know the smell of your own dead. Ours is sweet and nauseating and makes you retch, as I did. The doctor, apparently inured, didn't react but charged on, rattling through the details of each patient as he passed them.

This man's leg was blown off in a bomb blast and would probably die, he'd lost too much blood, they couldn't do anything for him. The bed groaned in pain.

This one had shrapnel lodged in his heart and needed a complicated operation none of the doctors were specialised in.

He would also die. The dead man's face, whiter than anything human I'd ever seen, stared up at us and blinked.

'I would like to ease their pain but we're running out of anaesthetic and even basic painkillers.'

This mummified form entirely wrapped in bandages was a boy approximately eight years of age whose mother and father had not yet been found, likely they were dead. The boy was unrecognisable even underneath the gauze, because he'd suffered 80 per cent burns, and so hadn't yet been claimed by his relatives, who probably thought he was dead too. The mummy boy didn't make a sound and I hoped he was unconscious. The doctor didn't stop but strode on calling out prognoses over his shoulder.

'At this point, most of the injuries that come in are fatal. The survivors are the unlucky ones. At least the dead don't have to live with the pain and the disabilities.'

He turned a corner and continued down another avenue of moaning stretchers. I'd stopped looking at the patients and was focusing instead on the blood splatters across the doctor's Crocs. My hot cigarette and coffee breath was steaming back onto my face in wet pants inside my surgical mask causing the paper to stick to my mouth. Nasser's mask took up almost all of his face and his tiny head nodded constantly in the direction of the doctor, hands clasping their beads tightly behind his back. I looked back at the mummified kid and thought about the life he was going to have when he woke up. If he woke up. Grotesquely messed-up face and body, no parents, or home, or school, maybe no friends, never any girlfriends or wives.

'Do you have any more questions for Dr. Al Shanti? Sara?'

Nasser was talking to me. No, I didn't have any more questions. I wanted to get away from the burning-eyed doctor and his inferno tour. I shook my head. We pushed out of the emergency room doors back into the chaos of the reception and Nasser pulled down his mask, thanking the doctor effusively, chatting and taking extra notes. I was searching for the blue sky through the swing doors when an almighty roar ripped through the air fabric. The sky had gasped for breath, suspending time in silence, then a huge blast shook the room. The hospital erupted in violent panic.

'They bombed the hospital? Nasser? Did they bomb us?' I shouted urgently over the screams and shouts of everyone else.

Nasser's voice came back weakly through my ear ringing: 'They hit the road outside the compound. We're fine.'

I sprung from my foetal crouch behind Nasser, clawing and elbowing my way out of the hospital building into a wall of car horns, ambulance sirens and screams. There was the security guard transformed, huge and angry, pushing the crowd back into the hospital building, keeping the entrance clear for the cars tearing up to its entrance. A surge of people thrust me towards him and he shoved me back hard with his large palm.

Behind him, yelling men were pulling a body out of the back seat of a car onto a stretcher. It came out backwards very close to my face, one flip-flop dangling from a dusty foot, skinny and bloody but intact. It was the face that was missing. Everything apart from a small clean section of lower left jaw had gone. A second smaller person pulled from the front seat was bundled along a chain of screaming men towards waiting medics. It was a boy, complete only until his naval, legs replaced by a tail of entrails that left a trail of viscera on the arms of his relatives.

A surge of cold electricity ran across my skull, down my neck spine and into my arms. My throat was closing, I could feel it closing. I couldn't breathe. I needed air. I tore through the mob around me until I burst free into the carpark and charged towards the big peeling tree.

'Hi there!'

The other jock American TV reporter was ambling towards the commotion, luminous white teeth flashing through his tan and hairspray smell.

'How you doing, Sara?' he beamed.

I lurched past him towards a closer, smaller, barely living shrub and began to retch in spasms until my ribs ached but produced nothing. I felt the TV guy's eyes on me. I let my diaphragm heave and I wondered if he would ever fuck me after seeing this because I had been thinking about him naked, tanned and muscular in cowboy boots. Then I started to count how many days into the war we were and how many days in a row I'd been looking at dead people. Then I realised the date and there in my head was my father. Then I didn't want anyone but Michael.

7
WHERE THE WILD BEASTS ARE

Dad died in St. Thomas' hospital on 19 November 2010. On 25 November, a manilla folder was delivered to us at home by his lawyer. It had an index, neatly written in Dad's red-ink spider hand, categorising his instructions for our bereavement.

Memorial Service
Church: Corpus Christi on Maiden Lane (guest list enclosed). 5pm, spring evening.
Eulogy: Martin Ferryman (contact details and draft enclosed).
Reading: Sara, Virgil, Eclogues (extract and direction enclosed).
Wake: El Vinos (6.30pm until late, wine list and canapé menu enclosed).
Miscellaneous: flowers, music, order of service etc.

Shortly before 5pm on 3 April 2011, Michael walked into Corpus Christi Church on Maiden Lane, his face framed by the feathers and felt domes of fascinator hats. I hadn't seen him in 14 months but it was just the same, his face. A little thinner. His hair was greyer but still thick, his body slimmer. He was wearing his navy suit, freshly shaven and alone, which made me smile even though he couldn't see me. My mother offered him a powdered cheek to kiss. I watched him place a compassionate hand on Cathy's arm and her shrug it off. I watched him, a chastened courtier, unsure what to do next, apologetically find a seat at the end of the third row on the opposite side of the church to Cathy and from me.

The retired editor Martin Ferryman, who was very, very old, told us that Dad had been *a Titan, sat proudly among the giants of Fleet Street*, and then curiously *a loving husband to his wife Sara and devoted father to his daughter Sue*. The church shifted in its seats but as I'd never met Martin Ferryman, I was unfazed.

'Few had the opportunity to read Bill's longer literary works, but those who did describe a rare mind. An unsung Hazlitt of his day,' the editor read haltingly, surprising even himself.

Michael was politely studying the gilded Mary and Jesus clutching each other opposite him, hands folded neatly in his lap. What had been his posthumous instruction? Mine had been succinct. *Sara: the reading is short but that doesn't mean race. Delivery should be slow and clear. NB No histrionics!*

I had bought a very low-cut black dress and an expensive push-up bra, which I wore with a lot of red lipstick. Under-lit at the marble lectern, I leaned towards the microphone and cleared my throat, engaging the congregation in a moment of generalised eye contact before starting to read in a low, soft voice.

I will be gone from here and sing my songs,
in the forest wilderness where the wild beasts are,

I paused to look up from my notes and find Michael's gaze, but he was looking down at the order of service.

And carve in letters on the little trees
The story of my love, and as the trees
Will grow letters too will grow, to cry

I allowed my voice to crack, and the congregation, including Michael, looked towards the pulpit. I curled the corners of my mouth and spoke only to him.

to cry
in a louder voice the story of my love.

El Vinos was packed and hot and I wanted urgently to be a lot drunker than I was. Michael wouldn't come to the wake if Cathy was there and there was Cathy in a hat welded to my mother. Cancer Cathy commanding my father's wake with her infinite sadness.

I decided to get so drunk that I would be unaccountable for

my behaviour. Having swiped three bottles of red wine from the bar, I retreated to the very back of the room to sit among the discarded overcoats and drink methodically. From the safety of my coat hide, I watched the wake milling and circling, clucking and fawning. The same people from our summer parties, only older. Very few of them had recognised me at the church and those that did had been unsure, edging around me as they would a stray dog.

'Sara! Yes of course! But Bill was so proud of you. No! He was! Especially your work in, yes, what *is* the situation in the Lebanon now? You really are *very* brave,' said Charles, Dad's stupid school friend with the facial psoriasis. Rejected from the armed services for failing the literacy test Charles.

'Diane and I want you to know that we're here for you and your mother, both of us. Really here. Whatever you need,' Laurel the essayist drawled, staining everyone she touched with her patchouli stink.

'*Such* a moving service and *such* a moving reading. But then, he was *such* an outstanding chap!' said the man whose name we always forgot but whose buck-toothed wife June flirted outrageously with Dad so was often invited to dinner.

'How you holding up there, girly?' asked Michael's voice.

There he was, standing over me, clutching his grey cashmere coat. Suddenly, we were together again, alone at the edge of a roaring room where no one could hear us.

'I'm so sorry. I miss him,' he said sincerely before flashing a strange new toothy smile.

'What have you done to your mouth?' I frowned up at him, but he didn't hear me over the roar and looked around uncomfortably.

'So, Jerusalem?' he persevered.

I nodded, staring up at him, drinking him in, and gulped some more of my wine. He nodded too.

'And you're writing for *The Tribune*?'

A smile tugged at the corners of my mouth at the thought of

him scouring the paper for my by-line and I nodded again. My eyes were stinging.

'Not thinking of going to Syria are you? It's too sad what's happening there, I adored Damascus.'

I allowed my stinging eyes to start crying because I was unaccountable.

'No. No, no, it's okay,' Michael hushed, dropping to his knees out of the party's line of sight.

'It's not okay, don't say it's okay!' I nearly yelled and watched his face morph into marble panic.

'Please, don't.'

'Don't what? Be sad at my father's wake?'

He grimaced. I tried a bit to stop crying but the combination of being so close to him that I could smell his cloakroom smell and that nearly finished second bottle of red wine in my hand made it too difficult. Also, I was unaccountable. I tasted snot.

'It's my dad's wake Michael!' I sobbed at him.

Michael, still crouching, patted at my knee.

'You're alright,' he patted. 'It's alright.'

He watched me cry and his clenched jaw twitched.

'You sharing that bottle you're clutching there or is it all for you?'

I wiped away more of the snot tears from my mouth, grabbed around for an almost empty glass and poured what was left of my bottle into it.

'Where's Mimi?' I asked, repeating her name into my glass as a mouse squeak.

'At home,' Michael sighed. 'I should get back really, but I wanted to see your poor mum. And see how you were doing of course.'

He patted me again and I grabbed his hand.

'I miss you.'

He wrenched his hand back quickly, faded blue eyes flashing sharply. I knew not to touch him like that in public but I was unaccountable. I wiped the tears from my cheeks with the heels of my hands and he turned to look behind him from his crouch, staring into the party edgily.

'I miss him a bit but mostly I miss you,' I admitted.

He sighed sadly again and studied the floor around our feet. Standing, he stared hard into his wine glass, drained it and put it back empty on the table. He dropped his coat on top of the coat pile.

'I have to go to the toilet. Do you have to go to the toilet?'

He raised his eyebrows and walked off towards the toilets. I waited for a few seconds then followed. The door of the first cubicle opened and he pulled me roughly inside. His big, hot hands were in my hair, under my dress, on my ass. His mouth was on mine and my heart felt like it would burst out of my chest and shower us in gory fireworks. I kissed him as deeply as I could. He pulled my head back by the hair and looked at me.

'This is just for tonight, okay? It's too hard.'

'Is it now?' I asked.

If I thought he meant it I would have made it better. I would have shown him that he couldn't live without my mouth any better than I could live without his, but I was drunk and it was too quick. Then I was washing him off my face and he was gone again.

8
DEADLINE

Nasser had been standing at a discreet distance in case I was actually sick, but when after a good 10 minutes of heaving I was not, he approached. I was grateful for his suggestion that we head back to the hotel to make some calls. We had more than enough material to be getting on with, he said, and he was right. Also I wanted very badly to not be around dead or dying people for a bit.

'Are you okay?' he asked as we walked to the car. 'Your face is sort of red white. And sweating a lot.'

'I'm fine,' I said, not feeling fine. 'Probably didn't drink enough water.'

Back at the hotel Nasser went off to pray and I went to my room, which hadn't been cleaned, took off my clothes and washed my face. I leaned in to study it in the mottled bathroom mirror. Under a map of raised, red blotches the canvas of my skin was so white it was almost green. My lips had no colour at all but the blues of my irises were insanely vivid, rimmed with cherry red lids like that.

I ran the cold water as cold as it would go, which wasn't very cold, and stuck my wrists under the tap until I began to feel less dizzy. I drenched a towel with tepid tap water and wrapped it around my head, where it warmed instantly. Dripping prodigiously, I sat down in nothing but my two day old underpants on the side of my unmade bed and called London.

'Foreign.'

Neil Devereaux answered the phone hoping to communicate as much disinterest as possible in whatever foreign matter was calling him. I said hello, it was Sara Byrne in Gaza.

'Yes,' Neil confirmed.

'I just wanted to let you know that I'm back safely. I'm sure the airstrike outside the Shifa hospital compound is already on the wires?'

'It is. Where is your copy?'

'The strike hit very close to the emergency room and we were right there when the first bodies were brought in. Lots of injuries and dead people. Dead kids with no legs.'

A stream of water seeping from my head towel, slipped past my temples towards my mouth.

'We've put through agency for now, but I'll need 500 words from you as soon as you can. We can update with a proper refile later but I'll tell you, Sara, it doesn't look great that we keep having to carry your story with wire copy. Seniors have noticed.'

'You'll have it within the hour,' I said.

'Thirty minutes please.'

He hung up. Like many cunts, Neil found it unnecessary to say goodbye.

The sweat from my neck and chest had mixed with the towel water. Pools in the depths of my clavicles were overflowing, forming gentle streams that ran through my blotchy cleavage. I watched the water run between my tits onto my stomach and into another pool in my belly button and I considered how I didn't have the statistics I needed on the hospitals. I didn't have a comment from the Israelis about the hospital bombing or there being no medical supplies for the bombed either. I sat observing my cleavage river a bit more. I was not going to meet my deadline, it was impossible. Doron knew I was at Shifa before the strike. Had he told anyone?

The crackle of a speaker switching on echoed through the room and the call to prayer rang out. The muezzin next to the hotel was on a normal day mournful and melodic but since the war started, his adhans had become increasingly deranged wails, wild and angry. Maybe it was a different man. Maybe the original muezzin was dead, which was why the new one was so deranged, with grief.

I was experiencing a weird sensation, like my brain was pouring in cold watery jelly out of my ears and nose and eye sockets. I needed it in working order inside my skull so took a quick tepid shower hoping it was just overheated. Dressed, I rushed out of my room to find Nasser and get to work but bumped directly into Jihad and his cleaning trolley. Had he been waiting outside my room? He smiled his three-eyed smile at me.

'Hi Jihad,' I said.

'*Mahabar* Jihad,' he corrected with a scowl. '*Salamtek* Sara.'

His huge body performed a slight, awkward bow. He had been developing a role-play in which he was a stern Arabic teacher and I was his lazy student. At that moment this game particularly delighted him and he presented my new vocabulary with a slow rolling delivery. A small, hard face popped up above the stack of clean, white towels, evidently unimpressed by the theatrics. The two Jihads: the beaming cyclops and his dour ancient son.

'*Salamtek* Jihads,' I said, moving past them and down the broad tiled staircase to the lobby.

Already 15 minutes gone without any writing. The restaurant was empty. The other journalists were elsewhere and all the waiters, except handsome Mohammed, were praying. The only other people in the vast room were a cluster of middle-aged, fair-haired men in suits drinking coffee. Diplomats, Scandinavian almost certainly, talking more loudly than was necessary.

I called Mohammed over and asked him please for a coffee and had he seen Nasser. He had not but thought he was probably praying, and I thought not for the first time about how much constructive work time is lost to prayer and had an economist somewhere worked out how much exactly and is it any wonder capitalism is godless. The cursor blinked on my blank screen. I would lead of course with the airstrike outside the hospital.

The Israeli F16 (??) jet dropped its bomb on the street outside the Gaza Strip's main hospital shortly before midday on Monday, I typed.

The stream of corpses had started to pour into the Shifa Hospital emergency room before the dust from the blast had cleared. One was a young man whose head had been blown clean from his neck, the next a child trailing organs from his severed torso.

It wasn't clean though, was it? There was that bit of jaw. The Fin-Danes erupted in great Nordic booms of laughter. What could possibly be that funny in this lobby in a war. I deleted the corpse paragraph. Where the fuck was Nasser?

The target of the airstrike was just metres from the entrance to Gaza City's already overwhelmed Shifa Hospital. Even before the smoke from the blast had cleared, the bodies started to arrive, announced by a chorus of sirens and car horns.

A small boy trailed his guts over the arms of the relatives carrying him into the emergency room. A man whose face was lost apart from a small, clean fragment of jaw wore only one flip-flop. And the bodies kept on coming, bringing their stench of blood and gore.

I stared at a smeared fingerprint smudge on my laptop screen and deleted the section about the blood and gore. One of the larger Dane-Swedes raised his voice to be heard above the others.

'Ze emphasis of ze visit must be on communicating our advocacy messaging, not just establishing grrreater humanitarian access,' he argued emphatically.

It was 45 minutes since I'd hung-up from Neil and Mohammed arrived bearing my coffee on his large tray. He shifted my notebooks aside carefully to make way for the ceremony of cup, saucer, milk and sugar, as if his coffee service were more important than my deadline. As if he didn't know by now that I didn't take my coffee with either milk or sugar.

'Leave them!' I barked over my notes.

Mohammed startled but the coffee remained perfectly poised on his platter. Embarrassed to have barked at nice Mohammed but still in no mood for time wasting rituals, I smiled, thanking him with bared teeth and jerked the cup and saucer from his tray myself spilling black coffee over my open notebooks. Mohammed exclaimed sadly and I decided not to notice.

The other journalists were seeping back into the hotel bringing their hubbub. There was the small, silk-scarfed Italian correspondent with his neatly cuffed linen shirt and his vast, silent, pony-tailed photographer. Jane Sawyer, cool and crisp. Nasser took his place beside me and opened his tiny notebook to reveal pages of his small, neat script punctuated with numbers and percentages.

'So,' he said, 'I was just on the phone to the morgue. 10 have died so far in the Shifa airstrike, including three children. The numbers of injured are . . . '

'What?'

I couldn't hear his soft voice over the grandstanding diplomats.

'WOULD YOU MIND KEEPING YOUR VOICE DOWN?' I shouted towards the loudest of the Fin-Danes who raised his eyebrows in surprise. 'Can you speak up please Nasser, I can't hear a thing you're saying.'

Nasser tensed.

'Did you find out how many doctors were on duty?' I asked him.

'Usually they have six, but today it was five.'

'And what is the hospital running out of, aside from doctors?'

'That fluid they use to sterilise tools for surgery, gauze, anaesthetic and pain killers.'

I typed steadily with Nasser beside me and he watched as I worked, calling out figures and quotes from his notebook. Mohammed hovered, waiting for Nasser's order but as usual he wanted nothing and Mohammed glided away. The Israelis had issued a statement, which Nasser read out from his phone.

'*While Hamas actively exploits and endangers their civilians, COGAT's activities are . . .*'

'Who?'

'COGAT. Coordination of Government Activities in the Territories—occupation forces basically. *COGAT's activities are yet another example of the measures that Israel takes to minimise casualties and harm amongst that very same population that . . .*' he trailed off in silent search of something interesting.

'There's stuff about food. Can't see anything about medical supplies. Ah wait, here. *COGAT has placed special emphasis on prioritising health-related requests, whether supply requests or exit permits for treatment in Israel.*'

The harder I concentrated on understanding what he was saying, the less the words meant.

'Nasser, just read out slowly and loudly what I should be writing!' I instructed, raising my voice so as to be understood.

Nasser repeated the bit about medical supplies, having to raise his voice to a near yell above the extraordinary din of those fucking Nords.

'JESUS FUCKING CHRIST WOULD YOU SHUT THE FUCK UP!' I slammed both palms down on either side of my laptop, sending the coffee leaping from its cup and back down to drench my already splattered notebooks.

The diplomatic huddle jumped. Jane Sawyer and the Italian looked up. Nasser froze. My temples pulsed with anger.

'Excuse me, Nasser. I'm going to have to finish this in my room,' I said.

I gathered my belongings and set off at a brisk half-walk, half-run back through the lobby and up the big, stone staircase. Jihad's cleaning trolley was still parked outside my open room and I swung the door open violently, exposing him, mop in hand.

'I need my room back now, please.'

Jihad smiled.

'*Mish mushkila,* Sara, just 10 minutes more.'

The Bold and the Beautiful was playing on my television and his small, shadow son was crouched on the floor near my bed watching it. His dried face turned from the screen to stare at me with its green snake eyes.

'Now! I need the room *now,* Jihad!'

Little Jihad moved first, standing with solemn dignity to turn off the television. He then stalked out of the room ahead of his harassed father who was apologising and wheeling his bucket and trolley with sloppy haste.

My wet notes were indecipherable, so I sat in the damp musk of my half-cleaned bedroom and finished the last few paragraphs from memory. I didn't read the piece through because it was more than an hour late but hit send immediately after typing the last word, which happened to be jews. There you go Neil, some fresh, unpasteurised news. News of the Jews. As I sank back in my chair, fatigue fell over me like a lead blanket. It was an irresistible tiredness and so, fully clothed, I crawled into my unmade bed and let my head sink into the pillow.

9
Dad

I jerked into semi-wakefulness, unsettled to find myself in a resort on the River Styx at some unknown time of the day. A manky bird perched on the low wall of my balcony was eye-balling me. I didn't like the way that bird was looking at me. I lay still on my polyester pillow and stared past it to the water.

Room 22 was on the second floor and had wide sliding windows onto a tiled balcony that looked directly out to sea. From the bed, which was white and wide and covered with too many small, lurid green cushions, I could see up the full length of the beach to the deserted harbour. By late Autumn, Gaza's sun was too weak to rise from its low orbit even at noon. In the mornings especially, it cast a cold, milky light from the horizon that refracted eerily off the sea and the dust and salt mist.

I had dreamt about Dad again. Dying Dad, his frail frame moving nimbly through rubble towards a bombed house that was both our old house on the park and some generic, half-built, concrete Gaza building. I knew that if he reached the building it would explode so I screamed at him to watch out. He snapped his head around and in the place of his face was a bloody, skinless jaw that yapped back, '*YOU* watch out!' Even awake with my eyes wide open I couldn't shift the image of his snapping skull jaw. I blinked a few times rapidly and stared hard at the beach.

A gang of boys were chasing a football along the sand, pushing and shoving at each other athletically. A lone child perched on an upturned fishing boat was watching their game, knees crunched into a ball at his chest. At the harbour end, by the empty moored fishing boats, a couple walked barefoot slowly along the water's edge, the woman resting her covered head comfortably on the man's shoulder. Closer to the hotel, an old man was standing knee deep in water, his trousers rolled up, trying to fish. None of these beach people were paying any attention to the humming of the surveillance drones above them or the chain of war ships along the horizon.

The boy on the upturned boat cupped his hand to his mouth and called out some instruction or encouragement to the football boys, prompting the largest in the boy gang to stride away from the game and punch him hard in the face. The others laughed as the punched boy got to his feet, trudging back through the sand towards the hotel. It looked like the cleaner's weird son. He tripped in the sand and the football boys doubled over laughing again.

I'd slept too long and my head still throbbed with Dad's yapping skull. He was ash now, gone. The instructions in his manilla folder had been explicit.

The cremation: family only.

Cremation ceremony: no readings, no eulogies—these at the memorial (CF memorial folder).

Music: Kozlovsky Requiem in E-flat minor, USSR Symphony Orchestra (CD enclosed).

Flowers: white peonies.

Casket: wicker is fine.

My father would have been as appalled by people coming to Croydon to watch his body pass through an incinerator as if we'd thrown a viewing party for his autopsy. He had always been repulsed by matters corporeal. *Pulvis et umbra sumus.* The manager of the Mitcham Road Crematorium did not know this about him.

Geoff, a translucently pale man in his late forties, carried out his work with sad seriousness and an uncomfortable Steampunk sensibility. In the little he misunderstood of my father he had found a kindred spirit and strove to bring the solemnity and occasion to Dad's cremation he believed he would have wanted and that we, his family, were incapable of providing. Or worse, were refusing to attempt.

A devoted, ashen-faced death groom, Geoff stood next to the ancient CD player at the front of the west chapel, hands clasped in front of him, waiting. As per his instruction, my father's arrival was announced with a bone-shaking blast of Soviet horns. Too loud. Geoff, wincing, lunged towards the elderly stereo to adjust the volume, then resumed his post, dropping his head to his chest. In the front row, Ma and I stood up as the rich low voices of the Moscow State Choir filled the room. In his wicker coffin under a blanket of white peonies, Dad was carried slowly up the aisle, parting a sea of empty blue office chairs. Geoff stood rigid with attention.

As the grey-suited, gently sweating funeral directors laid him on the wooden planks of the short, coffin conveyor belt, the chorus of Russian tenors, sopranos and strings climaxed, straining the speakers of Geoff's ghetto blaster. The CD started to skip and Geoff spun in horror. As Dad's coffin began to move on its electric belt, sopranos looped like banshees screaming in terror of the looming furnace. Ma delivered a sharp elbow to my ribs.

'Stop it!' she growled, but I couldn't stop giggling any more than Dad could delay his roll towards the inevitable incinerator.

Two heavy, burgundy curtains moved on their electronic rails, ready to shield us from his meeting with the furnace, but in an extraordinary flourish of bad luck for Geoff, the mechanism stuck and then jammed uncannily in time with the stuck CD. I lost my balance and had to sit down as Geoff leapt into an unwinnable battle with the spasming drape and Dad continued his unshielded progress towards what I remember to be very visible flames and what Ma insists was just a room stacked with other coffins.

'It's alright Geoff! For God's sake don't hurt yourself!' Ma called out over the hysterically syncopating orchestra.

'Pull yourself together Sara!' she hissed down at me.

I tried to pull myself together, for Geoff's sake, and almost did when an unexpected crash of timpani made me squeal.

'I don't understand it! This has never! Mrs Byrne, Ms Byrne, I'm so *deeply* sorry!' Geoff whimpered as he made grunting tugs at the stubborn fabric, then issued a deep sobbing sigh of relief as the curtain mechanism finally clicked back into action.

The choir was back too, thundering at full force, but I missed Dad's disappearance because I had laughed myself blind.

In the unseasonably warm gardens of remembrance, Geoff took uncertain sips of tea. Raising the paper cup to his thin lips with a trembling, veiny hand, he told me quietly that grief-induced hysteria was not uncommon. Laughing is so close to crying, in animal terms, he observed. I had absolutely nothing to be embarrassed about, my father would certainly have understood. A crumb of custard cream biscuit that had been stuck in the corner of his mouth fell loose to join a dusting of dandruff on his lapel. He brushed it deftly away.

Dad's angry skull face definitely did not understand. I closed my eyes firmly and tried to summon his normal face but only found it dead in the funeral home. I'd not wanted to sit alone with him but Ma said I should, so I could say anything to him privately that I would regret not having said. His cancer sunken cheeks had caused his bird nose and cheek bones to jut out like crags. His white, thin lips had vanished entirely. But his overall expression, neutralised by the Madame Tussauds process he had been through, looked softer than usual and it wasn't unpleasant sitting with him. He looked like the death mask of some rich Roman, which he would have loved. Roman epitaphs were his favourite. I tried composing one for him.

'Spirits of the dead, this is my father,' I announced. 'He was a journalist and often bad-tempered. He had a wife and a daughter.'

'He could be funny,' I added, because that was also true. 'Bye Dad.'

I stood up to leave and wondered if I should touch him. We almost never touched in life but he was dead now so I bent to kiss his forehead, which I hadn't done since I was a child. I felt the white wisps of his hair brittle with hairspray, his cold skin tacky like plasticine, inhaled his death chemicals, and wished I hadn't.

I glared through Room 22's small bathroom window out into the street and down the sandy bombed main boulevard. A man wearing a garish knitted jumper and tracksuit bottoms was methodically sweeping up the ruins of the top floor of a building that had been knocked off. Huge blocks of masonry and piles of rocks sprawled out into the road like guts out of road kill. It was an impossible thing for one man to clear up with a single broom. Why was he trying?

Then I saw my father alive. It was summer in the old house and we were sitting opposite each other in silence: me on the big, stained sofa drinking wine, Dad in his red armchair reading. The living room smelled of roasting lamb and cut grass. He had just mown the lawn and was fresh from the shower. I was in an old bikini top I'd found down the back of my underwear draw and pyjama bottoms and had not washed. His wine was delicious and I was drinking a lot of it. I was home on my first visit from Jerusalem where the wine I could afford was not delicious. Ma was humming along to the opera she had playing in the kitchen.

Dad was as tanned as he could ever be, dense clusters of auburn freckles smeared up his forearms and along his high, fragile cheekbones. They had just come back from Istanbul, which was pretty close to East Jerusalem where I was living at the time but which they had refused to visit. Ma would not travel through Israel, because she was boycotting it. Dad did not support the boycott—*when has collective ostracisation ever encouraged constructive dialogue*—but still said there were many places in the region he'd prefer to visit, like Constantinople.

'What Europe has right about the AKP is that it's a populist movement. Of course it is. What I cannot entertain is this hysteria that Erdogan is an autocrat. To say he's anything *like* Saddam is just brain-dead, liberal tub-thumping. What he is, is a Europhile. A pragmatist! Getting rid of him now, with all that's going on in Syria, would be catastrophic.'

There were only two of us in the room but it was unclear whether he was talking to me or just talking. Since losing his column to that not unattractive Asian Tory MP, he had taken to delivering snippets of unwritten columns in conversation, the lost souls of unborn pieces. Having spent the first half of his career fixated on Northern Ireland, he was now fixated on the Middle East. Michael had told him his essay *Why a Liberated Iraq Will Embrace the West* was a work of genius and he had appeared on *Newsnight* to defend it. Shortly afterwards he made a trip to Jermyn Street where he purchased two hats—a Fedora, which he wore in the summer, and an Irish tweed flat cap for winter.

'What's the take in Israel, Sara?'

I looked up. His dark triangle eyes were glinting with interest and trained on me. He even smiled.

'Huh?'

'What does your Netanyahu make of Erdogan?'

He smiled again. So fucking like him. To choose that moment, my mind a swamp of hay-fever pills and tannins, to ask for my opinion. It was a trap, obviously, and I needed to tread carefully. I strained my brain for thoughts but it hummed blankly. Did I know *anything* about Turkey? Nasser liked Turks. Why did Nasser like Turks?

'Ah, well, it's quite interesting actually. Other Arabs hate Palestinians. The Egyptians, the Lebanese, the Egyptians in particular *really* hate them, like as much as they hate black people. But the Turks! Maybe it's because they aren't actually Arabs, they're something else, Persian is it? But Turkish people love Palestine, so Ankara has no choice but to be officially pro it really. Pro Gaza definitely.'

'The Turkish people are Turkic,' Dad corrected, knitting his fine eyebrows.

'Right. But that doesn't stop Erdogan donating gazillions to the Israeli war effort.'

I laughed Nasser's bitter, informed laugh. He had found this betrayal particularly egregious and ranted for an entire car journey about it through a weird rigor mortis smile. I'd thought I had tuned him out, but apparently not. Dad winced.

'*Erdowan*. It's a *yumuşak* g. And where did you read that?'

'About the gazillions? I didn't *read* it. If you'd gone to Gaza— if you'd ever bothered to go *anywhere*—any kid on the street would tell you. Sure, Turkey sends the odd rickety boat of old guns to Gaza. But meanwhile, Israel is sending *huuuuge* ships with all sorts of high-tech weapons to Turkey because Erdogan is paying Israel gazillions of dollars for them. Presumably to kill Greeks, or disobedient Turks. Kurds? Anyway, Israel pumps all those Turkish gazillions straight back into making even more high-tech weapons to kill more Palestinians. Which is why, in answer to your original question Dad, I'm pretty sure Netanyahu, despite all appearances, is quite delighted with your *Erdowwwan*!'

I finished the wine in my glass, pleased with what I had been able to dredge from my memory on the topic of Turkey despite never having been or paying much attention to it. The apple hadn't fallen so far from the Bill Byrne tree after all!

'Is there more of this?'

My father looked down his long, fine nose at me, weak jaw and high, feminine cheek bones intact. His face was flushed, so alive with disapproval I briefly forgot he was sick and no longer drinking.

'The burgundy?' he asked sourly.

I shrugged because I didn't know if it was burgundy or not. The interest that had flickered briefly in his deep, grey eye sockets was extinguished and they returned their dead, watery focus to the heavy book open on his lap.

'If there's any left, it will be in the rack. You might want to watch that drinking Sara, it's been like having late-stage Oliver Reed to stay.'

'*Le donnnnna ay mobilllllaaaaayyyy,*' Ma sang from the kitchen.

10
Unbelievable News

I knocked back two paracetamol and glared moodily out onto the beach road. There was a new, deep, black-smouldering hole in the plot of empty ground behind the hotel. It looked like a bomb crater but it couldn't have been a bomb crater because I wouldn't have slept through a bomb that big dropping that close by. I reached instinctively for my depression pills and found the packet missing because I had taken the last pill on day two of the war.

I'd been taking the pills ever since I came back from Dad's wake to the Jerusalem shoilet and found myself unable to get out of bed. Ron my landlord liked to call in early most mornings to read me the best examples of antisemitism from the previous day's English-speaking papers. After 10 days, my unavailability for this ritual had started to annoy him and he ordered me to see his doctor. The doctor had a pot belly and a dirty shirt. He asked me what a healthy young woman like me was doing being depressed. Parents die, that's life. I was attractive *enough*, young *enough*, what could be so wrong? Had I been raped? I told him yes I had been raped because for fuck's sake what a question.

His pills had helped get me out of bed but I didn't need them. I hadn't been raped, not really. So I thought good riddance and stared out the window at the new hole a bit more. My phone beeped with Nasser telling me that his asthma kid was sick in hospital and that he would be late again, which was lucky because I had just remembered that I needed to meet Fadi.

I was already halfway into the great Thunder Dome of a

restaurant headed for my usual table by the sea when I realised the room was totally deserted. Waiter Mohammed's matinee idol head popped out of the kitchen and called to me urgently.

'Miss Byrne! The restaurant is closed. Miss Byrne! Please! It's not safe!'

'What happened?' I asked.

He had joined me in the middle of the vast room in a flash of quick light steps. I noticed then an entire row of the largest of the windowpanes overlooking the beach had shattered and the bulky form of one-eyed Jihad sweeping a carpet of glass.

'You didn't hear the airstrike?'

He raised his arched eyebrows in amazement.

'Don't worry, you can be sure they weren't trying to hit us, but the shells landed quite close.'

He pouted towards the shattered windows.

'The restaurant is not safe now, so please, we are serving food in the lobby for the time being.'

I didn't like the lobby. It felt like a theme park version of Aladdin's cave—synthetic, stuffy, viewless. Resentfully, I took a seat in the only empty corner. By 9.30, I'd had my breakfast omelette, four of waiter Mohammed's sweet grainy Arabic coffees, served with the usual fussy ceremony, and smoked almost all of my American cigarettes.

Even with the paracetamols my head hurt, a dull pounding ache that thudded up from my neck to my temples and sat like a sadist jackhammering at my eye nerves, forcing me to squint. The pain plus the nauseating generator fumes were making me agitated. I'd sent Fadi three texts, and he hadn't answered one of them. I'd cleared a morning for him when the story of my career was literally blowing up around me and he was sleeping in like a teenager. It made me sick. Was I sick?

I fished my very last precious American cigarette from its packet with a shaky hand and took it out to the courtyard to smoke with some air. Mo was having an intense conversation with his two receptionists, front desk Mohammed and the rude Ukrainian. Nasser told me the Ukrainian had married a Palestinian she met when he was studying in Kiev, and probably very hot, and had followed him back to Palestine like an idiot. Now she was trapped like everyone else in Gaza, living with his mother and helping Mohammed at reception. Her normal face was a blue eyeshadow mask of bitterness but in that courtyard huddle she looked even more miserable than usual.

They were in some kind of crisis talks. Mo was sweating in shimmering sheets from the top of his smooth head and the receptionists were wide-eyed and tense. He spoke in English for the Ukrainian's benefit, even though Nasser said she spoke perfectly fine Arabic.

'When they ask, you say it will be open again in a few days.'

Mo was huffing breathlessly, punctuating every sentence with a karate chop of his hand.

'When they come this afternoon, Mohammed, you answer their questions, like always. *Mish mushkila*. Ilyana, you say nothing. *Nichts!*'

Mo made a zipping gesture across his mouth. Spotting me, he issued a tight smile. I smiled back and moved to the far side of the courtyard to smoke my cigarette by the potted palm and spy more discreetly, nearly tripping over Jihad's strange son who was crouched sweeping a perfectly clean section of tiles with a dustpan and broom. There was a large particularly filthy cat next to him and they both glared up at me with wild, green animal eyes. The matted white tom cat started to yowl lowly. They looked related.

'Hello down there!' I said.

The cat's manky tail flicked ferociously and it continued yowling. I tried to smile kindly at the cleaner's kid reminding myself that even weird children with old man faces were children and required adult kindness. I noticed an angry purple and yellow swelling distorting his cheek bone and struggled to supress a wince.

'Is that your cat?'

The child looked up at me and said nothing. He probably didn't speak English. Maybe he was an adult with some kind of gene disease. I'd been to the hospitals, there was a lot of inbreeding.

I sucked hard on my cigarette. What if Fadi was hurt? Or dead? How would I know? I'd sent him off chasing after a terrorist commander at a time when any old fighter was a clay pigeon to Israeli drone operators. I texted him a smiley face just in case he was too embarrassed to say the whole uncle thing hadn't worked out. Then I sent a row of question marks because I didn't want him to think he didn't have to tell me it hadn't worked out.

It was past 10. If he hadn't arrived in 15 minutes, I'd tell him not to bother coming. I stubbed out my cigarette in the pot plant near Little Jihad's unsettling head and went back to my waiting spot in the lobby. It was 10.20 when Fadi finally bowled through the door, walking purposefully and jabbering into a phone pinned to his ear with his shoulder bone. He loomed over the table, one hand digging deep into his tight jean pockets for a pack of cigarettes, the other raising an index finger indicating that I should wait. He sat down opposite me on a low stool, throwing his skinny legs wide.

'*Yani.*'

I hadn't learned Arabic, but I recognised some sounds. Okay, okay, *mashi, mashi*. Something else that sounded like *uptick, yallah*. Okay! *Yallah*! Okay *mmm-bye. Yallah-bye.* Bye. He hung up and with a beseeching look extended both palms towards me.

'Sara!'

'Fadi! You have your phone!'

My voice sounded tighter than I wanted.

'When you didn't reply to any of my texts, I assumed you had lost it. Or were dead.'

He looked at his phone despairingly.

'No credit!'

'You're an hour and a half late.'

Fadi ignored this chastisement and threw a cigarette into the corner of his mouth then offered me one, which I declined curtly.

'So,' he said with a dramatic pause, raising a thick eyebrow. 'I saw my uncle.'

'Yes?'

'Yes.'

He lit his cigarette and exhaled his first puff slowly.

'And?'

'Well, it's good news and bad news,' he said, taking another slow puff from the corner of his mouth Wild West style.

I didn't like this cocky Fadi. He narrowed his eyes, waiting for me to respond, smoking dramatically. Jesus Christ. It was like watching a slow kid with a magic kit.

'Just tell me, Fadi!'

He leant in close towards my face, wafting his perfume and gel smell, right leg pumping energetically.

'I talked to my uncle about you. I told him you're a big British journalist who wants to meet the commander and I said we could trust you.' Fadi lowered his voice. 'I didn't tell him your name because I didn't want him nervous. You're a Jew, right?'

'No.'

'So why have you got a Jew name?' he asked with a sly knowing look.

'Sara is not a Jewish name, it's just a name. What about the tunnels?'

Fadi eyed me with distrust.

'I told him your name is Kate.'

I gesticulated irritably for him to continue.

'We didn't talk so long, he needed to get some rest. It was a big night for the resistance. He said he'd think about it. But believe me Sara, with me and my uncle, not saying no means yes.'

There was a pause as we both thought. I took one of his shitty Egyptian cigarettes and lit it.

'I can get this for you, Sara, it's just right now everyone's feeling very on the edge.'

Finally, maybe I had something, possibly. I leaned back into the deep red, nylon lobby cushion and looked at Fadi who was still wearing his *I Heart Brooklyn* t-shirt. He had recently wet his hair and slicked it back. He either hadn't been home or only had one t-shirt. He suddenly looked very tired and very young.

'Okay Fadi,' I smoked. 'You promised me tunnels, that was the deal, and I still want the terror tunnels. Anything less and I won't be able to pay you, it's not worth it. You understand?'

Fadi was nodding earnestly. I needed him to leave before Nasser arrived, so I gathered my laptop and stood up so quickly I felt woozy. Fadi followed my cue and gathered his skinny limbs to stand. I fished 20 shekels from my pocket and handed it to him.

'Get credit for your phone. I'll call you tonight for an update and what will you do, Fadi? Yes? You will answer!'

Before he could take the crumpled note from my hand, Stuart Finch had blown into the lobby and was gesticulating broadly next to us.

'Unbelievable news, Simon!' he shouted through his nose into his phone, unloading his dusty flak and notebook heavily onto our neighbouring table.

Unburdened, he stood there, sweaty and grinning, one hand resting jauntily on his belt.

'You know the Hamas border patrol guys I was with yesterday . . . . yeah, that one, their only border patrol . . . Yes, you have it. You do have it! Mate! Mark got the copy last night . . . Anyway, listen! The story just got so much better. They all just got blown up! . . . YES! All of them! . . . I know! Drove right over an unexploded shell and boom! No more Hamas border patrol!'

He laughed with shoulder-pumping booms. Fadi slowly took the note from my hand and put it in his pocket, fixing Stuart with an uneasy stare.

'I will get credit for my phone,' he said. 'Thank you, Sara.'

11
CHILD MONSTERS

A man was picking his way through the smouldering ruins of the Ministry for Information and Technology, pieces of official-looking paper in various states of burn floating in the air around him. He stepped through a charred window frame on his march across the blackened terrain muttering *Allahu Akbar, Allahu Akbar, Allahu Akbar* over and over again. On the opposite side of the road to the bombed government complex, a row of shops was scorched: a pharmacist, a kebab shop, a place that sold sunglasses. The juice place in particular looked like it had been firebombed. The windows of the mosque next to it were blown out.

'What did this? An F16? Bomb?'

I was not good on weaponry.

'They're saying it was eight rockets fired from a naval ship.'

I picked up one of the fluttering documents and showed it to Nasser, who narrowed his eyes to read it.

'It's a time log,' he deciphered. 'Employees in, employees out.'

He handed it back to me. I had enough war souvenirs, so I threw the paper back into the smoky bureaucratic apocalypse and we stood looking around for a bit. Nasser kicked a bit of window frame.

'I guess we should talk to some people,' I said.

'Sure,' he said.

We found a man sweeping inside the sunglasses shop. A lot of this war seemed to be middle-aged men calmly sweeping up their exploded lives but this one was sweeping half-heartedly and turned out to be very happy to stop and talk. This was the first time he'd been able to come and check on his business because it was the first moment of peace, he said. He'd been too terrified to go outside his home until now and just look at what he'd found! He gestured to his broken shop with his broom. His wife and kids had stayed inside their flat because they were still too terrified to leave.

'You can't run a business in a war. I've been closed since Al Jabari was killed. There's been big financial damage. Big. It'll take a long time to recover,' he said, shaking his head and leaning on his broom.

Possible economic story, I supposed. The guy went on talking about his business until even Nasser was bored.

'He's saying all the banks are closed, the businesses are closed... shortage of currency... we hope there's a truce... he really hopes there's a truce... there's no currency... his business can't open...'

'Thank you, sir!' I said to the man, who was still talking as we started our walk back to the car.

The man stood leaning on his broom watching us go and I thought how boring people will be boring even when extraordinary things happen to them. It was only when we walked past the burned pharmacy sign that I remembered Nasser's sick kid.

'Nasser! How's your kid doing?' I said, quick as I could, because my question was already hours late.

'Better, thank you,' Nasser said, chewing on his sunken cheeks as he stalked along.

'Really? That's good.'

'Yes, the doctors say he's stable.'

Stable was not good. It sounded good but it actually meant not yet dead. Dad's stable had lasted four days before he died, by which time I had left the country owing to the doctor's having told us he was stable. I stopped in my tracks.

'What's wrong with him?'

'They don't know yet,' he said, tight mouth twitching. 'He

has a fever and was having fits. You know, seizures. But they've stopped now.'

'Fits?'

I made a face. Fits really didn't sound good.

'He's not in Shifa, is he?'

I could smell the blood-steeped corridors and felt instantly queasy.

'No. I took him to a private one. My cousin's a doctor there.'

'Is it any good?'

'I hope so,' he said.

'What sort of fits?'

Nasser's mouth disappeared into a thin line, and he said he didn't want to talk about it anymore, so I said okay and got in the car feeling like total shit because Nasser's son looked like he might die and I hadn't even thought to ask after him. Of course Nasser couldn't have spared us that awkwardness and just told me like a normal person.

We started off to the UN school where families evacuated from the border areas were now living, and almost immediately hit a funeral procession on the road. It was a small one, only 20 or so men and a few weeping women following a Palestinian flag-draped body. The grieving group was pretty much contained to my side of the pavement, but I wanted to distract Nasser in case it got him thinking dark thoughts about his probably dying son so when the jazzy orientalised jingle that signalled breaking news came on the radio, I asked him to translate.

Almost 80 rockets had been fired out of Gaza so far that day, he said, including two towards Jerusalem. Only 50 of the rockets Hamas fired this war had so far managed to hit anything in Israel hurting no one other than that rabbi and his family. We drove passed the dead body and onto clear road.

'Did they land on anything?' I asked.

'They're saying one hit a Bedouin guy in southern Israel.'

'Did he die?'

'They don't know yet.'

'Shit! What are the odds? Another miraculous own goal for Hamas. What about Jerusalem? Very ambitious! Get anywhere close?'

'No. They hit a Palestinian village in the West Bank.'

'Fuck off! You're fucking kidding.'

I laughed a lot. Nasser wasn't laughing.

'What? Oh come on Nasser, it's a bit funny. Hamas have to be the worst terrorists ever!'

'No, I don't find Hamas funny.'

Nasser's lips had gone all white and tight again. I apologised but only because of the state his kid was in.

'Do you know any Italian photographers?' he asked.

I said almost all the photographers were Italian. I knew who they were but I didn't *know* them. Total sluts every one of them, riddled with communicable disease. The shahid anthems had come back on and he turned the radio down. There was an Italian photographer with the Hamas border patrol when it was blown up, Nasser said. He died from his injuries waiting to be evacuated to Israel.

My limbs flushed cold. It must have been one of the scarfed lobby guys. There was no network coverage so I couldn't check. Journalists didn't die in Gaza, they died in Afghanistan and Iraq. I hadn't once considered dying in Gaza. Even when F16s had smashed up the streets next to the Al Jabari funeral and Nasser and everyone else had run and hid, I kept walking down the middle of the road because I knew the bombs weren't meant for me. A kid had screamed in English for me to get out of the street, crazy woman, but I really hadn't seen the need.

We drove into another bigger funeral procession, this one green with Hamas flags. It quickly engulfed our car, letting out a volley of yips and *takbirs*. The radio was playing a happy military song and bursts of machine-gun and Kalashnikov fire erupted around us. Instinctively, I tried to drop, squeezing myself down in front of my seat even though a shitty Japanese car door would do nothing to protect me from machine gun bullets.

'Why do they do that? It's so fucking stupid!' I shouted angrily from my awkward squat.

I was much too big to fit more than my legs into the footwell, particularly in my flak jacket. Nasser looked around the car in a mime of searching for the bullets raining down on us but not finding any.

'It's tradition,' he said, once he'd finished miming.

'A tradition since when? How long have machine guns been around in Gaza?'

We drove past the white form of a body bobbing around in the middle of the still firing funeral party.

'Does anyone ever get hit?'

'Hit?'

'By the bullets they fire into the air? They have to come back down somewhere, because of gravity. Do they land on people?'

'Yes, occasionally.'

Punctilious truthfulness made arguments difficult for Nasser.

'There was a girl killed last year when her brother fired off some rounds celebrating his exam grades,' he admitted. 'But that's unusual. Usually they come down half a mile away and don't hit anyone.'

'A Spring Break *shahid*? Can you tell me that's not fucking stupid?'

I scowled out the closed window at the masked guys and their Kalashnikovs. Some outliers were looking in at me crouching, curious through their black face masks, so I slithered back up into my seat.

'It's a cultural thing,' Nasser said quietly.

'Cultural? It's not fucking bullet art! They're not making beautiful bullet ballets!'

Nasser was driving close past the front runners of the funeral group who let off another enthusiastic few rounds into the air above us.

'Like your culture is never stupid,' he muttered.

'Not *that* stupid.'

'No, they just give away countries that aren't theirs to give starting wars that spread across the world and burn for generations,' he snapped, glaring at the road. 'Sykes-Picot. Kissinger. Things like that.'

I tutted and he accelerated, driving on in silence until we reached a bright blue UN building with a huge white and blue sign that said New Gaza Preparatory School. Nasser's car was pinned between a truck piled high with mattresses and another truck jammed full, mostly of children and confused looking old people clutching bundles. The old faces looked bewildered to be packed into the back of a truck outside a preparatory school. Neither of the trucks was moving.

As the trucks didn't seem to be going anywhere, a swarm of kids had surrounded them and now our car yelling and playing some version of football. Their game involved a lot of very loud shouting and passing the ball through the truck wheels and around mattresses and piles of bags. Behind them a plume of black smoke rose in the sky from the crater of the bombed ministry.

'Where are we?'

'El Nasser Neighbourhood.'

'Ha! Nasser in El Nasser!' I joked, but Nasser's bird head was out of the window, straining to see if there was a way past the trucks, which there wasn't.

'What does Nasser mean again? It means Egyptian, doesn't it?' I raised my voice so he could hear.

'No,' he said.

'What does it mean?'

'Winner.'

Was that a Nasser joke? I didn't think so, he was huffing. He abandoned trying to navigate around the truck, switched off the engine and busily began winding up his window. Apparently, we were just going to leave the car in the middle of the street.

I opened my door into a writhing pit of children. There were tens of them, all pulling and pushing at each other. Kid mobs are unpredictable and uncontrollable and make me very uncomfortable. Individually, a kid might be normal, even shy, but in a pack they are emboldened. Unclean hydras with head lice and one or two English phrases they chant over and over again in a creepy singsong while pushing and shoving and trying to get close to you.

'Hello what is your name?'
'How are youuuu?'
'Hellooo!'
'What is your name?'
'How are youuuu?'

The child monsters laughed hysterically at nothing funny. I walked as quickly as I could through them, trying my best to behave as though they didn't exist. But I'd forgotten Nasser's thing with children; they always seemed to like him. You'd have thought his pointy eagle face would put them off, but he was kid catnip. As we strode towards the school building, a subgroup that had broken off from the pack bounded along next to us, pulling at Nasser's elbows and laughing at whatever it was he was saying to them.

Inside the school, the hallways and stairwells were swarming with people. Mattresses were being carried in and out of classrooms. Piles of blankets and bags and the interiors of kitchens lined the corridors. Someone had brought their TV and was sleeping slumped across it. The school acoustics amplified the chaos into a claustrophobic clamour.

We found a hive of pale teachers huddled in the headmaster's office. They were meant to be managing things but clearly were not. I couldn't really hear what anyone was saying above the noise. An intense looking woman in her 30s wearing a green hijab, started shouting at me in English: *300 families here so far, 1800 or so people in total, most from Beit Lahiya and Shejaiya.* Nasser was talking to another teacher in Arabic who seemed to be listing names of families and he began to pass this useless information on to me.

'The Tambora family is here, they all came in a rush last night after the Israelis dropped leaflets telling them to leave. Some of them didn't know to come last night so slept in the street and are only turning up now.'

I felt a sharp nudge in my lower back and turned to see an ancient woman with a deeply vexed expression and a basket of clothes on her head pushing to get past me. The weight of living had at some point folded her body completely in half and as she went by, the edge of her clothes basket almost skewered my kidney through the gap in my flak. I yelped but she didn't care or notice because she was so old and vexed. Now my back hurt.

Nasser had made friends with the teacher in the green hijab and wanted us to go with her on a tour of the classrooms. I could find no reasonable argument against the idea and so walked slowly behind them, rubbing my bruised lower back. We walked up staircases crowded with baskets, shopping bags, prone bodies and carpets, and entered a particularly crowded room where several old people were lying on mattresses on the floor and a pregnant woman sat at a school desk surrounded by children of various ages. Something about the set-up looked unsanitary even though they had probably only been there a few hours. The green hijab teacher approached the pregnant woman. These couldn't all be her children, there were about 12 of them and she was no older than 30.

'They're from Al Atara neighbourhood, behind Beit Lahiya... They slept on the street last night...' Nasser started translating. 'She doesn't know where they slept exactly but it was near here, next to a mosque.'

I pointed out that every other block in Gaza has a mosque.

'They just had clothes with them, and they used them to protect the children... the children were crying, they hugged the children . . . they told them stories . . . bombs were still dropping nearby . . . they came with nothing.'

Except a lot of children and televisions. We went into four crowded classrooms and heard various versions of this same story. One room with posters of plates divided into fruit, grains, meat and cheese on the walls had five families in it. All of them had arrived during the night. I asked if any of them had a copy of the leaflet the Israelis had airdropped but no one did. I still hadn't seen one even though there had apparently been thousands. What did it say exactly?

'The kids tore them all up,' one of the mothers said.

Having experienced first-hand the ferocity of the children, this rang true.

'When they started falling, we panicked and grabbed the most precious things and . . . '

'Why is this happening?' a short angry man interrupted in English.

The way the mother fell silent and looked exhausted led me to believe this man was her husband. Nasser fell silent too. Suddenly the room was hushed and tense. The short angry man had bloodshot eyes and a Saddam Hussein moustache. He would have been threatening if he weren't quite so short.

'Why is the international community letting this happen?' he shouted in furious falsetto, glaring into my eyes, jabbing his finger at me.

The international community? Who was that? Apparently, it was me for this man and now for everyone in the classroom.

'It's America who's to blame! Where are the Americans now? Who gave Obama his victory in the last elections? The Zionists! Is Barak Obama stopping them dropping bombs on us? No! He is *sending* the bombs! What did my children do? Does he look like a terrorist to you?'

The angry man pointed at a blushing teenage boy with vivid facial acne who was presumably his son and abruptly abandoned his pursuit of answers. His jaw closed into a clench and his jabbing finger fell back to his side. He wandered off morosely towards the empty back row of desks to stroke his moustache. I wanted to leave the school now.

Grabbing Nasser by the elbow, I told him in a low voice it was time to leave. He said something in a whisper to the teacher and we followed the back of her green head down the stairs, against an upward stream of bodies, bags and mattresses. We passed through the big swing-doors and out into the bright heat of the sandy courtyard where we were immediately surrounded again by children, dripping from Nasser like syrup.

From above our heads the thundering whine of jets then the unnatural silence. I now knew what was coming and dropped to the playground dirt as the first bomb landed. The ear-splitting cry of a hundred children screaming and after a long moment, a tidal wave of bodies propelled by tearing arms and legs. I had my eyes shut tightly against the bomb dust but I could feel them around me, bony limbs clawing towards the school steps and the shelter of the building. Another blast. Then quickly two more. More screaming, more pummelling from the child waves.

I counted four blasts. When I was fairly sure there were no more coming, I opened my eyes. No one around me was hurt so the bombs must have hit a nearby street. Car alarms were screaming like a flock of blinded birds. I saw Nasser crouching next to me. He looked at me, it was time for us to run. We set off in a low scramble towards the car. Inside, the screams of the UN school were muted. The trucks had vanished. Nasser started the engine and I saw that his hands were shaking. I looked at my own hands, they were perfectly steady.

12
Jiminy Cricket

Only Arabs come into Gaza through Egypt. For foreign journalists, the end of the world theatre at Erez Crossing is unavoidable. That great concrete wall at Israel's vast unmanned citadel clunks open and you are ejected down the lonely one and a half kilometres of caged pathway through the apocalypse-scape of the borderlands towards the way too narrow turnstile at Fatah's Hamza-Hamza checkpoint to be sprung finally from Israel's militarised womb into Palestinian Death World. Like any birth, it's at best disorientating, at worst an existential rupture.

Nasser's no idiot. He knew this. He knew each time I came to Gaza he'd be the first person I'd see, standing by the *Informers Will Be Executed* poster, all sphynx-ish in his pressed jeans and sports shirts, arms folded, holding my Hamas press credentials like a passport to the Underworld. More spirit guide than human fixer, he levitated past the Hamas checkpoint that upset my underwear in its hunt for illegal booze, through the Mad Hatter insanity of the Hamas ministries, to emerge without a glitch on a sofa in some widow's living room. He had access to everyone and entry anywhere, the ghost of Gaza past and present. It was uncanny but as Gaza itself proves, the unthinkable can quickly become ordinary.

The Tribune's multiple-award-winning Middle East correspondent Anthony Harper, like most staff correspondents, did not want to go to Gaza. Why would he? Editors and readers didn't want to hear about it unless it was being substantially destroyed. It was an almighty pain in the ass getting in and out, and the migraine-inducing diesel air, lack of alcohol and general normalised horror of Gaza life meant it wasn't much fun once you were in. But Anthony covered the Israeli-Palestinian conflict and Gaza is a significant slither of Palestine, so what to do? Find a lackey prepared to spend any length of time there in exchange for a by-line is what he did, which was smart.

Whenever Hamas started up with its simmering and spitting of rockets into Israel, or Oxfam released one of its reports about kids in Gaza drinking raw sewage because Israel had systematically bombed its sewage treatment plants, Anthony magnanimously dispatched me through the strip-searching Israeli interrogation merry-go-round at Erez Crossing into this boozeless, airless, electricity-starved slice of conflict so that I might try to make a name for myself and he could be left on his bar stool in Jerusalem, poised to cover the greater Middle East. In the two years since I'd met Anthony, he had been to Gaza no times. I had been more than 10, and as Nasser was *The Tribune*'s contracted fixer in Gaza, I always worked with him.

But it wasn't until my fourth trip that I got the measure of him. We'd already spent hours alone together, driving in his too hot car, accepting glass after glass of sweet fizzy drinks and sugar-thick tea from sad mothers and subdued daughters. I knew that he never ate anything before noon and that he was self-conscious of, even revolted by, his own feet so always wore socks. He saw himself as spiritual but not dogmatic and absolutely not conservative, despite being both. He could recite books of Arabic poetry and privately thought himself quite a fine poet. I asked to hear some of his poetry but he said it didn't translate well. English is a very basic language, he said. Like Spanish. Arabic, on the other hand, has more than 20 words for lion: *noble lion, sly lion, proud lion.*

One of his kids was sickly so we were forever stopping at pharmacies. His wife thought the boy needed meat, so Nasser often made us stop by the butcher in the old city market that made me think strange thoughts about mortality with its huge, flayed cow carcasses, tails still on the big, bloody, skinless bodies. But I was never invited to Nasser's home. It was Anthony Harper who had been asked to his apartment, who'd met his family. I knew this because Nasser told me about it repeatedly and always with that wet, wistful look that said, 'God those were great times when Anthony Harper came to my house and met my kids and let my wife cook for him. Those may have been some of the best of times.'

Nasser hardly even spoke to me about his family. He didn't mention them at all until my fourth visit, when we were stuck in traffic on the long drive back from Rafah to Gaza City. We'd been doing the story about Libyan jeeps being smuggled into Gaza through the smuggling tunnels from Egypt and had met a man in a white tracksuit and a lot of gold chains who was selling cars with blood still on the drivers' seats from where the previous owners had been shot dead in Tripoli. It was a good story, and we were both upbeat. We were on the road somewhere just past Deir al Balah—I remember because of the shit-smell cloud that hangs over Deir al Balah—and had reached that confessional point you get to after hours spent in a car with anyone. I was trying not to breath in through my nose and Nasser was asking me how it was that I had passed 30 and not had children. He asked me if I didn't want kids and I said I didn't know, maybe someday. He asked me what I was doing about it and I shrugged. He asked if he could be honest with me and I told him okay and he said that my big problem was a lack of self-worth.

'Excuse me Sara but I see it,' he said. 'It's clear.'

He then told me the story of how he met his wife as a parable about self-worth. Nasser had been teaching journalism at the Islamic University of Gaza, which made total sense, Nasser being a teacher. He first saw her in a crowd of students. She was laughing at something a friend had said and there was something in her eyes, he knew right away he was going to marry her. I told him that in the UK he would have been sacked for professional misconduct and he laughed heartily to himself about crazy Western double standards.

His future wife's dad was a pharmacist who smoked heavily and would eventually die of emphysema. The dad had thought his daughter was too young to marry, she'd never even had a boyfriend before, she needed to finish university first, and he refused Nasser's proposal. But Nasser persevered. Why did Nasser do this? Because he trusted his instincts. He knew he was right.

He visited her family every Saturday at their home until eventually the father allowed Nasser to take his daughter out alone for coffee. He discovered her sweet tooth and started to bring her the syrupy cakes every afternoon that made her happy. Then after four years of coffee and a lot of sugar, her father the pharmacist, who was by this point very sick, gave in and agreed to the marriage. She was 24, Nasser was 33. The pharmacist died on their first wedding anniversary.

'We've been married 10 years and have two beautiful children, *alhamdulillah*.'

He turned to look at me, his sharp face, briefly illuminated by the headlights of an oncoming motorbike, loaded with foreboding.

'How old are you, Sara?'

I was 32 and didn't get the point of his story. If I were less of a slut, I would be easier to spot in a crowd? If only I had a stronger sense of self, I too might spend four years obsessively persuading a man to love me using cake? His message wasn't clear, but his tone was judgemental and spoke of regret that I was already old and used and at this rate unlikely to attract any sort of man. What I also took from it was that after 10 years of fucking his wife, Nasser cared a lot less about her happiness—we hadn't stopped at a bakery even once. But he cared a lot about his moral high ground. Maybe his wife was obese now, or diabetic.

By my sixth visit, Nasser seemed to think he had the measure of me. We had gone to interview a widower who was handsome in that particular grey-haired, Roman-nosed, twinkly Michael sort of way, even though this man's twinkle was the weary kind that had clearly fought hard to survive. His wife had just died of cancer. Breast cancer is very common in Gaza, but they can't treat it, Nasser told me on the drive there. They don't have they drugs or the equipment so patients have to get permission from the Israelis to leave for treatment in Israeli hospitals. The wife had fought a long battle, years, and then finally didn't get permission in time to leave for a round of treatment and died.

'It's the children I worry about,' the man said, looking rumpled and attractive over a plate of inedible stale biscuits. 'How can I fill the hole she's left in their lives?'

I don't offer opinions in interviews, interviews are for the opinions of interviewees, but this man's story really annoyed me.

'And what, you're just accepting this is your life?' I exploded.

Nasser looked at me sharply. He was struggling to form what I'd said into an acceptable question when tears rushed into my eyes. Then I was crying, properly crying. Nasser noticed and was further thrown off his translating game. We'd met dying orphaned kids, interviewed weeping 60-year-old hospital directors and homeless widows, and I'd never so much as welled up. Gaza's mind-bending new dimension of misery had taken getting used to but it had never ever made me cry before. Nasser was dumbfounded.

'It's okay,' the handsome widower said in faltering English, smiling and offering me a tissue from a large, ornate tissue box. 'God has His plan for each of us.'

I excused myself from the widower's flat to sob in his concrete hallway. I'd had episodes like this before. I just needed to be alone until the crying spasm passed, then the numb hollowness would come and everything would be back to normal. I recovered enough to say goodbye to the confused, attractive man and we left. In the car on the way back to the hotel, Nasser's quiet was unusually tender. He looked over a few times to examine me, slumped in the passenger seat.

'You know, it's not weak to get upset. Sometimes it shows strength. It means you're still human,' he said.

I nodded and chewed my lip.

'Keep that humanity, Sara. So many who come here have already lost it.'

I nodded again.

'Was it the kids?' he asked, softly.

I shook my head.

'That poor man.'

'He was very brave,' Nasser said, then let the engine sound fill the car again.

'Brave? He gave up years of his life to be the husband of a dying woman. Now she's dead and he's trapped himself again as the dutiful father.'

As I talked, I got angrier.

'That's not brave, it's a stupid waste of a life. You heard what he said about it all being okay, it being God's plan or whatever? A man like that doesn't believe in shit like that, he's just saying what he's expected to say.

'I bet he didn't even love her in the first place, probably got forced into it. What sort of businessman is he? If he were *brave*, he would leave those kids with her family, get a permit, get out. Go to Germany or somewhere, live his life, find someone he actually likes!'

The air around Nasser hardened. He lowered his window and leaned his arm outside, making a sucking noise with his tight little mouth.

'What?' I asked.

He clicked his tongue against the back of his teeth and jerked his head back, indicating that he had nothing to say.

'Don't tut at me. What is it?' I demanded.

Nasser continued his cheek sucking out the window for some time before deciding to answer.

'Okay. If you want to hear it, I was thinking that I've never ever met such a cynical person. Never, and it's my job to work with foreign journalists.'

'Cynical? I'm *not* cynical,' I argued, flushed with indignation. 'That man's life is over because he hasn't left his kids for a German woman? He never loved his dead wife?'

I guffawed.

'That's not cynicism, it's realism. You just don't want to admit it.'

'No!' Nasser was close to shouting. 'What's real is that people love their families. Here we have faith and community and that gives us strength. But you can't admit that because *you* don't have any of it and probably never will!'

He narrowed his eyes on the darkening road, reading the shadowy potholes like runes. We hit one and the car jumped.

'You know, you'll need to be honest with yourself Sara at some point. If you ever want to be happy,' he said finally, voice hushed with judgement.

'Wow! That's nice. Quite the mean little fortune cookie, aren't we Nasser?'

'We're what?'

'Don't worry about it. I'll just sit here, trying to be honest with myself.'

We continued our drive back to the hotel in disturbed silence, me dark with fury, him an anguished Jiminy Cricket hunched over the wheel with his spiky insect body. Cynical? Nasser had no idea.

13
Cancer Cathy

'Bob, it's just so awful. How could a person be that cruel? And to *Cathy*? Poor Cath! SHE DIDN'T EVEN HAVE HER WIG ON!'

Ma was making an apple pie wearing her appalled face unaware that smears of white flour across her cheeks, nose and forehead were undermining the gravity of whatever was so appalling her. This was the face she reserved for life-altering accidents or moral depravity so gross they could only be purged through detailed re-telling. It was usually a signal for me to walk away or tune out, except when the awful thing had been done to her friend Cathy by Cathy's husband Michael.

'Oh Bob, you're cutting sideways? Always cut lengthways!'

'What's so awful? Ma?'

'Do you ever cook, sweetheart? Are you watching?'

Ma stole the paring knife from my hand and with her best maternal forbearing, demonstrated how to correctly dissect a potato for roasting. Handling the slippery vegetable deftly, she skinned it then dropped long quarters into a large pot of salted water on the counter. My mutilated potato was dispatched with prim disappointment into the bin.

'Some people just halve the potato, which is fine, but then you absolutely need to score it.'

'Ma! What was the awful thing that happened to Cathy when she didn't have her wig on?'

Ma returned to sucking in her big, flat cheeks with disbelieving sadness and rolling out her short crust with a pin as heavy as her heart.

'She's had her suspicions, of course, for a while. She's so

private Cathy, she barely hinted at them, even to me. Imagine having to pickpocket your own husband's phone! Well, Cathy wouldn't, not without good reason.'

The rolling pin was levelled threateningly at my face, dripping flaps of shortcrust.

'This goes nowhere, Sara. Do you hear me? Not a word, even to your father. Cathy is *such* a private woman. The humiliation would kill her quicker than the cancer.'

Prickling heat flushed from my chest, up my neck and into my cheeks. Ma flipped the pastry disc violently and dusted it with a dismayed handful of flour.

'What did she suspect, Ma?'

Ma shook her head at the dough and resumed her pummelling.

'The business dinners that lasted until 2am, the weekend conferences. I love her, I do, but honestly Bob, a conference of literary agents in Paris? In August? Who is ever in Paris in August?'

I shrugged. Michael and I had actually never been to Paris. We had only ever managed to go abroad together once and that was to Amsterdam for that weekend when he got us the Colombian massage girl I hadn't been so sure about. And that was in April.

'I mean we all *assumed* he was cheating. You need to take one look at the man.'

Ma shuddered as if she hadn't been flirting shamelessly with Michael for decades. She broke off her heavy-handed rolling to push a frizzy forelock of fringe back from her forehead with her wrist. Her flirting was aggressive and had mostly involved her calling him a shit while glinting at him coquettishly.

'Roll my sleeves up for me, will you Bob?'

She held out her hands, webbed with butter and pastry, and I obediently reached over the counter to fold her sleeves above her elbows, freeing an old tissue from her cuff to float gently onto my chopping board.

'It's only your father who can't see it. Won't hear a bad word about *Dear Michael Frazer*, not since he called him a genius.'

Ma snorted and the snotty tissue was sent to the bin to join my mauled potato.

'You remember that Bob? When Michael Frazer gushed about one of Bill's essays being *genius* and your father suddenly started wearing hats? Forget that Michael never actually sells anything your father writes. How that man manages to get people to swallow *quite* so much bullshit . . .'

I threw the last slithers of my potatoes into the pot and stabbed the paring knife into the chopping board.

'Ma! What happened to Cathy?'

Ma sighed deeply and swivelled her pastry disc.

'So, there she was naked in the bath, vulnerable, mastectomy scars on display, no wig. And he, Michael, was cleaning his teeth, in his boxer shorts. And she was looking at him from the bath, the man she's shared a home with for 25 years, the father of her children.'

That stung. Cathy may not fuck Michael but she still got him every morning, brushing his teeth, putting on his socks, drinking his coffee. And then she had the kids and the cancer that meant he would never leave. She got the holidays, the house, his mother's ring. Cancer Cathy with Everything.

'It's *so* humiliating! A proud woman like Cathy, who's been so brave. She took his phone when he was in the shower and read just as much as she could stomach. Sara, these messages were filth! The utter *filth* in that man's head!'

My heart thudded blood to my cheeks. I hadn't heard from him for months, even after her treatment ended. It all made sense now, she had found us out. She had his phone!

'So, she spent the whole morning crying and crying, but by the time he came home that evening, she'd had the day to calm down. Think it through. She had made a life with this man, 25 years, two children. If she told him calmly that she had found out about the affair and asked him with dignity, without drama, to end it for the sake of their marriage, for her health, she was sure he would.'

When had this happened? Did Cathy know it was me? Did Ma know? My face burned. No, he would have warned me. And even if she knew, Cathy wouldn't have told Ma. Would she? Jesus Christ, did Ma *know*? I looked at her, busily pressing the edges of her pastry disk onto her pie with a fork. She winced and bit her lip as a slip released a spurt of purple blackberry juice across the pie's pristine whiteness. No, she didn't know. Dabbing the blackberry gore off with a piece of kitchen towel, she shot me a sly look. Did she?

'With who, Ma? Who was he messaging?'

'With *whom*. With *whom* was he messaging. So for some reason, God knows why, she decides to confront him when she's naked and hairless in the bath. She admits she took his phone. She tells him that she's seen the messages, she knows about the affair and asks him please, for the sake of the kids, for her health, to just end it.'

Ma dropped her berry-blooded fork and placed her giant flour hands dramatically on her wide hips.

'And can you guess what that man says to her? To his wife of almost 30 years, to the cancer victim naked in the bath in front of him? Can you guess?'

It was 30 years now. No, I could not guess.

'He turned to look at her.'

Ma turned to look at me.

'He looked her square in the face.'

She looked me square in the face, eyebrows arched in the attitude of a Lothario.

'And he told her: *You have no idea how hard your cancer has been for me. I can't take it anymore. I'm leaving.*'

What?

'So, there she is, naked, hairless in the bath. Stunned! She tells him she still loves him, that she can forgive him, they'll work it out, and he tells her, cold as ice, "But Cathy, I don't love you. I don't think I ever have."

'Sara! It's not funny! Why are you laughing? *You have no idea how hard your cancer has been for me? I don't think I ever loved you?* It's the most awful thing I've ever heard!'

I hadn't realised I was laughing. I tried to stop by covering my mouth with my hand.

'Sorry! It's just so awful. I'm laughing at how awful it is.'

Why hadn't he told me? Was it a surprise? Would he want to be *together* now? What about those weird sad kids? I wrenched my features into a frown.

'Who is she? Does Cathy know?'

'Oh Bobs, it's so predictable. Cath actually met her countless times but never even noticed. One of the baby agents at his office, a little mouse type girl, very ordinary. But 26! Can you imagine? TWENTY-SIX, Bobs! Half his age! Really, it's disgusting.'

A surge of dread uncertainty made me suddenly nauseous. I was exactly half his age, 26 was less than half his age.

'Really? What's her name?'

'You won't know her. I don't know, it's Poppy or something. No. Something that screams Sloaney hussy. Nessie? No, wait. Mimi! That's it, she's called Mimi! Can you imagine being left for a Mimi?'

'Mimi?'

'I know! It's too awful.'

I sat down heavily on the high stool at the kitchen counter and chewed distractedly on an apple core. *Mimi?*

'Bob, don't eat the cores! You're scoffing like a fat child, stop it. He's already moved out of the house. The boys have met her, without even asking Cath, can you imagine? She's basically their age. All in less than a month! Totally ludicrous, some pathetic late midlife crisis. Obviously, poor Cathy's in bits. I saw her today and Bob, I couldn't believe how thin.'

Ma's voice suddenly softened and she wiped her sticky

hands on her filthy apron, peering at me as though I were a deep, murky well.

'Bobs? Why are you breathing like that? Did it go down the wrong way? Should I help you?'

Ma regarded me with distant alarm from across the counter. Who the fuck was Mimi?

'Bill? BILL! Quickly! I think Sara's choking again!'

14
THE BOLD AND THE BEAUTIFUL

'Sara, you're sick?'

Front desk Mohammed's face was a tragic mask of concern.

'No, I'm fine.'

I smiled at him normally.

'But your face! You're not sleeping? Is it the bombs?'

He raised a delicate hand to touch his own round face.

'No, I'm sleeping fine. That's just my face.'

I stopped smiling. I had put on lip gloss, I looked nice. Had he seen his own face? It was a perfect perspiring circle. He looked like the Man in the Moon if the Man in the Moon had cholera, but was I telling him that?

'Oh Good!'

Mohammed beamed anxiously at me but I was no longer in a smiling mood. I scanned the lobby for Italians. The desk wanted a story about the dead photographer. The American TV crews were back in their usual spot at the tables closest to the TVs, delivering sincere and detailed food orders to the small, fat waiter who was sweating prodigiously. The generators were screaming. The alcoves were full and noisy, but I couldn't see any Italians.

'Mohammed, have you seen any of the Italians?'

'Oh my so sad. So, so sad.'

His features reformed into their tragedy mask.

'Poor Massimo. Poor, poor Massimo.'

I said yes it was very sad and asked him if he had seen any of Massimo's friends as I'd like to offer my sympathies. Mohammed seemed relieved by this suggestion and said actually yes, Marco,

Alessandro, Carolina were all still here. Lovely people, always in the courtyard smoking. He laughed at this as though smoking in the courtyard was one of the funniest things Marco, Alessandro and Carolina could think to do. I left him shaking his head affectionately at the crazy smoking Italians.

Sure enough the surviving photographers were huddled together by the potted palms in the restaurant courtyard under a fog of cigarette smoke like mosquitoes under a streetlamp. I paused in the doorway, undecided as to which one to approach. Obviously not the woman. There was a blond stocky one who seemed to be crying already. His broad shoulders were heaving and his face was covered with a blue cotton scarf. I moved slowly to stand close beside him and pressed my glossed lips together to plump them.

'Hi,' I said gently at first, then louder because he didn't respond. 'Hello!'

The squat blond figure raised his enormous head to reveal two bulging, wet, blue eyes. They regarded me wide with shock, looking to see who had disturbed their weeping.

'Hi. I just wanted to say how sorry I was to hear about your friend.'

The eyes quickly crinkled again and resumed their deep, silent sobbing into the damp scarf. I placed a comforting hand gently on the Italian's muscular, blond forearm.

'I'm really sorry,' I said.

He choked with distress and nodded. After some minutes standing like that in the courtyard, he agreed mutely to my suggestion that we move to a table in the lobby and get a coffee. I led him to the darkest table in the most private alcove and ordered our coffees from the fat unfriendly waiter.

The Italian sat like a giant sad puffin, heavy tears falling in unimpeded torrents down either side of his large beaked nose. I watched him as he cried and smoked, lighting every cigarette before he had extinguished the last, each papery stick soon becoming soggy with snot and spit and tears. Two packs of

Marlboro Reds sat stacked on the low table in front of him like comforters. I took one and lit it. He wiped his big nose with the back of his big, square hands, which were carpeted with thick white hairs, and slowly began to talk with glassy puffin eyes.

'He was my brother. Really. You know how that goes, when you see enough death with another person, feel that fear together, all the moments of joy, they become family. You know?'

Did I know that? Did Nasser think I was his family? Was Nasser my family? No he was not. Alessandro had met Massimo in Afghanistan where they were rivals, he told me. Both newswire photographers, one working for Reuters the other for AFP. They had grown up streets away from each other in Rome but never met until they were both embedded with the same US army unit in Helmand.

'We were chasing the same girl in Kabul, this beautiful, sexy Spanish with the UN.'

He chuckled, his eyes shining with laughing tears.

'Max went so crazy for her. He stood outside her window screaming he would kill himself with the bottle of wine he'd brought her if she didn't let him in. He didn't know I was inside with her.'

The Italian began to laugh until he sobbed.

'We fucked her together in the end.'

He took a deep long sigh, lost in that memory.

'I'm sorry, you don't mind me talking like this, do you? I don't even know your name.'

'It's Sara. And no, I don't mind.'

I smiled at him with the look of a woman who could hear a lot of talk about people fucking and not mind.

'*Saaraa*,' he repeated my name, making it Italian and put his big clammy hand heavily over mine, squeezing it tightly before letting go.

So did Max have a wife? A girlfriend? Alessandro laughed loudly at the ludicrousness of this idea. Max? Max could not have one woman! He was too free, too beautiful. No one could expect such a person to live the conventional life. To settle down? Not Max, no way. He was the *world's* lover, an artist, a nomad. But Max's mother, he worshipped her, and she worshipped him. He was so good to her. And kind. The night before he died, he was saying that when he got back from Gaza, he was going to start a charity for football kids in war zones. So excited. Massimo's story dissolved here in his friend's heavy tears.

I looked up suddenly, feeling the sharp psychic prod of someone looking at me and found the cleaner's son was squatting on the lowest stair of the lobby staircase, watching our table the way normal people watch television. He didn't look away when I caught his eye.

'Alessandro,' I persevered, trying to unsee our audience.

'Sandro. Friends call me Sandro.'

Alessandro smiled winsomely at me with his big bloodshot eyes.

'Sandro,' I smiled back with my glossy lips. 'I'm here with *The Tribune*. I think it would be nice to write a profile about Max, a tribute. Do you think his mother would speak to me? It would have to be this evening, unfortunately.'

Alessandro wiped his dripping nose with the flat palm of his hand, which he then rubbed thoughtfully on his thigh. He said that maybe she would. He'd spent some weeks at her home two summers ago with Max, after Afghanistan. Yes, he would call Signora Giordano, he must. Why hadn't he already? Che cazzo! *Che cazzo vero!* He smacked the table violently with his open palm then went back out to the courtyard to call his dead friend's mother.

I went to the toilets behind reception to apply more sticky peach lip gloss. I took my time about it, following the contours of my mouth with thick swathes of the pearly, shimmering goop. I tucked my t-shirt into my jeans, smoothed my hair down, picturing how the Italian's cock would look in my mouth.

I went back out into the lobby the small face still following me with its hard, unblinking eyes. Was that weird child smirking? I glared at him furiously and he looked back impassively. This gawping offensive would have to stop. I pivoted, walked up to the boy purposefully and asked him slowly and deliberately what he thought he was looking at. He blinked but didn't answer.

'DO YOU UNDERSTAND ENGLISH?' I enunciated.

'Yes, of course I understand English.'

The voice that emerged from the wizened child's head was startling. Deep and gravelly, it had the fluid confidence of a well-educated man.

'Whereas *you* don't seem to speak more than two words of Arabic.'

The boy allowed himself a snort of amusement. I told him coldly that his English was very good and asked why that was. He asked in return if I had ever watched Arab television, raised a thick, dark, sardonic eyebrow, crinkling his burnt parchment forehead, and issued another derisive snort.

'My mother likes *The Bold and the Beautiful*, it's one of the few American shows they broadcast here. Gaza gets a lot more Turkish television in general, but we watch *The Bold and the Beautiful*. I suppose I do read a fair amount of English writers too, like Charles Dickens. *Great Expectations* is my favourite of his books, I've read it twice. So yes, I suppose, I speak English quite well but my Turkish is better. Also I have some Hebrew and a bit of Russian. I plan to learn French. *Parles vous français*? It would be better if you spoke *something*.'

Even stranger than the pompous, perfectly pronounced English pouring from the mouth of a one-eyed Palestinian cleaner's child was the impression that the words didn't seem to be the point at all. They were gushing out like rose-scented water from a storm drain while some crueller train of thought ran on in his head. His imp eyes twinkled with amusement.

'I speak German,' I lied.

The boy shrugged his bony shoulders as if German didn't count as a language.

'Why are you watching me?' I asked.
'Why have you got all that stuff on your mouth? What is it?'
'How old are you?'
'11 and a half.'
'Really? I thought you were younger,' I said, spitefully.

His thick brow shot up again, triggering another ripple of papery wrinkles.

'Sara?'

Alessandro was striding back into the lobby from the courtyard, pulling at his thick blond ringlets with his large fists.

'I'm here, Sandro!' I called.

Little Jihad smirked. I turned on my heel and walked self-consciously back to our table, stray strands of wispy hair sticking to my gloss. Alessandro was panting with short nicotiney breaths.

'I spoke with her, the mother. She says Max will be buried next to his father. I told her I would bring his cameras back for the funeral. I'll take the newest one for myself, he would want it, but the rest he needs with him. They were his *swworwds.*'

His what?

'He lived by them, he died by them. He should be buried with them.'

Oh, his *swords*. Alessandro's big shoulder blades heaved inside his linen shirt and I laid a large hand reassuringly on his arm. Feeling Jihad's smirk broaden, I retracted it.

'Did she say anything else?'

Alessandro raised his confused, wet face.

'His mother. Does she blame anyone for his death? Is she angry?' I prompted.

'Oh. No. She just says she hopes the Israelis will let him through quick. Every day her boy isn't in Roman soil is a day that brings her closer to death.'

'She said that?'

'*Si*,' he wept.

As far as grieving mum quotes went, it was poor. It didn't

even make sense. Whether her son was in Roman soil or an Israeli terminal building, every day was bringing her closer to death anyway. I squeezed his hand.

'Do you think she might have some pictures of Max as a child? Something she would like to share with us? Or maybe you, Sandro? Do you have any pictures of Max doing his work? Doing what he did best?'

Alessandro sniffed loudly and stopped crying. After a moment's thought he said that yes maybe he did but he would have to look through the hard drives in his room. I kept my hand on his and he sniffed thoughtfully. But of course he would have to be paid for the use of his images. I said I was sure that would be fine, and we sat in silence for a bit as he wiped his broad cheeks with the palm of his hand and shook his golden head disbelievingly. I took my hand back and lit another of his Marlboros.

'I'd better get up there and get started on this piece. Thank you Sandro. Max really was beautiful.'

Alessandro nodded into his cigarette smoke. From the corner of my eye I saw Jihad had leant forward, apparently straining to hear better. I walked out of the lobby leaving the Italian with his large head in his hands and stuck my middle finger up at the obnoxious little spy as I passed his stare, which the fat waiter clocked and seemed to think was for him. The waiter reacted furiously and little Jihad sniggered as I walked heavily upstairs to write my third piece of the day.

15
Understanden

By the time I finished my piece the Israeli gun boats had taken up their nightly tenderising of the northern coastline. I was happy with it.

Massimo Giordano, the first foreign journalist to be killed in this latest outbreak of violence in the Gaza Strip, was prepared to die for his work.

"If you go to war, be ready to bleed," the 36-year-old conflict photographer had often told his colleagues in the field.

It was a motto he believed in so deeply he planned to have it inked permanently onto his chest when he returned to his native Rome. Tragically, it will now be written on his gravestone.

Alessandro had told me that Max was addicted to tattoos and had more than 20. The biggest was a sketch of Michael Jackson's face on his groin with *Thriller* inked underneath it. He liked to ventriloquise with this one while he fucked, Alessandro said.

The deranged bird that had been terrorising my balcony was apparently building a nest, mostly of its own feathers and crap. It was hostile and unsanitary. Jihad would have to kill it. I glared with displeasure at the possibly health endangering shit nest through the open balcony doors then went in search of missing Jihad. The lobby was on deadline and the American TV reporter was circling the foot of the stairs in tight steps, rehearsing a piece to camera in full body armour, creating a vortex of hairspray smell that spiralled up to the first floor.

'Today, Anne, the secretary of state will break from her busy schedule in Cambodia to take a call with Benjamin Nitanyihau . . . Binymin Netanyahu . . . Binyamain Nit . . . .

'Anne, Secretary of State Clinton knows better than anyone that Israel must do whatever it takes to defend its citizens. But I'm hearing she will break from her schedule in Cambodia today to call the Israeli prime minister and warn him that any further escalation . . . '

No sign of Jihad or his trolly. The red-bereted blogger was hosting some sort of live web debate with headset in place and much performative eye-rolling in the direction of Steve Sweeney and Jane Sawyer, who were sitting side by side at the table opposite him, typing with concentration, not noticing.

'Kyle, you think we can't hear the Zionist propaganda in your argument?' Red Beret told an unseen panellist, scouring the lobby greedily for an available face to eyeroll at.

He glowed with delight at the atmospheric soundtrack of the call to prayer ringing out in time for this crescendo in his debate and I walked as quickly as I could in the opposite direction. Reception was unmanned, so I stormed back up the wide stone staircase, increasingly irritated by how hard it was to find a member of hotel staff to help me. I turned towards that unpleasant bit of the first floor with the unused meeting rooms and Steve Sweeney's odd little garret room. It would be just like Jihad to be lost cleaning this entirely unnecessary part of the hotel when he was urgently needed elsewhere.

The heavy door to the largest, never-used meeting room was ajar. I pushed it open and sure enough, there were the two mismatched forms of giant Jihad and little Jihad. Their backs were to me, one subdued bear, one shrunken acrobat, shoulder to hip, heads bowed to their chests. They had prayer carpets rolled out in front of them and Jihad was carefully leading his sprite son in ritual movement.

I was about to call out but stopped and watched instead. Little Jihad was uncharacteristically compliant, a physical echo of his huge father. Hands behind his ears, bending towards his mat, then on his knees, forehead touching the ground. I realised that Jihad's third eye was a faith tattoo, grazed into permanence by devotion. His son would have one too, a spiritual umbilical cord. The boy husked his prayers as an incantation.

Neither Jihad reacted when the door slammed noisily against the wall and I felt a sudden, deep uneasiness, like I was trespassing in some vast, strange, sacred place. I allowed the door to swing back and close in my face and felt a restless emptiness, as if my soul needed scratching. I would go and get something to eat.

Taking a table in the potted palm courtyard outside the blogger's field of vision, I sat feeling odd. Unable to rouse myself even to order food, I stared at my phone instead. It had received nothing other than a missed call from Ma. She had already requested by email and then text message that I call her but I couldn't face it. I would text Fadi. *You promised news*, I wrote. Why hadn't he called? I stared hard at my phone and made a silent deal with God that if Fadi delivered me the commander, I would call my mother.

'And here I am with news! Just like how I promised!'

I jumped wildly in my seat, sending Fadi into fits of theatrical giggles. He laughed hammily, doubling over and wiping imaginary tears from his eyes. He had sprung out of actual thin air. Was Fadi a message from God? Did I now actually have to call my mother? A new squat person was sniggering close behind him, a boy about twice his width and half his height but dressed in almost identical clothes. Skinny jeans did not suit this boy's physique. Squashed Fadi was grinning at me sheepishly. He had huge chocolate brown eyes and the rosy, chubby cheeks of a boy whose mother loved him too much.

'Fadi, you're *here*! And you brought a friend,' I told him, pointedly ignoring his painful clowning.

Fadi gasped for breath, leaning heavily on the back of my chair.

'A bit on the edge Sara? Sorry, *Kate*,' he giggled. 'No? Okay, so this is Sami, my colleague.'

Sami smiled uncomprehendingly on hearing his name. He clearly didn't understand anything that was being said.

'Your colleague?'

'Yeah, our driver. He has a car and he's going to drive us.'

'Drive us where, Fadi?'

Fadi hiked up the jeans that had begun to sag off his even skinnier hips. His leg had started to bounce jerkily.

'This is my news! The commander's father wants to meet us!'

He grinned broadly, his left eye squinting in spasms.

'The commander says we should meet him before he will agree to any interview. I guess they need to make sure you're not a Mossad spy or something.'

He laughed heartily at this, triggering a Pavlovian response in Sami who also started to laugh heartily. Who did this twitchy skinny fuck think he was, independently agreeing to terrorist father meetings? I was dizzy. I needed to eat.

'Two things, Fadi. No, three things.'

I struggled to control the level of my voice and Fadi's blinks accelerated.

'Number one, do not turn up at this hotel without asking me first, particularly not bringing *colleagues*. Serious journalists are working here trying to report on a war, it's not a fucking youth club.'

The angry talking was making my head spin, so I took a breath and lowered my voice to a spitty whisper.

'Secondly, never hire people—like non-English speaking drivers—without asking me. How much am I paying Sami out of interest? And lastly, never arrange meetings for me with terror cells in the middle of the night in the middle of a war without my explicit instruction!'

I was hearing the world from inside a thick bubble, acid rising obnoxiously in my throat. Fadi's face was red, embarrassed or angry or both, I didn't care. I cared about what I was going to do now. I would of course have to go and meet this terrorist's dad, which meant no time for supper. And I would have to tell someone before heading out into the heavily bombed night with two idiot teenagers. But who? Definitely not Nasser. And Desk Mohammed would only tell Nasser, snitch-face Mohammed. *Gay* Mohammed? At that moment, Alessandro bowled past on his short-legged swagger.

'Hey Sara, you good? You look not good. Are you good?' he asked me, staring hard at Fadi.

'I'm fine. I just need a smoke.'

I grabbed him by the elbow and led him away to the furthest corner of the courtyard. Alessandro looked at me intently with his bulging, blue eyes as I told him about my need to get across town to meet a contact and that no, I was sure I didn't need him to come with me. He looked down at his huge diver's watch.

'It's seven now. If I don't hear from you by 10, then I start to make calls.'

Who would he be calling? He locked me again in intense eye contact, raising his fist to his heart and placing his other hand heavily on my shoulder.

'Wear your flak and your helmet and don't be too brave. *Va bene? Basta morti!*'

I patted my own heart at a loss for any other response and swallowed a mouthful of bile.

'Okay,' I said.

The streets were black and empty, and Sami drove quickly. We passed the big checkpoint at the roundabout near the hotel and headed up the main street towards downtown and the house of the terrorist commander's father. Fadi had his window open, and the cool night air smelled of sea salt and sewage. Sami's car had the chemical, clean feel of a conscientious taxi driver's but it had no seatbelts and I had to hold my heavy body upright against the violent swings of his driving by my index finger, which was hooked into the tiny coat hook on the side of the door. It hurt. I was the only one wearing a flak jacket and helmet.

'We'll use the back streets. The coast road is too dangerous now,' Fadi told me over his shoulder.

'Okay,' I said.

Sami turned his Egyptian pop up and we drove past the swings in the square that hung still. All but a few streetlights were out and all the shops were closed, their shutters down. I looked at my hand resting in my lap and watched it change colour as we drove through the stray beams of streetlights. That same hand would at some point have no skin or flesh on it. It would just be bone and then it would be dust. Unless I was burned like Dad, then it would be dust immediately.

Sami took corners at speed. I asked Fadi if he knew that most journalists killed in war zones died in car accidents, and then pointed out that this is exactly how a militant would drive if he were speeding from a tunnel to a rocket launching site. He didn't answer. It was pointless to look for drones, you could never see them at night. Two old men passed us on a motorbike, one clinging to the other, their headlight on full beam.

'Fadi? Are we lost?' I asked from the back.

We had pulled over and Sami was looking out into the darkness while Fadi yelled at him.

'No we're not lost. We're looking for the right street.'

He yelled again violently at Sami in Arabic, who remained unfazed.

'Don't you guys have the address?'

Our voices strained to be heard over the music and through the sound bubble thickening in my ears.

'There are no addresses around here, you just have to know,' Fadi barked.

Sami made a sharp U-turn and sped back along the dark street. He braked hard outside the one shop that had its lights on and one shutter open. A very old man sat outside under a green, fluorescent light on a plastic chair in a thick woollen jumper, a dusty pinstripe blazer and flip-flops. Fadi yelled out the window at him and the old man issued a series of low growls in response, raising a bony, woollen arm and pointing a long finger. We tore off again in the direction of his finger and after a few minutes stopped abruptly outside a tall apartment building. The street was very, very dark. The moon was missing.

'Are we here?'

'Yes, we're here.'

Fadi turned around to smile at me.

'You're sure?'

Fadi grinned.

'I'm sure I'm sure.'

Sami turned the engine off, and the sound of drones leapt out of the sky. Psycho robot cicadas. Fadi stuck a hand out of the car window to wave at them.

'*Shalom Moshi! Shalom Chaim!* There's more of them here because we're close to the border,' he explained over his shoulder.

Slamming the car door behind him, he strode off down a sandy alleyway into the pitch blackness towards the towering apartment block. A large shade emerged from the gloom and the two forms greeted each other with chummy back slaps. Sami was indicating with smiling urgency for me to follow Fadi out of the car. I felt heavy with not wanting to, but Sami's smiles were insistent.

We all walked into a pitch-black stairwell that smelled strongly of damp and Fadi turned on the torch on his mobile phone, illuminating disjointed patches of water-stained concrete. Half beacon, half praying mantis, he launched himself into the darkness and reluctantly, I climbed slowly after him. Their soft voices pressed on ahead of me passing the eighth floor with no sign of slowing or stopping. I whimpered for the group to slow down, resting my hand on the cold, sticky wall, but they either didn't hear me or chose not to. At the tenth floor, when I was about to curl up in the dank dark and give up, a door opened and I found myself panting outside a well-lit, sparsely decorated apartment.

A man in a smart red sports shirt stood in the doorway. His broad face was split through one eyebrow with a wide, white scar. He was probably in his seventies and among the handsomest men of any age I have ever seen. Even his hands were handsome. A generator hummed pleasantly.

'There you are! We thought we'd lost you. Come in, please. Take a seat,' he twinkled. 'What can I get you? Tea? Coffee?'

Fadi was already lounging in one of the man's comfortable low armchairs, twitchy legs splayed. Sami had taken himself off towards an enormous television playing *Al Jazeera* Arabic on mute and lay down on the carpet in front of it like a fat concubine, not even slightly out of breath. They both seemed very at home. A tea might be just the thing I said, wiping sweat from my hairline, and our host looked delighted.

'Tea! So British, that's perfect,' he beamed.

I removed my helmet and flak allowing delicious cool air to rush at the sweat patches on my head and back and sank into the armchair next to Fadi's. The incredibly attractive old man soon returned carrying a golden tray that he placed on the low table in front of me. On it was a large golden teapot, elegant gold-leafed glasses and a gold-leaf glass plate piled high with dates, biscuits, radishes and a small dish of salt crystals.

'It's Kate, isn't it? I'm Abu Yasser, nice to meet you. I love radishes. Delicious. Good for the heart too,' he said with a merry chuckle.

'Are they? I love radishes too!' I exclaimed.

Abu Yasser was sorry his wife wasn't home to do a better job of receiving us, but he was alone in the apartment for the time being. He had sent his family to stay at his brother's house, not far from The Beach Hotel actually. It was crowded there and his wife was complaining about having to share a bathroom. But better to share a toilet than be bombed on your own bidet, right? Fadi and I giggled.

His wife must have taken most of the flat with her. The place was bare, not a photo in sight. It had a cosy feeling though and I happily chomped on the radishes Abu Yasser insisted I coat in salt flakes, drank his sweet tea and listened to him talk. He had studied in Dublin in the 70s and worked in a pub. The people were funny, drunks of course, but funny. His first love had actually been a blonde from Cork named Moira. Moira had broken his heart by running off with a bookie called Brian whom he later heard died in a bar fight. Stabbed, apparently. Fadi and I laughed at the ludicrous idea of this silly, drunk Moira leaving Abu Yasser for a Brian and I noticed I was feeling a lot better.

The sound bubble in my head had thinned and the dizziness was all but gone. I reached for a date and Abu Yasser told me how one date contains everything a body needs to survive and that it's actually possible to live for some time entirely on dates and water. This is why you break your fast with dates during the holy month of Ramadan. I had not known this about dates.

'So Kate, you want to meet a commander. Why?'

The question came softly but abruptly and Abu Yasser's handsome, scar-lined face was suddenly serious.

'Well,' I started, chewing rapidly to get rid of the date in my mouth.

Fadi shifted uncomfortably next to me, but I wasn't daunted. I knew instinctively this was a man I could be straight with.

'Well,' I swallowed hard. 'As you know, I'm a British journalist and I work for an important British newspaper. Pretty right-wing. *The Tribune*? Of course you know it. So I've been here in Gaza for what, a week? Trying to cover the war here and in all that time, the only Palestinians I've been allowed to speak to are people in bombed houses or hospital beds. Victims, basically.'

Abu Yasser was looking at me steadily. Fadi's leg jiggled.

'And every day I've been here, a captain in the Israeli army has called me. He's from Philadelphia and his name is Doron.

Always sounds like he's fighting a cold. Seems like the type to own a Segway.'

Abu Yasser indicated his confusion with a head shake.

'A Segway? Those big electric unicycle things, make everyone look disabled?'

He shook his head again and looked towards Fadi who shrugged. I sipped at my tea.

'They're everywhere in Tel Aviv. Not important. So, this Doron calls me every day, all chummy, asking how I am. He sounds normal, like Starbucks normal, and gets me all the quotes from Israeli field commanders I need for my pieces. His office emails me press releases early every morning before I send my story list to London, telling me how Israeli dogs are being traumatised by air-raid sirens. That kindergartens are having to close in the kibbutzes, *kibbutzim,* but the Israeli army is still doing all it can to help Palestinians. He calls you *Aravim* actually.'

Abu Yasser raised a scarred eyebrow.

'Meanwhile, I'm here in Gaza where even the kindergartens don't have air-raid sirens and dogs are flattened in their bombed houses and the closest I've come to the Palestinian military is a tiny sweating man in a shiny suit hiding in a hospital car park talking about hell fire. I know better what generals are thinking in Tel Aviv than in Gaza City. It makes me think: what I am doing here?'

Abu Yasser held me with his soft brown eyes, and I reached for another date. They were very good, juicy. The room was either unusually quiet or the sound bubble was back. I popped the date in my mouth and kept talking, hoping the chewing would clear it.

'Every war is a propaganda war, you know that. And yet here I am, the Western media, maybe the world's most powerful propaganda weapon, eating your dates—they're so good, thank you—unused on your sofa!'

I chewed thoughtfully.

'Listen, as far as the West sees it, this is a war between Jews and Arabs. Right? A few million Jews versus hundreds of millions of Muslims. It's cowboys and Indians. And it's there, in the cultural mind, that Israel is winning.'

I tapped my index finger against my temple and Abu Yasser continued to study me silently.

'Can you name one sitcom on an American network about a bunch of kooky Muslim mates? How many Jews do you see driving passenger jets into American skyscrapers?'

'Who says they don't?' Fadi edged forward in his seat, eyes wide.

'Excuse me?' I asked, annoyed by the interruption.

'You think it's a coincidence the Jews did so well out of those towers going down?'

'What *Jews,* Fadi? You mean the Israeli government?' Abu Yasser broke his silence irritably, scar slicing through his furrowed forehead.

'I mean, show me a Muslim life that got better after 9/11!' he replied, wide-eyed, both legs pumping wildly.

We both turned away from Fadi.

'My point is, if you want the West to help Palestinians, you can't keep relying on dead kids and bombed buildings. How many years have you been doing that? You see anyone doing anything about it? No. Because after a while, one dead kid blurs into 10 dead kids, 20, 100. Then it's just random sad numbers.'

I spat the date stone as delicately as I could into one of the neat stacks of red paper napkins on the coffee table.

'Meanwhile, telegenic Israelis with cute Delaware accents are telling us *We didn't mean to kill those poor kids, Hamas made us do it! Look! Look how they keep firing rockets at our kindergartens! They don't value human life!* And then, sure enough, when we do hear from Hamas it's all *Death to Israel! Burning hellfire!* And firing rockets into kindergartens.'

All that sweet tea had made me speedy. I didn't feel my message was landing.

'Listen, you're clearly a very intelligent man. You don't need me to tell you that *understanding* someone is the key to sympathising with them. And popular sympathy means popular support for the politicians who are sympathetic to you, which means financial and diplomatic support for you, which is what you need to win a war. Right?'

Both Abu Yasser's eyebrows had been raised for some time.

'Do you know where the word *understanding* comes from? It comes from the Old English word, *Understanden*. It means *to stand in the middle of* something. My point is, you should let me stand in the middle of you, in your tunnels. Let the people hear what you have to say!

'Why do you think the British didn't let the BBC broadcast Gerry Adams' voice all those years? Like you, Gerry Adams happens to have a very nice speaking voice.'

I opened my jaw widely a few times trying to force my ears to pop. Fadi was gripping his jiggling knees with both hands. Abu Yasser put his glass of tea down gently on its saucer, tugged his trousers up an inch at the knees and leaned forward.

'Okay, Kate. Katie?'

I nodded, pleased to have a fake name he could make affectionate.

'You want to get into the fighting tunnels. Obviously, this can't happen, it's too risky for us, too risky for you. If I've understood you correctly, Palestinian fighters getting a nice lady journalist killed somewhere underground in Gaza would not be a smart tactic in our media war.'

He smiled wryly and I smiled broadly back. He'd got it! He really was very charming.

'So here's what we're going to do. You will meet the commander tomorrow evening at 7pm at the cemetery in Beit Lahiya. You will ask him all about why we fight, what we want, why we traumatise Israeli dogs.'

As he talked, he pushed radish stalks around the low coffee table with his index finger, troops on his sand table. There was no pause for argument or negotiation, he was delivering the plan. It was impressive. He was a good 10 years older than Michael, but I would still fuck him. Or wished he was my dad. Either or. I clicked my jaw.

'The meeting will last no longer than 10 minutes and there will be no photographs.'

'Okay,' I agreed.

This was a start. If it went well with this commander, I'd win their trust, the tunnels would follow. Sami had turned up the volume of the television and was calling Fadi over to look. The plasma screen was Gaza City illuminated with tracer bullets and fire balls.

'Is that happening now?' I asked.

No one answered.

'Is that a ground invasion? Is that now?'

Fadi jumped to his feet, a giant hummingbird, and kicked Sami hard in the ankles.

'The Israelis are destroying Shejaiya. Dropping leaflets telling people to evacuate Jabalia Camp,' he told me.

Sami winced but rose to his feet without complaint. I stared at the television trying to make out from the skyline where the bombs were falling but failing to recognise anything.

'Are we in Jabalia Camp? Fadi?' I asked.

Fadi ignored me.

'Yes we're in Jabalia, you need to go,' Abu Yasser said. 'But don't panic, put your big jacket and hat on and when you get to the car, keep down on the floor. You'll be fine. He may not look it but Sami's a pro. Aren't you Sami?'

He grinned and patted Sami heavily on the shoulders. Sami gurgled uncomprehendingly. Abu Yasser stood and waved at us from his doorway as we hustled into the pitch-black stairwell.

'You're not coming?' I called back.

'Don't worry about me, I'm indestructible,' he smiled with his handsome teeth and winked, scar deepening into a lightning bolt. 'Nice to meet you Kate.'

We scrambled, stumbling in the sand, to get to the car. The

formerly very dark empty street was now flooded with torch and phone lights and shouting people carrying screaming children, mattresses, televisions and bags. I had barely got my helmet on when Sami lurched into reverse, his hand on the horn forcing the crowd to clear. I wedged myself between the back of Sami's seat and the floor as best I could and closed my eyes. We jerked and beeped and Fadi screamed out of the window until we accelerated onto a clear road. The car shook with the blasts erupting in nearby streets. My eyes shut tightly, I was flying at speed just inches above the road. Then the blasts were further away and soon the only noise was our tyres speeding along tarmac. I heard Fadi wind down his window and light a cigarette. Sami turned his Egyptian pop songs up loud again and Fadi laughed with relief.

'You can get up now *Katie*. We're clear,' Fadi called into the back.

But I didn't want to get up. I stayed on the clean floor of Sami's car, thinking. I rotated slowly onto my side to look up through the rear window to see an almost full moon keeping pace with our car. It had found me.

I'd asked Dad once how it was that the moon was always able to keep up with our car. Dozing against the cold, hard window in the backseat, I'd call out when I thought we'd lost it, but we never had. Sooner or later its great white face would beam out through some balding tree or around the corner of a shadowy building. Was it after me? Watching out for me? Dad had issued one of his dark private laughs but didn't answer.

In Gaza, the moon was always huge. Why would the moon look any bigger in one place than anywhere else? Was it looking harder?

16
KIDS ARE ANNOYING

Michael arched his pale hips just high enough to pull his crisp white boxer shorts on, which he did quickly. At some point he had started fucking me with his pants around his ankles, pulling them up immediately after coming as though sex were a wasp that needed trapping. I was lying as still as I could on my belly on the scratchy carpet in my living room, hoping my ass looked hot in the silver moonlight beaming through the steamed up window onto it.

It was the first time we'd had sex in weeks and it had taken days of persistent and explicit messages about what I was doing to myself and what I was going to do to him to get him to come over. When he had finally arrived, he looked tired and barely managed to get hard. He didn't react to the new underwear I'd spent too much money on and I'd had to take off myself. Now he lay still and quiet on the floor next to me. I also lay still and quiet, pinning both my hands to the floor with my chin thinking about how for more than a year now he'd only wanted to fuck me from behind whereas in the beginning he was always telling me to look him in the eyes. Had something happened to my face?

'Cathy starts a round of radiotherapy tomorrow,' his voice was bald and flat in the moony darkness.

'Oh,' I laughed dryly. 'I see.'

Treatment meant he would be gone for months. When she'd had chemo he'd disappeared for almost a year. My heart pumped hard against the hard rugged floor and we lay in silence again for a while.

'I kissed Tom when I left for work this morning and he

flinched. He's grown up, and I don't think he likes me very much.'

Michael sighed and I watched his old chest empty.

'I don't like him very much most of the time. He's so like her,' he confessed to the tree shadows flirting with each other on my ceiling.

I hated it when he talked about his children. Cathy's teenage tennis boys, her adolescent replicas. They even had her haircut. It gave me the creeps. I turned onto my side to look at him better and sighed. He was at his most handsome in profile. His thick hair almost completely grey, his eyebrows greying, face pale and tired, he looked like bleached marble. Pentelic Pontius Pilate. I reached out to squeeze his hand.

'That's okay. Kids are annoying.'

Michael issued a half-hearted laugh towards the flickering shadows, which pleased me. I rolled onto my back and stroked the length of his smooth arm.

'Ours would be perfect though, owing to our perfect genes.'

I stretched my legs into the silver light in a siren pose and threw my head back alluringly. I opened my eyes to find Michael's face and kiss it, then hopefully have him fuck me again but he was sitting bolt upright, soberly buttoning-up his shirt.

'I should get going. I told Cath I'd be home to eat with the family.'

Planting a chaste kiss near my mouth, he stood and moved with quick socked feet from the living room to the kitchen counter where his trousers lay in a heap on the floor.

'But I made chicken!' I sat up.

Michael looked towards the charred bird sitting on my countertop as if he'd only just recognised it as food, then at me. His face was difficult to read. Standing under the ugly, low-hanging lamp in my kitchen, his features were distorted by dramatic shadow. He pulled on his trousers.

'Girly, you do know that's never going to happen right?'

'Dinner?'

He sighed deeply again, the weight of his many responsibilities apparently crushing all the air and humour from his body.

'Children. I can't have any more, won't. I wouldn't survive a whole new person to disappoint.'

His old face was solemn and aggravatingly serious. I was 28 and until that moment, hadn't given children much thought other than finding other people's irritating. But suddenly, now he'd said that, I needed one of my own. I needed one of his. He couldn't have two with her and none with me, it was ridiculous.

'I was joking! Remember jokes? Look at me! Do I look like the maternal type to you?'

Michael watched me expressionless as I used the discarded red silk nightie I only wore for him to wipe the come from my ass with a burlesque flourish. He fastened his belt.

'Maybe,' he said.

Fully dressed now with his hands on his snake hips, he studied me, Caesar sitting in judgement. I laughed, trying to dispel the churning unease in my stomach.

'Girly, do you see anyone?' he asked, his voice low and grave.

'What do you mean? Like a shrink?'

I laughed again automatically and pulled on my come-damp nightie, not wanting to be naked anymore.

'Boys. You don't talk about your boyfriends.'

What was he doing? I didn't talk about them because there weren't any. He must have known that. Since we'd started together, I'd had other *encounters*, I wasn't a *nun*, but they were always brief and usually bad. Usually drunken and almost always when Michael was going through one of his absent phases. I was his, always had been, like he was mine. That was unsaid. I smirked enigmatically.

'Wouldn't you like a nice boyfriend? Someone to stay and eat your chicken?'

He had to search for the word chicken. I smiled up at him through the deep pain suddenly puncturing my solar plexus.

'Eat my chicken? If that's 70s slang for being fucked, yes, I do very much want someone to eat my chicken. I thought that's why you were here.'

He let out a humourless laugh and studied me a bit more with his new remoteness. He reached for his coat, which was cashmere and grey and expensive. By the time I'd stood up, his hand was already on the latch of my front door, green scarf skimming his loosening jowls. I walked towards him. Under the glare of the LED light in my shabby hallway, against the bold of his emerald scarf, his face looked even more pale and drawn.

'I'm sure you've got contenders lined up around the block,' he said grimly.

'Well, there's always contenders,' I lied and smiled coldly, leaning against the door frame as seductively as I could manage.

He hesitated, considering the stained brown carpet in my hallway.

'You should get going. Cathy's waiting,' I told him.

I didn't move to kiss him. He should have wanted to kiss me, but he didn't.

'Right. See you then girly,' he said.

'See ya,' I said, and flicked the door shut.

It slammed. After a second, the pad of his hard-soled Italian shoes. I listened to them walk away until they were gone and I was alone again with the steely moon and the dried-out chicken in my empty, cheap little flat.

17
THE GATEKEEPERS

I didn't want to live in West Jerusalem, I wanted to live in *East* Jerusalem, which yes being occupied and Palestinian was the poorest and most violence-prone bit of the city, but that was sort of the point. It looked closest to what I expected *the cradle of civilisation, riven by conflict* to look like.

On the whole Jerusalem was nothing like what I thought it should be. It looked like a council estate on a space station if that space station had been built on a drought-ravaged penal planet by the survivors of some gruesome intergalactic war. Where I expected ancient olive groves to be growing on Jesus' bones, there were monolithic malls with fury hate-filled underground car parks. The one or two stone temples worn smooth by the feet of holy men were buried inside a spaghetti tangle of highways in perpetual tourist-coach gridlock with the angriest people in the world living around them. There was no spiritual charge in the air. No soul-elevating frescos on ancient city stones, just advertising billboards with the women painted out so as not to offend the ultraorthodox. A fuse box of the world's hate, it was a very unpleasant city.

East Jerusalem at least had the yelling Arabs pushing wooden carts full of herbs over cobblestones through crowds of tourists—let's call them pilgrims—towards ancient stone gateways into the Old City. Forgetting for a minute that inside its walls, the Old City was teaming with twitchy, heavily armed teenage Israeli soldiers, fast-moving settlers and sunburned tour groups haggling with dead-eyed Palestinian stall owners over Magen David t-shirts with *God Loves Guns* slogans on them. 'Pat, you gotta barter with these people. That's the point!' cried the heat and dust stressed Americans. 'Stu just paid $15 for a pomegranate juice! They'll rob you blind if you let 'em!'

My original flat had been in East Jerusalem, on the third floor of Mrs Ayyoub's building, opposite the drug-dealing barber, just behind the Salafi butcher on Salahadin street. It was a five-minute walk from the Old City wall, a few blocks east of the racist traffic light that marked the threshold of West Jerusalem by only turning green for Israeli cars, and a few blocks west of the corner where Palestinian kids threw rocks and Molotov cocktails at Israeli soldiers every Friday. It was the perfect location.

And the flat was nice because Mrs Ayyoub made sure it was kept nice by the cleaner who came around at unpredictable hours to escape her violent husband and who I sometimes found napping or weeping in my bed. The flat also came with Mrs Ayyoub's seven year-old grandson who had very neatly combed black hair and played in my living room whenever he chose. He carried a small yellow bird about with him in a blue metal cage.

On one of the Ayyoub boy's unannounced early morning visits, he and the bird found the art student in my bed. Mrs Ayyoub herself was in the room within minutes, hair curlers and pressure stockings still in place. No one bought my story that the student was a German tourist, mostly because he kept apologising to Mrs Ayyoub in Hebrew and checkpoint Arabic. The embarrassed Israeli and I were instructed to leave the building immediately and forever, and the only place the student could help me find on his social media on my sort of budget on a day's notice was the Orthodox American man's shoilet.

It was in the part of West Jerusalem that had been intellectual and bohemian until its recent colonisation by the ultra-religious, and my new landlord's stuttering Hebrew, like his English, came out in a thick Williamsburg drawl. He showed me and the student, compelled by misdirected guilt to see me safely rehomed, around the room with its walls yellowed by years of undisturbed dirt and its stained, sagging mattress. He pointed out the rusted shower head that hung directly above the toilet, which was just next to the kitchen, which was a folddown plastic counter with a toaster oven on it.

'It's a shoilet,' Ron the landlord explained when he saw me gawping.

I had never seen a shoilet before. The student left. Ron required a month's rent up front in cash, which was the last of my cash, and hurried off muttering fretfully about a daughter's wedding and then, louder, a final urgent instruction not to use the shower when the toaster oven was on.

'Never do it. *Ever!*'

I urgently needed to make money. In almost six months of pitching to editors at every English-speaking newspaper, even sending unsolicited, fully-written stories, I had received only a handful of replies all of which said more or less the same thing.

Thank you for contacting us with your story/ story idea but we already have a Jerusalem correspondent whose salary we're paying, whose rent we're paying, whose car rental and living expenses we're paying, not to mention the school fees of their children and the fees and expenses of their fixers. So even if your story/ story idea wasn't one we'd heard a thousand times before, even if it was in any way new or good or interesting, we'd just get our very experienced, really expensive Jerusalem correspondent to write it. More vicious editors added a kicker: *but good luck placing your story elsewhere.*

It was only after sweating through a whole summer in the shoilet that I worked out I was never going to get anywhere with the editors in London. It was the correspondents who were the gatekeepers to Jerusalem. And as the Palestinian-American Christian who was paying me poorly to poorly write her charity's fundraising reports had told me, they could be easily found most evenings at the bars of The Affry Hotel.

Tactfully tucked just over the city's invisible border in

occupied East Jerusalem, and owned as it was by Swiss, The Affry was the city's grandest and most neutral place to drink. Its heavy sandstone walls, artisan-tiled swimming pool and vined courtyards jingled with moneyed power. A disgraced former British prime minister and his entourage occupied the hotel's entire west wing enjoying their exile from domestic politics in the company of Israeli billionaires and $25 cocktails. Every evening, its various bars filled with expatriate media.

A glass of house wine at The Affry was my food budget for two days. So, on Wednesdays and Fridays I slept and fasted until sunset, put on my pharmacy red lipstick and went there to breakfast on free nuts, trying to make a single glass of wine last several hours with tiny, agonised sips. It was three weeks before the big British broadcast correspondent approached me and demanded to be told the name of the most attractive woman in the bar.

'It's Sara Byrne,' I said.

I was the only woman in the bar. It was just me, the broadcast correspondent and Anthony Harper perched on three stools in the hotel's incongruously themed tiki bar. It was a quiet Wednesday.

'No relation of Bill Byrne?' a sun-grazed Anthony Harper chipped in amiably, little legs dangling from his seat, brushing the pebbled ground with the tips of his evening loafers.

Despite a lifetime of his name-dropping, I never expected anyone to actually know my father and my surprise must have registered.

'Ha! For God's sake!' Anthony chortled in amazement.

'I'm his daughter, actually.'

'Ha! Well fancy that! Pete! Did you hear?'

Pete the broadcast correspondent was explaining carefully to the Palestinian barman what cask strength was and why it was impossible that a bar like his didn't have a better whiskey to offer.

'Just look at the colour of that!'

Pete held a glass of amber liquid up to a tiki torch for the barman to inspect.

'It's anaemic! That is not a whiskey. That is a ginger ale with a blood disorder.'

'Hey! Peter! Did you hear? This is Bill Byrne's daughter! Sophie!'

'Sara,' I said.

'Sara!' Anthony beamed.

'What?' Pete frowned impatiently at Anthony, mirroring the barman's expression almost exactly.

'Bill Byrne! You know! The lefty foreign affairs sage. Hats! Big old hats and big old *opinions*.'

Anthony looked to me for confirmation, which I nodded. He actually hadn't written anything much since losing his column, other than the mystery book into which years had been poured without a single page being produced. It was variously described as an autobiography and a treatise on war. The premise was that all civilisations are born, grow and eventually die through conflict.

'Of course you know him Peter, the lone lefty hawk! Got into a total balls-up over Iraq. *Sorry* Sophie, but he *did* a bit, didn't he?'

I smiled indulgently and Pete looked blank. This had nothing to do with sex or whiskey.

'You *must* know Peter! Had those big old summer parties, in Clapham was it?'

'Battersea,' I said.

'Battersea! That's it! You *must* have gone to one of those.'

Pushed over the edge of disinterest by this mention of parties he hadn't gone to, Peter turned his back on Anthony and returned to instructing the barman. Chortling at his friend's beguiling rudeness, Anthony swivelled back to face me and asked politely what had brought me to the Holy Land.

'*Un*holy *waste*land!' he stage-whispered, chuckling at his own wickedness before settling back into his stool and asking in his usual car showroom voice if I was a guest at the hotel. 'Not part of the PM's mob, are you?' he pulled a convivial revolted expression.

Anthony had sunk a few beers.

'No, I'm a journalist too actually.'

'Oh, you are?'

I understood from the long hours I'd spent sitting unnoticed at that same bar that young female journalists were more Pete's bag. I hadn't realised that Anthony wasn't just uninterested but actually phobic of them. His face tightened visibly and he shot an anxious glance towards his star pal.

'Longer format stuff, for American outlets mostly,' I lied boldly.

'Oh right, gosh! Peter!'

Anthony tugged at his friend's shirt sleeve.

'Pete, did you hear? Sophie here is a fellow member of the Fourth Estate! Living right here in Jerusalem, poor thing!'

'Sara,' Pete corrected smoothly.

He spun back to face us, sipping on a fresh whiskey and winked. An improved drink had radically transformed his mood and he was now grinning seductively, but even this playful Pete was not attractive. He had one of those faces that really did look like boiled potatoes in a wet muslin sack. The girls in matching black dresses I'd watched following him around the hotel's bars like a school of tadpoles in a porn pond had to be very ambitious. I wondered if they also lived in shoilets.

'Longer format? *New Yorker* type stuff, is it? Very grand. Very serious. But I'd expect nothing less of Billy Byrne's girl! Christmas lunch at yours must be a riot!'

We all laughed politely. No one had ever called my father Billy. Anthony exhaled a last chortle, then a conclusive sigh and pivoted away from me hopefully with an: 'Oh well'. But it was too late, Pete had scented his discomfort.

'So, young Sara,' he gulped, causing his ice cubes to jangle. 'What brings such a bright, young spark to Jerusalem just as everyone else is leaving? Know something we don't?'

I'd heard about this from the bitter charity woman. After decades of violent fertility, the news well in Jerusalem was drying up owing to an irreversible shrinking of global interest and rapidly diminishing news budgets. The press herd was moving on, with half already lost to Beirut or Cairo. I told the stem of my wine glass evasively that I guess I just liked the idea of having the cradle of civilisation to myself for a while.

'Oh, but that's adorable! You're about 600 miles off course sweetheart!' Pete roared.

Anthony chortled, thrilled to be back on the laughing team, and my cheeks flushed disobediently.

'The cradle of our civilisation is Iraq, or what's left of it, if you believe Ms Segal. You've not read *Where the Tigris Ran Red?*'

Pete pronounced the title in a grand dame voice. I shrugged to indicate that I may or may not have read it. I hadn't.

'I'll save you the bother. She tells us that it's we Brits who destroyed your cradle, causing the pandemonium we see here today. Like so many angry ladies, she manages to blame poor old Churchill for pretty much everything.'

I snorted at this, and Pete grinned back.

'I'm sure your Pa has hooked you up with all the big movers and shakers out here has he?'

I avoided answering by drawing deeply on my wine and narrowing my eyes. My father's only intervention had been advice to visit Petra. *The only buildings worth seeing in those parts.*

'I'm sure daily news is way too grubby for your high brow, but if you *did* happen to be looking for some side-line meat and potatoes, Anthony here is in the market for a deputy. Aren't you Anthony?'

Anthony's eyebrows reached for his receding hairline in panic. Pete glowed demonically and ploughed on.

'Anthony, as I'm sure you're aware, is *The Tribune*'s award-winning Middle East correspondent. Aren't you Anthony? An award-winning correspondent who at this very moment happens to be in the market for a sharp young deputy?'

Pete grinned insanely.

'Well,' Anthony demurred then chortled.

Slapping his friend heartily on the back, Pete explained that Anthony had become quite the greedy little vulture and was itching to spread his wings glory hunting in Syria and Libya and *The Tribune* was in need of someone to step in and mind the empty shop in Jerusalem while he was away

'Look at that fluffy little vulture head,' Pete teased with a pout, ruffling the few downy whisps left on Anthony's scalp.

I ignored Anthony's squirming and coolly asked Pete if he also planned to go to Syria.

'Me? No way! Another totally saturated conflict. Bleugh!'

He stuck out a nicotine-stained tongue, and allowed his face to fall in pantomime melancholy into the palm of his hand.

'You know Sara, you wouldn't think it looking at this place now, but Jerusalem used to be fun. Back in the Intifada days. Naked cocaine orgies at the consulate pool fun.'

Pete exhaled wistfully through his fleshy nose.

'But this dump is drier than a nun's cooch now. I'm shipping back out to Afghanistan soon as I can. Way better drugs out there anyways,' he said, downing his whiskey.

'Peter!'

Anthony flushed with delight at the outrageousness of his exciting friend but Pete was looking at his phone, bored again.

'Okay you two, better exchange numbers,' he monotoned, scrolling through the messages in his Blackberry. 'This round's on *The Tribune*, right pal?'

After a bemused moment, Anthony Harper agreed that yes indeed it was and looked around anxiously for the missing barman. Slipping his little legs off his bar stool, he stalked off into the night in search of the bill, motioning for it with a rolling wrist.

'There you go, *Sophie*. Entirely up to you what you make of that,' Pete said, not looking up from his phone screen. 'Nice tits by the way.'

18
In the Manner of an Animal

I lay in bed in the old robe from the bathroom, eating chocolate and flicking through cable channels. I skipped past the news stations reporting on the airstrikes outside until I found an Egyptian shopping network. I'd been sick when I got to the room but was starting to feel better. Having eaten all of Jihad's chocolates, I was starting on the previously untouched mini-bar chocolates. The Egyptian television women wore white foundation and sparkly pink eyeshadow and were handling a lot of gold jewellery with their long, pink fingernailed, hands. They looked like large, taloned birds. I wished very much I could be drunk.

My phone rang again and I ignored it again, not wanting to be interrupted while I watched the neon talons fingering varying lengths of gold chain. It rang and rang until reluctantly, I answered.

'Sara, it's Neil.'

'Yes, Neil.'

The women were trying on diamond rings shaped like seashells and displaying them to the camera. I didn't like the rings as much as the gold chains.

'I've been trying to reach you for over an hour! I need you to get to the Gaza hospital. *The Mail* has an incredible story. A boy was rushed into the emergency room at,' he was reading. 'Schafer hospital. The surgeon only realised the boy was his son when he died on his operating table.'

'Ha!' I spat, taking a bite out of a tiny Mars bar. 'Incredible is right.'

A bit of wet chocolate flew from my mouth onto the robe. I

tried to brush it off but succeeded only in smearing brown even deeper into the dirty white towelling.

'Shit!'

'Sara?'

'There's no way that happened, Neil. *The Mail* doesn't even have a reporter out here. And even if it wasn't bullshit, there's airstrikes all over Gaza City now. I'm not going anywhere.'

There was a pause on the other end of the line.

'You are refusing to go?'

Neil's voice was strangled.

'If you're asking me to wake up Nasser and go out into airstrikes to chase a bullshit *Mail* story, then yes, I refuse to go.'

I opened the coconut chocolate regretfully because who likes coconut, really? There was another pause on Neil's end of the line.

'Hello? Neil? I can explain all this to Jason if you like. Is he there?'

Jason Argent, the actual foreign editor, was a reasonable man. Not attractive, but reasonable.

'Dammit! You clearly have *no idea* the stress we're under here Sara!' Neil exploded, then his line went dead.

The coconut chocolate wasn't so bad. There was that knocking again. It'd been going on for an hour now, nonstop fucking knocking when I was trying to watch the nail ladies. It had better not be Jihad offering me more soap. I opened the door the width of a bar of soap and peered out. There standing squatly in front of me in his flak jacket, strapped like a suicide bomber with cameras and lenses, was the Italian.

'*Porca miseria*! You're okay. Thank God. You didn't hear knocking?'

His eyes bulged.

'*Madonna*! You didn't text! We said 10, *no*? It's past midnight!'

Alessandro ran his hands agitatedly through his thick, dusty wedge of blond hair and craned over my shoulder through the crack in the door. What was he looking for?

'I'm sorry. I was writing. I didn't hear.'

I licked the chocolate from my teeth.

'Fuck! It's okay. I'm happy you're okay.'

His huge forlorn eyes had grown even more bloodshot and buggy since I last saw them.

'I guess I'm a bit crazy after Max.'

He peered past my shoulder again. If he was trying to see the strikes outside, he wouldn't be able to because I'd closed all the doors and curtains against them and that hostile bird, which was back squatting on my balcony. Did he think I had another photographer in my room?

'Can I come in? For a minute. I'm so stress.'

I didn't want him to come in. My bed was covered in chocolate wrappers and the muted shopping channel was on the TV. Also, if we were going to have sex, I hadn't shaved my legs or pussy in weeks. Unable to think of a valid reason to turn him away, I told him of course he could come in and as he stepped into the room, I loosened the dirty robe. If I was going to have to fuck him, I'd need to do it quickly, before he noticed the chocolate wrappers and the hair. I reached for his hand and pulled him close to me.

'I'm happy you came to check on me Sandro,' I lied.

I was definitely going to have to fuck him. I placed his big bristly blond hand on my left tit and kissed him, pushing my tongue deep into his mouth. He tasted of stale cigarettes and his hair smelled of sand and metallic sweat.

'Fuck! Sara!' he said, when my tongue wasn't in his mouth.

He pushed me back to look at me dumbly and I leaned in to kiss him again, not wanting this to drag on. It took him a moment but this time he kissed back, forcefully, tearing open my grubby robe. I stood as confidently as I could naked as he took off his cameras, biting his lip with his nicotine teeth and making a mewling noise. Grabbing the robe belt, he pulled me towards him roughly, kissing and biting my lips and neck, pulling off the rest of his clothes as he kissed and bit. I hate being bitten, but I moaned encouragingly.

Undressed he had little skinny bowed legs and a hard, barrel-chested torso covered in coarse, blond fur and tattoos. That was a lot of tattoos. I reached for his cock through his jeans and found it exactly as I thought it would be: stout. He bit my nipple hard and put his fingers inside me. If he were to believe my pussy, any man would think he were a god, Michael always said.

'Fuck, that pussy *wantsss* me,' the Italian whispered in my ear in hot breaths.

I moved to kneel and suck his cock, like I'd pictured in the lobby bathroom, but he pushed me hard onto my back on the bed and knelt in front of me, stroking himself. I looked at him because he seemed to want me to. He had shaved his pubic hair creating a dark shadow of stubble down his upper thighs. He looked at my tits, slack-jawed with his dick in his hands for a while, then fell forward, forcing my thighs wide apart and pushing himself into me. Leaning back again, he watched his cock fuck me, holding my legs wide apart at the thighs. The stubble on his groin rubbed against my pussy like sandpaper.

He fucked me like that for ages until my legs began to ache and then shake. At some point I tried to flip over so he could fuck me from behind and maybe come quicker, but he held me down tighter, so I gave up wriggling and just lay there. Finally he pulled out of me and started to wank furiously, his eyes tightly closed, until he came with a groan in hot spurts over my thighs and belly. Still on his knees, he leaned back and opened his eyes to look admiringly at what he'd produced, smiled, then collapsed on his back next to me.

'You mind if I smoke?' he panted.

'No,' I said.

Still panting, he reached over to grope for his cigarettes in the crumpled pile of jeans and clothes on the floor and I walked to the bathroom to wash. I was sore. In general, my pussy didn't agree with being fucked by anyone but Michael, and I hadn't been fucked by anyone at all in almost three months. The last guy had been the barman in Tel Aviv who'd spent the evening feeding me tequila shots and boasting about his military service at a checkpoint in Jenin. 'The best years of his life,' he'd said. He wanted to keep the bedroom lights on and the windows open when we fucked and asked me if the Arabs were watching us over and over again with his hand over my mouth. He punched me in the face when he came, but even that sex hadn't left me this sore. It must have been the groin stubble. I splashed some water on my face and between my legs and came back to the bed feeling cleaner and cooler but definitely injured. Alessandro had bunched up all the pillows behind his head and was lying on them smoking.

'Come here.'

He extended his arm so that I could lie on his chest, which was also shaved and scratched my cheek.

'*Grazie* Sara. Sometimes we need reminding that we're animals. That we're alive.'

He mewled and bit into my hair in the manner of an animal. I tried to cover my nakedness, with as much sheet as I could pull from under his body. I don't like eye contact in general but during or after sex especially not and I could feel him boring into me with his puppy gaze. Rather than meet his searching eyes, I studied the tattoos on his torso. Italian phrases mostly, written in gothic script, and sequences of numbers that ran across his shoulders and down his arms.

'You're looking at my ink,' he said, also looking at it. 'Those are latitude and longitude points, places where the most important things happened in my life. This is where I was born. Here is my first assignment for AP. That one's Helmand.'

He pointed to a string of numbers running down his sinewy forearm, then he pointed to an empty spot at the base of his ribs.

'I'll get the numbers for Gaza here. For Max. Underneath them: *If you go to war, be ready to bleed.*'

This idea moved him and tears rushed back into his big wet eyes. I didn't say anything because it seemed like a stupid phrase to get permanently written on yourself, particularly given what had happened to his friend, but I squeezed his hand. He brushed a large tear off his nose with his big coarse fingers, then cupped my tit with them, squeezing it hard.

'You know, Sara, you are not a beautiful woman but you are sexy. I find you sexy.'

He squeezed my other tit harder.

'There's something, I don't know, a bit crazy, a bit animal.'

Having run out of words, he mewled again.

'Thank you,' I said.

He bit his lip and rubbed his cock against my thigh. He rubbed and mewled like that until he was hard, then he fucked me again on the chocolate wrappers while the muted, pink-taloned, white-faced shopping channel women watched. I thought about Abu Yasser and his scar and his handsome hands. Why hadn't he evacuated like everyone else?

19
SPIES GET EXECUTED

Sometime around lunchtime eight men were executed. Middle-aged, in dusty t-shirts with potbellies, they were pushed out of a van onto a busy street corner in the middle of Gaza City and made to kneel in a row. One extremely fat man struggled to get to his knees so was kicked down. Then two guys in balaclavas shot them each in the back of the head, one by one. I knew this because mobile phone footage of the executions and a motorbike dragging one of the bodies through the streets was playing on loop on the TV in the lobby. The body reminded me of the flayed cows at the Old City butchers.

The deranged stalker bird had now claimed my balcony and busied itself with territorial eyeballing whenever I opened my curtains. It had developed some sort of obsession with me, or its reflection, and had taken to staring and then pecking at the glass in flurried assaults so violent that it was impossible to be in the room. Luckily, the lobby was empty. Nasser was at the hospital with his still sick kid and everyone else was out, even the Americans. The waiter Mohammed brought me another herbal tea with honey, which I hadn't asked for.

'What did they do?' I asked him as he placed the steamy cup in front of me, pointing towards the television and the executed men.

'Spying for Israel, so says Hamas.'

Mohammed's pretty features contorted in bitter disgust and he shook his tidy head.

'Usually, *spies* get executed when Hamas is afraid.'

He stood behind me and we watched the crowd kicking the dead fat man in the head.

'Would you like me to change the channel?' he asked.

'I would actually like some hummus,' I said.

Mohammed already had the remote in his hand and was flicking through the local news channels, all showing the same grainy footage of the public executions, until we landed on an American channel. A cry of indignation rang out from a dark corner of the lobby.

'Hey!'

I jumped in my seat and Mohammed let out a mild shriek of shock. Neither of us had noticed the cleaner's son glowering in the dark corner. Furious at having revealed himself, little Jihad sank back into his shadow, glaring ferociously at the jock reporter who had a headline running underneath his desert boots: *Cairo peace talks collapse as Hamas terrorists fire rockets at Israeli school.* I knew exactly the spot where the reporter was standing because it was on the street directly outside the hotel, just up from the Hamas roundabout checkpoint. Aside from Shifa Hospital, it marked the furthest point American TV crews ever ventured inside Gaza City.

'Anne, it's at times like this when Israel will be asking our secretary of state how can anyone be expected to make peace with these people?'

'HOW CAN YOU MAKE ANY SORT OF DEAL WITH PEOPLE YOU'RE REFUSING TO TALK TO?'

I shouted at the television, hoping my voice would carry out onto the street and onto their live feed.

'They don't want peace, Sara.'

Mohammed jabbed the remote control spitefully in the direction of the screen, where the Israeli defence minister and a negotiator from the Palestinian Authority in the West Bank were walking grim-faced towards their respective blackened Mercedes.

'If there's peace *here*, those big men *there* would be out of a job.'

Mohammed stood looking hotly at the television. When

after a good few minutes he made no move towards the kitchen, I asked him if any men at The Beach Hotel would be out of a job if I didn't get my lunch. He put the remote down and walked quickly away. I hit refresh on *The Tribune* website. My Italian photographer piece was no longer among the most-read stories.

'You went out with Fadi last night, not Nasser. Why?'

I snapped my head around, prompting a wave of nauseating dizziness.

'Fuck! Jihad!'

Little Jihad's face was centimetres from mine, his hard, skinny little body tucked into a crouch on one of the low, cushioned lobby chairs. He grinned and his face crinkled up with freckles and lines. It was the first time I'd seen him smile that long and that close. His serrated teeth were much too big and square for his face.

'Why are you always crouching and hiding? It's weird. You're such a weird kid,' I told him.

'I'm not hiding. I'm sitting.'

'I don't think you know the difference.'

I turned my entire body so that I could look at him sternly more comfortably.

'How do you know Fadi?' I asked.

'What were you doing out so late last night?' he countered.

'Why do you care so much what I was doing?'

The boy shrugged his skinny, brutish shoulders.

'You would only care that I care if there was something to care about,' he said.

His small, tough face was set in its hardest expression. What a strange little life, I thought, his whole child world absorbed by hotel drama. He must see a lot.

'*Okaaay,*' I exhaled, as though thoroughly bested by the power of his 11-year-old argument. 'I went out to meet a fisherman that Fadi knows. I wanted to go out on his fishing boat for the night to see the Israeli war ships but the guy said no, it's too dangerous. And I need to keep it a secret because I don't want Nasser to know I tried when he already told me no. Happy?'

Jihad narrowed his thuggish cat eyes.

'Now, you tell me what you know about Fadi,' I directed.

Little Jihad paused and scanned my face warily before answering.

'I know there is darkness behind his buffoonery. And if I were you, I wouldn't go out with him at night.'

'Darkness behind his buffoonery! What is that, Tolkien? Are you riddling?'

The boy huffed, exasperated.

'Everyone knows Fadi, he's famous! At least his family is.'

I snorted. Famous in Gaza is hardly famous, I said, and Jihad's eyes narrowed further.

'They're famous killers, not just resistance. Actual killers.'

I raised an amused eyebrow.

'*Actual* killers?'

'His grandfather's brother is Abu Yasser. You know Abu Yasser? Fatah leader, killed his other brother in 2007 in the civil war. Snapped his neck with his bare hands, like *that*.'

Jihad clicked his grubby fingers with a sharp snap.

'Oh, *really*?' I drawled.

Jihad rolled his eyes.

'Everyone knows the Abu Yasser stories! The one where he stabbed his son-in-law at his own daughter's wedding? And when he stabbed that Israeli guy in the neck in broad daylight in the middle of the street, went to Ofer prison then stabbed a bunch of Islamic Jihad guys in there? Even Hamas is scared of him!'

'So why did they let him out then, if he's so stabby?'

'Fatah did! Prisoner swap!'

Jihad searched my face earnestly for recognition of these fables of the killer Abu Yasser. No, I hadn't heard of him but I had eaten his dates. Maybe. I concentrated on keeping my face as still as possible. It could, of course, be a different Abu

Yasser. There had to be as many Abu Yassers in Gaza as there were Steves in Stevenage. Jihad scrutinised me with his ancient eyeballs.

'Every foreign journalist who comes to this hotel goes out on the fishing boats and they never have any trouble. Why didn't they let you go?'

'I'm very heavy,' I said.

I had no interest in our game anymore and sat back in my chair to think, watching little Jihad's expression fall into a surly glower as he realised he had been duped. I wondered what Abu Yasser's brother had done to deserve his neck snapping.

20
Do You Know Birds?

The English dial tone rang and crackled for a long time, and I was about to hang up when she answered. The sound of her remote voice dragged me instantly into her living room. It sounded like Twiglets and Radio 4 and that grotesque sofa and I immediately regretted calling.

'Hi Ma,' I said, sitting on the edge of the bed in my unlit room with the curtains drawn, feeling very small for a large woman.

'Who's that?'

'Who else calls you Ma?'

'Bob! Sweetheart! Isn't it weird how you always manage to call just when I've put food on the table? It's uncanny.'

There was a pause. I had called, was that enough?

'I'll call back,' I said with relief.

'No, no. Don't be silly. Are you still in Gaza?'

She sounded uncomfortable.

'Yes, Ma.'

'And how is it going there? Are you okay?'

'Yes, it's going well, busy. Sorry, I've not had a moment to call.'

'I'm sure darling. I just wanted proof of life, that's all, so I might finally get some sleep. Are you being careful?'

'Yes.'

She had clearly not read a single one of my articles. Her Battersea Community Action Group's media integrity subgroup was calling for a boycott of *The Tribune* owing to its stance on immigration. There was a shifty silence.

'But it's so odd you should call now. Really odd. Did I tell you what happened yesterday?'

She seemed to be pretending that we hadn't not spoken in weeks.

'Well, it was late in the afternoon, I was doing the washing up and *The Archers* was on. I've been totally engrossed of course, what with poor Arthur's death. Are you following it darling?'

'No Ma, I'm not following it.'

'Oh.'

She allowed a moment for this disappointment to register.

'Well *I'm* engrossed and I was listening doing the washing-up when a small, neurotic looking bird landed right on the kitchen window ledge. I think it was a wren, but it could have been a sparrow. I've not got a clue about birds. Do you know birds? Anyway, it was this jittery little thing with angry eyes, pecking at the glass. I screamed, quite loudly because it gave me a shock, but it didn't budge. It just stood there, pecking and glaring.'

She paused to reflect on this small bird's unprovoked aggression and I sat in the darkness thinking about the large bird that was at that moment stalking the balcony on the other side of my drawn, faux-velvet curtains.

'You know darling, you'll think I'm losing my mind, but I could have sworn that bird had a look of your father. The eyes, or maybe it was the expression. Angry. Judging.'

I stared at the floor next to my bed, following the green veins pulsing through the fake marble tiles. Was my mother losing her mind?

'Did you say anything to him?'

'Who?'

'The bird. Dad.'

'Say anything? What a strange idea. Why would I talk to a bird? No darling, but I looked at it and it looked back at me furiously for a good while, ages it seemed, then it just flew off. I can't work out if it's a good or a bad sign but it definitely felt like some sort of omen. And with no word from you, you can imagine where my mind went.'

I considered telling her about my own hostile bird I was at

that moment cowering from in the darkness but my throat had started doing this strange contracting thing, like it was trying to strangle itself. So instead, I said nothing.

'Sara? Are you there?'

'It's two years since Dad died, isn't it?' I said, forcing out a thick, alien voice.

'Can you speak up Bob, I can't hear you! Oh dear. Are you there?'

I swallowed hard several times.

'OF COURSE HE'S ON YOUR MIND BECAUSE HE FUCKING DIED THE OTHER DAY! IT'S HIS SECOND FUCKING DEATH-VERSARY!' I shouted into the phone, hoarse and terrifying.

'My God Sara! You're screeching like a gorgon!'

'Sorry.'

'Good Lord!'

I coughed hard to clear my throat and we were both quiet for a while.

'Ma?' I asked the darkness. 'Was Dad angry with me?'

'Angry? Of course, he was angry. He was always angry.'

A rapping of hard beak on glass signalled the resumption of the deranged bird's attack.

'But was he angry with *me*, Ma? When he died.'

'Why would he be angry with you?'

A feathered thud as it hurled its body against the closed balcony doors, which it sometimes did.

'For coming back to Jerusalem. For leaving him when he was dying.'

Was she laughing? What the fuck was funny about that? Why did she only ever laugh at the wrongest possible moments?

'Oh Bobby, darling! I don't think he noticed when you were there! Don't you remember? He was out of it, totally out of it. Kept talking about armies of hats on the march and a missing briefcase. When he was conscious he was busy conjugating made-up Latin verbs or assaulting nurses. He kept accusing that nice Scott of being Pol Pot, do you remember? Scott's heritage is *Vietnamese* of course.'

There was another pause as Ma explored her most unpleasant memories of my dying father.

'God, he was awful to those poor nurses. I told you, didn't I? How he shouted and carried on when they were changing his nappies and tubes and so forth.'

She sighed bitterly at these recollections of her late incontinent husband's mortifying behaviour.

'But no, he didn't ask for you, darling. Not once. So I shouldn't give that another thought. I'm sure you have plenty of more important things to be worrying about.'

My cheeks had become wet, and I wiped them with the mound of my thumb in the dark, roomy silence. The balcony had fallen silent. The line clicked and crackled.

'Bob? Are you there?'

'Yes,' I said.

'You keep disappearing, it's quite difficult. But it's a good thing you called. I've been meaning to ask you about your father's watch. You don't want it, do you? I was wearing it for a bit but the wristband is all tacky and stinky. It's just a bit too revolting. I'll give it to charity.'

'DON'T!' I shouted, then added more softly, 'I'll have it.'

'Fine! It's yours!'

She was offended again. Dad had been asleep when I last saw him alive. He reeked of acrid chemical even from the armchair furthest from his hospital bed. Ma was telling me that as much as she wanted to chat, her food was now stone cold and even if she didn't feel like eating, she probably should because people kept telling her how thin she looked.

'And frankly Sara, I'm exhausted. We've just had Black History Month, of course, and I've been more or less living at the centre. You know I'm happy to do what I can, really I am, but it would be good if just *one* of them could read or write. You know Bob, this next generation is totally illiterate? Another

Tory tragedy. I don't think one of these kids could spell *decolonisation* if their life depended on it, which of course it does. It's terrifying to think what's to come. So of course it's all on me, the press releases, the briefings, the posters. The Facebooking!'

She pause to sigh pitifully.

'And then today, my first free afternoon in weeks, and I spent it with Cathy. I *know*, of all the people, but she's been so down since Michael had the new baby, and I'm sympathetic, really I am. But Bob, the woman doesn't even draw breath. It's just one long monologue, all about herself, absolutely *no* interest in anything or anyone else. Do you know, she didn't ask me a single question in four hours. Not one! Four hours!'

She exhaled heavily into the receiver.

'I love Cathy, but she *is* exhausting.'

'*Michael* had a baby?'

'You know what I mean, Bob, don't be a pedant. The girl, Mimi. Since *Mimi* had *their* baby. No flies on that little minx. I told Cath to brace herself, who knows how many more she'll pop out, she's still only 12.'

'What?' I said.

'I know! *Poor* old Cath. I told you, Bob, how very down she's been throughout the entire pregnancy. Well, it's somehow even worse now the baby's out, if you can imagine. And she just wants to talk and talk and talk.'

Was I going to be sick? I was.

'So darling, I'll let you go now. Try not to be too morbid. And for God's sake be careful! There's only two of us left now. How awful if it were just me!'

I vomited and my bare legs goose-bumped and trembled against the cold porcelain toilet bowl. My pussy hurt a lot. I shuddered and vomited again. That nasty bird's claws clipped on the balcony tiles outside. How had he let this happen? Why was he such a fucking idiot?

21
THE COMMANDER

Outside the air was fresher than it had been in days. A cool breeze blowing in from the sea washed over my face with a flush of dusky sunlight. A formation of swallows screamed and fanned over the dried blood red of the hotel's domed roof as Fadi hustled us into the car. Even more agitated than usual, he smoked and bitched at Sami, his skinny left thigh jiggling animatedly in the passenger seat, screaming like a girl when Sami turned a corner too quickly. Sami didn't react. He just kept on driving calmly through the empty streets. Sami was a professional. I too was a professional, here for the job, regardless of personal challenges. I asked Fadi preparatory questions as we drove.

'How old is the commander, Fadi?'

'No idea.'

'Does he have a job, outside of terrorism?'

'*Terrrorrrism*,' Fadi rolled to Sami, apparently mimicking an Israeli Elmer Fudd.

This made Sami belly-laugh and he too said it several times. '*Terrrorrrriiism*! Hahaha. *Terrrorrrism*.'

But it sounded nothing like the English word terrorism when he said it, and no one was laughing but him. Fadi was once again distracted by his phone, which was issuing a series of dings.

'Fadi?' I prompted.

'I think he's 30. Thirty something.'

'Why were you allowed to bring a phone and I wasn't?'

'Maybe coz they don't want your Israeli buddies tracking you?' he said nastily in a dumb American voice, still texting busily, face illuminated by the light of his mobile phone screen, a mean spectre.

'So what kind of reputation does the commander have?' I persevered.

'What do you mean?'

'Ugh, Fadi! What do you mean, what do I mean? What do people say about him? Is he brutal? Brave? Insane?'

'I dunno, Sara. He's the head of a military faction, I guess so.'

'You guess so what?'

Fadi said nothing, he was typing into his phone.

'WHICH ONE, FADI?'

Fadi hit the roof of the car hard with the palm of his hand.

'*Faaadi! Faaadi!* Stop saying my fucking name like that! Fuck!'

More dings.

'This is one annoying woman,' he muttered to himself.

'You think I'm annoying, *Fadi*? You don't think a teenager in skinny jeans texting his girlfriend while we're on our way to meet a TERRORIST COMMANDER isn't annoying? FADI!' I screamed back.

'This the last time we work together,' I said more quietly, shaking with anger. 'This will be the last time you work with any foreign journalist in Gaza, believe me. I'll make sure of it.'

We sat in rageful silence for the rest of the drive through the darkening, dusty streets to the cemetery, the ding of Fadi's phone and the occasional screech of a swallow, or starling, the only noise in the car. Sami pulled up close to the entrance of the cemetery, which was a narrow entry in a stone wall covered with the low-hanging branches of eucalyptus trees. He stayed in his seat, cheerful as usual, while Fadi and I stalked off together, me in my flak, desert boots and helmet, Fadi in his t-shirt, flip-flops and hair gel.

The graveyard was so crowded with graves there wasn't a patch of ground left to tread on without stepping on mounds of buried bodies. Fresh piles of dirt and old sandstone tombs jutted out of the ground at awkward angles, a skeleton mouth crowded with too many teeth. I stepped over a new grave that was just a smear of concrete with someone's name scrawled on it, but there were no living terrorists.

'They should be here! Where are they?' Fadi said, but not to me because we weren't talking.

I said nothing but wandered over to one of the higher tombstones and sat down, trying to stop my legs trembling. Fadi loped off with his mobile to his ear. His silhouette in the deepening dusk was so skinny he looked like a shade slipped out from one of the graves. I read over the questions I'd written for the commander in my notebook.

Who is your main supplier of arms and how are you getting them into Gaza?

Do you worry about dying?

Something was really spooking those starlings. I watched them dementing, screeching and swooping above the trees. Within seconds blasts erupted in the distance, signalling the start of the evening's strikes. The birds could feel them coming. Did birds get killed in airstrikes? Maybe their animal instincts could sense the threat. It would be dark any minute.

I looked down to find Fadi standing in front of me, phone dangling limply by his side. His face was pale and boyish, and his eyes wide and scared. Did he also know something was coming?

'So, what's your girlfriend saying?'

'He's not coming,' Fadi said.

'He?' I laughed.

'He the commander. He's dead.'

'What do you mean?'

'The commander died.'

'What?'

Fadi blinked at me, then looked back towards his phone.

'Fuck!' I screamed and the starlings screamed with me.

I turned and kicked the gravestone I had been sitting on hard with my desert boot until bits of it started to crumble off the side.

'FUCK!' I screamed again in agony because the kicking seemed to have torn my pussy in two.

The commander had been killed by a Qassam rocket. The theory was that it had exploded in his hands in the latter stages of construction, taking out half of his mother's kitchen and all of him. Rocket building is a fiddly business and even the most expert hands can be caught off guard, Fadi told me. It turns out Fadi knew quite a lot about rocket building.

He read me the updates from his phone as they beeped through, and I sat silent in the back of Sami's neat car in my flak jacket and too tight helmet listening to Fadi and looking at the airstrikes as they lit up the sky to our left. It was difficult to concentrate on details of the self-exploding commander or the airstrikes or anything other than my pussy because it was in so much pain that my hands had gone cold and were shaking. Something was very wrong with it.

We stopped at the Hamas checkpoint at the roundabout near the hotel and let the jumpy Hamas men look in our car boot. Then we rolled a further 50 metres down the road and pulled to a stop outside The Beach but I hesitated to move from the backseat as I was unsure what further physical damage moving may inflict. Fadi turned and looked between the two front head seats to see what I was doing.

'You know I can't pay you for a dead commander,' I told his pale, boy-band face. 'I'll pay Sami for his time and, you know, fuel. But I'm not paying for a dead commander who wasn't even going to show me any tunnels anyway.'

I wasn't entirely sure why I said that. It wasn't something I'd considered or planned to say, it just came out as I was so upset about whatever was going on with this pain on top of not having a story. I didn't want to continue with this unplanned conversation any further, so I lifted my torso up from the seat with my hands and slid it out, slamming the door behind me. Who did Fadi think he was with his moodiness and car roof thumping anyway?

Reception Mohammed was in position at his front desk. I could see him out of the corner of his eye smiling at me with concern, about to ask me where I'd been, out after sunset, but I wore the face of someone who did not want to be spoken to. I could see too that little Jihad was back, slumped in a chair behind the reception desk. Did that child ever sleep? I felt his hard stare follow me as I limped painfully up the stairs to my room, taking in this new information.

Emails pinged steadily into my inbox when I hit the refresh button. The first was a message from Neil, which had been sent three hours earlier. *We have a problem, call me immediately*. More messages from Neil and at least one from some new name, Kirsten Black. The phone I had left charging on my bedside table on the instruction of the terrorists had been called 12 times.

I couldn't face reading Neil's messages in agony and with a stomach full only of disappointment. I limped to the bathroom, necked a handful of paracetamols, had a pee the colour of tar that burned like molten lead, then ran a hand towel under a stream of tepid water and placed it gingerly on my injured pussy. I lay like this on the bed for some time before calling down to order hummus and an orange soda with ice, which front desk Mohammed warned may take some time to arrive owing to problems with electricity in the kitchen. I saw no point in returning Neil's calls until I had eaten.

22
Grave Concerns

It was the waiter Mohammed who eventually delivered the food to my room. He placed an assortment of plates on my coffee table with elaborate care and I gave him a 20 shekel tip, which was almost the last of my cash. I ate slowly and meticulously and only when I had wiped the bowl clean of hummus did I open my laptop and look properly at the email assault I had sustained. There were three messages from Neil and several from one Kirsten Black, who turned out to be a very shrill, very bold and particularly vengeful sub-editor. This Kirsten's emails had been sent to me, Neil, and around 20 other people, including every one of *The Tribune*'s foreign news editors, the foreign editor and the editor himself raising some sort of official complaint about my work.

She was not only a jobsworth, this much was obvious, but a deluded one. She wrote that my copy was *offensive* and quoted large illustrative chunks of my unedited pieces, pointing out in bold italics *pejorative* and *inappropriate* phrases. She found several of my descriptive paragraphs *disturbing* and was recommending that I be replaced by a more *stable and experienced* reporter, for fear of reputational damage to the paper. Having read the exchange several times, I stacked my empty plates in an orderly pile, smeared the olive oil from my laptop keyboard and called Neil.

'*Tribune*.'

Was that Neil? I couldn't tell. I asked please to speak with Neil Devereaux.

'Hi there Sara, this is Rob Buttwell.'

Rob was Scottish and friendly and the night editor. His name was not among those included in Black's slanderous email campaign. I guessed no one included the night editor in anything much, not even Kirsten Black.

'Neil's been gone a few hours now, it's past 8.30 here,' Rob breathed heavily into the phone through his nose.

Rob had sinus issues. I explained that I had just returned from an evening out reporting, where there was no mobile phone reception as he would understand, and come back to emails suggesting there was an issue with some copy I'd filed earlier. Had he any idea? I laughed the weary, breezy laugh of a stoic, humourful professional. Rob breathed hard through his nose and the line crackled.

'Hold on a sec there, Sara. I'm just looking.'

There was a pause and then a whistling nasal exhale.

'Your last piece is on the page for tomorrow's paper and yep, it looks fine up there on the site. Everything seems a-okay to me but I'll send Neil a message saying you called. He may still be wanting to speak with you.'

I was preparing myself a saltwater douche when the phone rang. I answered knowing that it was Neil, but in a tone that suggested any number of people could have been calling me.

'This is Sara Byrne.'

'Sara, it's Neil. Where have you been? I've been trying to reach you for hours. We have a serious problem.'

The line crackled.

'Sorry?'

'What?'

We chorused over each other.

'You go, Neil,' I said.

'Yes, so we have some serious issues. Not only did you disappear completely for several hours after filing your piece, but a formal complaint has been raised about the quality of your work. Sara, we have some very grave concerns.'

He paused here, waiting for the gravity of these concerns to travel from his sad flat, somewhere no doubt in Fulham or Putney, to land heavily on my bed in Gaza City.

'Clearly, this is a much larger news story than you're used to handling and I appreciate this has put you under a great deal of pressure. I've spoken with the senior editors here and we are sending Anthony Harper from Damascus to relieve you immediately.'

'Relieve me?' I repeated, amused.

'Yes Sara, relieve you. Take over. Your work has become increasingly erratic and we need a safe pair of hands on such a demanding and visible news event. You've had a good run.'

Now in his stride, Neil was talking like a junior school rugby coach. The veins in the marble tiles on the floor had begun to pulsate as if actual blue and red blood was running through them. They throbbed encouragingly.

'Sara are you there?'

'Yes, I'm here, Neil. The only thing I suppose I'm trying to understand is why you didn't raise these concerns about my reporting earlier. Particularly given that, as you say, this is such a *visible news event*. I'd imagine that you would get back to me immediately with any serious concerns before putting my copy through to the subs' desk.'

The line crackled, but Neil said nothing. Ha! He clearly hadn't taken so much as a peak at my pieces before shipping them off to that production line of hostile sub-editors. Tsk-tsk, Neil. Sloppy! The marble floor veins pulsed with delight.

'Sara, let me read one of your paragraphs back to you.'

There was a pause while Neil clicked around in his computer.

'Here!' he declared with satisfaction, having clearly hit upon a pleasing nugget of eraticism.

He read slowly and with emphasis.

'*The deranged, dirt-smeared, now homeless children clawed over each other as the bombs fell, a desperate, writhing mass. Four loud explosions, one after the other: Bang! Bang! Bang! Bang! The wretched displaced could not know they were not the target of the Israeli fire, not on this occasion, and their ignorant, fearful squeals tore the air.*'

Tore the air was hackneyed. That was annoying.

'If you were unhappy with my copy when you edited it, Neil, I do wish you had called to tell me. Tonight, when I heard nothing back, which is almost always the case after I file, I assumed I was in the clear to leave the hotel and pursue a very exciting exclusive. As you know, Neil, mobile phone reception is very bad across much of the Gaza Strip, particularly in the areas I was working . . . '

'Anthony arrives in Tel Aviv tomorrow and will be in Gaza as soon as we can coordinate his crossing with the Israelis . . . '

Neil was talking across me again.

'Neil, did you hear me? The connection here is very bad even at the hotel,' I shouted over him carefully. 'I'm saying that I have secured access to a terror tunnel, the underground base of the terror cell that kidnapped that Israeli soldier. The leadership has agreed to talk exclusively to me. They have not spoken to a journalist before. This is, I believe, a world exclusive.'

'Sara, can you hear me?'

Neil and I had stopped talking at the same moment. I started again, quickly.

'Neil, so the leader of the Al-Yasser Salah al-Deen Front has agreed to take me into the network of terror tunnels underneath Gaza City where their arsenal and leadership are hidden. I'm sure you know the group. I'm working with an award-winning Italian photographer who will get fantastic images, but if you're not interested, with Anthony arriving, I totally understand. I'll offer it elsewhere.'

There was a long pause on Neil's end of the line and I resumed my tracing of the pulsing marble veins until they were lost under the red and blue woven rug. Jihad hadn't left me a chocolate in days.

'Are you there, Neil?'

'Yes, I'm here. You should know it is absolutely unacceptable for a contracted stringer to be negotiating access to a terror cell on our behalf without our sanction. That is totally unacceptable.'

'I see. Having not worked for you during an active conflict before, I wasn't aware,' I said, noticing that I had been upgraded to stringer. 'Have I been contracted?'

'But if you've already gone ahead and secured the access on time we've been paying you for, I don't see what else we can do now but push ahead. You can aim for 1,200 words.'

'Okay Neil, that's fine,' I said. 'Once Anthony is here, I assume you won't be needing me for daily news?'

There was another pause on Neil's end of the line. I lay back on the bed and pushed my index finger in and out of my sweaty belly button, making a squelching noise. A torrent of sweat that had been pouring down my torso during the call was pooling in the depths of my naval cavity. Squelch, squelch.

'We can work all that out with Anthony when he arrives. He might want the support,' Neil said.

Squelch, squelch, squelch, the movement of my finger in and out of my belly button.

'Okay Neil. I'll make sure to keep you updated on any future movements.'

I woke up some hours later in a lot of pain. Swinging my legs off the bed, I moved slowly across the tiles towards the painkillers in the bathroom, whimpering. My phone beeped on the sink and I grabbed it. It wasn't Fadi.

'Ciao, sexy. I've been thinking about you. Winky face.'

Alessandro. I couldn't imagine what his thoughts might look like.

'Come here and show me what you've been thinking?' I texted back.

Why had I sent that? There was no way I could fuck him. I probably couldn't even manage a blow job without being sick or passing out. My phone beeped again.

'Where's here?'

Jesus Christ!

'My room. Winky face.'

Tap, tap, tap. Was that the fucking bird again? I threw my phone on the bed in disgust at how stupid my apparent lover was, marched to the balcony doors to close the curtains on that horrifying, tapping, shitting bird, then limped to the bathroom to apply thick layers of lip gloss. That angry marching had not been a good idea. I pulled my hair back tightly, smoothing it down with water, and applied layer after layer of gloss until my lips tingled. Watching myself in the mottled bathroom mirror, I slid my index finger in and out of my sticky mouth. It looked quite hot, but I was very pale and clammy.

There was a knock at the door and I put the gloss down. Alessandro had clearly just come in from outside and was sweating. He had his phone in his hand and was staring at it with confusion. I pushed my sticky lips into a pout, and he smiled leeringly with his tobacco teeth. Pulling him into the room, I shut the door behind him and lowered myself gently to my knees, triggering a rush of cold sweat to my forehead. He mewled, letting his arms fall down limply by his side. His cock was only half hard when I freed it from his jeans and put it in my sticky mouth. It tasted musty and sweaty. He put his big, thick arm around my head, forcing himself deep into the back of my mouth in quick, deep thrusts. My sticky gloss had got onto his reddish pubic stubble, which was grazing my face. I gagged.

'Come *on* my mouth,' I instructed when I realised how quickly he was going to and he immediately did with loud, feminine moans.

He didn't let go but stood for a long while panting, pressing my cheek to his stubbly groin so I wiped his come off my face with my shirt. The metallic saltiness of it mixed with the bubble gum flavour of the gloss was revolting and I retched, but he didn't seem to notice.

'I need to clean myself,' I said.

He released my hair and I moved carefully towards the bathroom. I could see him in the reflection of the bathroom mirror, standing in the middle of the bedroom with his trousers around his ankles gazing at his abdomen, his limp cock in the palm of his hand. I splashed water on my now corpse-pale face and smoothed my disturbed hair, feeling very much like I was going to puke.

'You're an unusual woman, Sara,' he called into the bathroom.

Unusual. I looked at myself. My mouth was red, my cheeks chaffed and my face whiter than I'd ever seen it before. The circles under my eyes had darkened to a deep purple. I needed to lie down before I passed out.

'Look at that big fat ass.'

Alessandro slapped his heavy hand on my ass as I lay on the tangled bed where he was also now lying, his pants still around his ankles. The pain from the ass slap shot down to my toes but I didn't scream, I pushed my face into the pillow.

'So,' I said, when the worst of the pain had passed and I was able to raise my head. 'I wanted to talk to you about a story I'm working on.'

Amused by this change of tone, the Italian smirked as he rested his huge head on one of his meaty arms.

'I want you to take the photographs, if you like.'

'Oh I like,' he cat-purred and squeezed my ass hard.

'I'm going to interview a commander of one of the factions with their weapons in their terror tunnel, and I want you to take pictures of all the fighters and the weapons they have stashed down there.'

'What? I didn't understand.'

His big nose face became dramatically serious.

'The Al-Yasser Salah al-Deen Front,' I explained patiently. 'The ones who blew up the Israeli tank. I'm going to interview their leader in their secret underground tunnel, and I want you to take the pictures.'

His expression was now both vacant and concerned.

'Who?'

'The group that kidnapped the soldier?'

'That was Hamas.'

'No, it was these guys and I've convinced them to give me access, but not through Nasser. He doesn't know so you can't tell him.'

He was thinking hard and in order to do this better, had raised himself up onto his square blond elbows.

'Nasser?'

The Italian raised a huge blond eyebrow quizzically. I wasn't sure how much more of this conversation I could survive.

'My fixer,' I said.

'So who are you working with if it's not your fixer? Not that skinny kid from the other night? I didn't like the looks of these kids. I don't trust them. This could be a dangerous game, Sara.'

A sudden officious rap at the door prompted him to jump to his feet. He grabbed a pillow to cover his nakedness rather than just pulling up his pants. I hoped it would be Jihad wanting to clean. I needed new towels and new sheets as mine were now filthy. He might also make Alessandro leave.

'Don't answer it,' the Italian pleaded like a terrified teenager.

'What? Why not?'

Picking up the discarded filthy robe and tying it tightly round me, I hobbled towards the door. Oddly, there was Nasser. He had never been to my room before and his face looked strange. Had his kid died?

'Sara!' he exclaimed.

'Nasser!' I exclaimed back.

I realised that I had no idea what time it was. Morning, surely. Nasser's quick hawk eyes took in my grazed, gloss-covered face and dirty robe and darted over my shoulder to where I assumed Alessandro was still standing with his modesty pillow. His pinched expression hardened, and he looked back to me, lips pursed.

'Sorry I disturbed you but we need to talk urgently and you weren't answering your phone.'

'Hey brother!' Alessandro called from behind me. 'I was just leaving.'

Nasser and I stood in silence in the doorway, watching Alessandro button his trousers and lace his desert boots, then gather up his scarf and cameras, all of which took an uncomfortably long time. We stood back to let him pass out the door and he shuffled his stocky frame between us. He nodded at Nasser, who did not nod back, and stalked off down the tiled corridor on his little, bandy cowboy legs, echoing as he trod.

'I've been waiting downstairs for you for more than an hour. I've been calling your phone,' Nasser hissed softly.

'I didn't hear! What time is it?' I asked, indicating for him to step into the room, which he did by one small step, stopping just inside the doorway and holding his small frame rigid and upright.

'Israel opened the border again and a whole lot of new correspondents arrived this morning. Everyone has agreed to work in groups with shared fixers. We are working in a team now, and ours is in the lobby wanting to get out.'

Nasser was spitting rather than talking.

'What do you mean *working in teams*? Who is our team?'

I did not want to work in a team. Nasser's expression was lodged somewhere between fury, disgust and pity, which I resented. I told him I would see him *and our team* in the lobby shortly and moved to close the door, but he blocked it with his hand.

'Sara, you need to pull yourself together,' he said in a low whisper.

Walking fully into the room without invitation, he strode over to the curtains and pulled them open, allowing bright, hot light to flood into the room. Flinging the glass doors open, he let in a blast of beach noise and air.

'Don't! The bird!' I shouted, looking anxiously towards the balcony. 'It needs to be killed. It's unhinged.'

But the terrifying crow or gull or whatever it had been was gone from the balcony. In its place stood an ordinary pigeon, which we had startled. It jerked its purple head out from under its wing, regarded us with blinking curiosity and cooed benignly.

'Sara, I'm going to be very straight with you. I don't think you're well,' Nasser said. 'This room stinks like a sick teenager. You have black circles under your eyes. The face is white and sweating. It seems you're unwell.'

I raised my eyebrows to indicate that this latest outburst of advice was not welcome, but Nasser continued.

'I know you're not going to like hearing this, but your behaviour is more and more worrying. You're getting crazy angry at little things. Not washing, I think. Listen, war is stressful, of course, especially when you're not used to it, but Sara, you've stopped making sense. You're afraid of birds? And now this!'

He indicated with a priestly gesture towards the bed. Was Nasser jealous I had fucked the Italian?

'I think maybe it's time for you to go home. You should be with family, people who love you.'

Ha! He knew I didn't have those. He had spoken to Neil! And Anthony too, probably. Monk-faced traitor! They all wanted me to leave! Was Anthony jealous? Was I getting too close to a story they didn't want told? Was Nasser Hamas? No! Not Hamas. Was Nasser an *Israeli* agent?

'Thank you, Nasser. I appreciate your concern. Really,' I said, in my lowest most controlled voice. 'You're right. I've let myself get overtired but I'm fine. I'll wash and change quick as I can and meet you downstairs. Please, apologise to the team for me.'

Nasser looked downcast as I ushered him out into the hallway and closed the door behind him. From the balcony, the pigeon struck up an ominous guttural chorus and it was quite right. I would have to proceed very carefully until I could be sure what I was dealing with.

23
LOVE

It was July and Cathy was in remission. She had taken the children to a resort in the Algarve where they played in tennis tournaments and she drank iced rosé with the other mothers of tennis playing children. She went to this resort every year to stay in the same very white villa on a golf course owned by another tennis mother's banker husband. She loved this villa, even though it was identical in every way to the resort's other 1,500 villas, all occupied by other families whose children knew each other from London's private schools. Its beach, tennis courts and all of the compound's 15 themed restaurants could be reached by golf buggy. Cathy and the kids would not pass its towering electric gates for seven days.

Michael could not join his family in Portugal. This was not, as Cathy accused, because he loathed her, the Algarve or the other tennis mothers who were her friends. Michael acknowledged that yes, the villa-owning banker was an unbearable ginger prick who in the course of one dinner had told him off for swearing and then informed Michael that he earned 'a penny or two more' than him. But no, this was not the issue. Michael was on a tight deadline to edit a hard-going manuscript, the second literary effort of a brilliant correspondent who, while brilliant, had written another book in bullet points that read very much like gunfire. Michael needed to flesh these out into a manuscript that could be presented to a publisher before the publisher went on holiday in August. He would be doing this at one of his other writer's wisteria-covered cottages in West Sussex because it was empty and because I had just quit my job at the women's supplement and we were giving my future some serious thought.

We had five days, four whole nights of sleeping tightly slotted together until he woke me by fucking me. We drank percolators of black coffee then drove to the village where Michael discussed our wine with the wine man and we searched second-hand bookshops for important novels for me to read while the book-shop owner, who assumed I was Michael's daughter, flirted coyly with him. We fucked in the sunshine in the garden to a soundtrack of small hovering bees and cooing wood pigeons watched by the shut-in neighbour who thought we couldn't see him behind his twitching net curtain.

Michael worked topless at a wrought iron table that was flaking dark green paint. He weighed his flighty papers down with wine glasses and white-washed stones borrowed from the garden wall and his bare chest skin darkened to a roast beef brown. He scratched at the manuscript he was annotating. With his head tilted back, he peered through his sweat-slippery reading glasses at his papers, and occasionally my ass, prodding the wire frame back into place with a long, well-formed index finger. I lay sprawled under an old apple tree on a rug in front of him, pale in my underwear, reading the books he'd bought me, drinking white wine from a tiny glass and eating warm cheese.

All the books he gave me were Russian because Michael couldn't believe I hadn't read any Russian writers. The all-time great, he said, was Nabokov but I would start with Bulgakov. Then Dostoyevsky. Reading Russians made me feel cultured and sipping at my wine, I laughed loudly at the funny bits for Michael's benefit. The garden air smelled of grass and honey. I was enjoying the sound of the scratch of his pencil, the allergic tickle of long grass against my legs, the feeling of his eyes on me until the scratching stopped altogether and I looked up. Michael had taken off his glasses and was rubbing his sweaty nose between his index finger and thumb, holding me with a strange misty look.

'What? You're too sweaty for glasses. You need a *pince nez?*' I called over.

'A *pance nay?* Are you suggesting I'm Koroviev Faggot?'

'Are you?'

I grinned, delighted at how erudite the Russians had made our flirting.

'Obviously I'm a Woland. Come here,' he commanded, extending a tanned, hairless arm towards me.

I put my book down and stood up obediently, carefully negotiating the rug of cheese between us, picking bits of dried grass from the damp skin on my ass. He pulled me onto his lap and pressed me close to his hot, clammy torso.

'You sure you're not a Faggot?'

'Kiss me,' he directed and I did.

He tasted of sunshine and salty sweat and kissed me deeply until I could feel him harden against my ass. He cupped my face in his big hands and sought out my eyes.

'You know, I love you Sara,' he whispered.

The birds fell silent. All the world was suddenly silent except my heart, which was beating too loudly and too quickly. The universe had vacuum packed around my chest creating an unbearable pressure. My ears popped and then started to ring. I squirmed on Michael's lap and he crinkled his eyes into deep wrinkles of amusement.

'It's okay girly, you don't have to say it back.'

He pulled my head down onto the damp bare skin of his chest and pressed it there.

My cheek was getting wet with his sweat and my neck was bent at an odd angle, so I wriggled to sit back upright on his knee.

'I do though. I love you too.'

I meant it but the words came out phlegmy and strangled.

'Sara, look at me.'

I tried to meet his gaze but found I couldn't, so rested my

eyes instead on his downy earlobe, which had a fleck of green table paint on it.

'Poor kid,' he laughed tightly and gave my shoulders a squeeze.

I shifted my gaze to his chin, where his dimple was covered in a short forest of greying stubble.

'I think you're more like the master actually. If he got old, and wasn't writing much anymore,' I tried, wanting to be loving.

'Oh God, it gets worse.'

He laughed again and clutched at his unruly grey hair. I shifted on his lap so that I could reach his cock but found it had gone soft as a sleeping gerbil. I licked his salty neck but his body stiffened uncomfortably so I stepped off and looked at him instead, blinking into the sun flares leaping through the branches behind his head. His hair, wet from temple sweat, had moulded into an undignified spike on top of his head.

'Should I fetch another bottle of wine?' I asked.

'Now there's a good idea,' he said, replacing his glasses and picking up his pencil.

I padded gingerly towards the kitchen, dry grass spiking the soles of my feet, and the wood pigeons resumed their cooing. A heavy grey cloud drifted in the way of the sun and the garden grew suddenly cold. I shivered.

'You feel okay after that pill?' he called after me.

'Yup,' I called back, pausing in the doorway.

'Not sicky like last time?'

'Nope.'

'Good girl. By the way, I heard back from my friend at the charity. He's still looking for journalists for that Congo trip if you're interested? It'd be great experience. Grab the red?'

'Sure!' I called back.

I did not like the sound of Congo. A sharp pain gnawed at my stomach and I shivered again. My guts growled and cramped and I wondered if taking that pill really could hurt your stomach if you took it too much. Every single pharmacist had enquired suspiciously about the last time I'd taken one, like they knew. I thought they were being judgy but maybe you really weren't meant to take them every month. I had also eaten a lot of cheese though. I needed a glass of wine.

24
ALWAYS SAY YES

The rude Ukrainian receptionist had been missing for days and front desk Mohammed was alone behind his counter. He wore his most nervous smile and was sweating from every part of his perfectly round face. He had a phone jammed between his ear and shoulder and piles of paper in front of him, which he was squaring and re-squaring into neater and neater piles. On the other side of the desk, he faced a dense reception of new journalists.

'The Beach Hotel never turns away a journalist,' was Mo's thing, Gaza's entrepreneurial champion of the free press. He repeated this slogan whenever a journalist was checking in and he happened to be about, which he hadn't been for days. But demand had never exceeded capacity before and with Mo removed to his home in Jordan and the Ukrainian absconded, reception Mohammed found himself alone, singlehandedly working to uphold the hotel's integrity against a deluge of roomless journalists. He spoke solicitously into his phone as I passed.

'No . . . Yes . . . Of course I understand . . . and The Beach Hotel also values your privacy, very much . . . '

Mohammed's large face was flushed so deeply red I wondered if the embarrassment might actually kill him. The waiting media pack pressed up against his counter, a listless, fresh-clothed huddle of neat luggage and blackberry-busy fingers. I squeezed passed the reception counter keeping my eyes fixed on the floor so as to avoid being drawn into any discussion about the unthinkable sharing of my room.

The lobby was also packed with reporters, crews and

cameras. Paula Miranda was at her usual table, slurping coffee and jabbering into the newly arrived ear of a correspondent from LA. I recognised him from Jerusalem, where he always wore a neatly pressed, light-blue Ralph Lauren linen shirt. In Gaza, he wore a navy-blue Ralph Lauren polo shirt and navy-blue Ralph Lauren baseball cap. His cold, grey robot eyes scanned their new environment. To his left sat the woman from the political magazine who looked like she made her own yoghurt and beside her was Ashraf, who was on his phone. Fixer Group One, I supposed.

Jane and Steve sat with their old, blind, lame Jim. They had also taken on a new addition, a very young, very wet looking journalist from a financial newspaper. I'd met him at a few Jerusalem press conferences and seen him at The Affry's bars, Harry or Barney. Somehow it was well-known that he had received a double first from Cambridge. He was trembling. Group Two.

In the far corner of the lobby, Nasser sat at a table with our group, which was apparently Stuart Finch and the quiet, angry Dane. They weren't even new arrivals but Nasser explained that as both their fixers had dumped them to work with rich American network crews, they'd asked if we could work together, which was pretty convenient for Nasser. How much was he going to make out of all of this?

'So how's this going to work?' I asked him in a low voice while Stuart and the Dane, whose name was Jan Petersson, talked about the last time they'd seen each other in Iraq; someone's safe house had been blown up. 'We share quotes? We take turns asking questions? Who gets to choose what story we do?'

Nasser low-talked back saying he wasn't too happy about this new set up either because his job was now settling arguments between three giant children.

'In Gaza, in a war, we pull together. But that's not something you people seem able to do,' he whispered, meanly.

I said nothing because I actually didn't care about what we were going to do. I needed to concentrate all my effort on making up with Fadi and getting my tunnels story back on track, which was more than enough to be getting on with while dealing with this horrific pussy pain. So I decided then and there that my new team persona was going to be quiet and accommodating.

The Dane was also mostly silent. He, like me, had a big red face and big, sad, uncomfortable blue eyes, which had fixed themselves dolefully on his coffee while Stuart whined on. The four of us should head out to sea with the fishermen, Stuart was saying. Us four would be on a little fishing boat as it tried to fish while being shot at by those big fuck-off Israeli war ships.

'No one's done it! Imagine the fucking images we'd get!' Stuart nasaled.

Stuart pitched himself as a photographer-reporter and insisted that editors illustrate his pieces only with his own pictures. A few days earlier, a big deal Serbian photographer had slammed his hand in a car door outside a bombed building, claiming Stuart had been trying to steal his angle. Stuart's slammed hand was now in a bandage and had blackened at the fingernails. His camera with its enormous lens hung around his neck. Nasser had been nodding along in apparent agreement with Stuart.

'That's a very strong idea,' he said.

But we should also know there had been an airstrike on a strawberry farm near the border overnight. A baby had been killed. Hamas said it was an Israeli airstrike, but the Israelis said the farm had been destroyed by a Hamas rocket that had fallen short. Nasser had spoken with the neighbours of the strawberry farmers and they would be happy to meet with us. If, for whatever reason, there was an issue with the fishermen, we could always go there.

'I'm not good on boats,' the Dane said, speaking for the first time.

Stuart puckered. I also voted for the strawberry farm story in my new meek way. Hours at sea in a fishing boat with my injuries while trying to reach Fadi was not going to work.

'I learned I wasn't good on boats when I did the Gaza fishermen story four years ago,' the Dane continued. 'And I reminded myself every time I did the Gaza fishermen story since then that I'm not good on boats. Every one of the five times I've done that story, I've told myself, "Jan, you're not good on boats, you shouldn't do this story again."'

He spoke slowly and deliberately. Stuart glared at him then looked to Nasser for back up but Nasser was fastidiously packing his notebooks into his shoulder bag and unavailable for eye contact.

'But you haven't done the story in a fucking war, have you mate, because no one fucking has!' Stuart hissed back at the Dane.

'*Die Zeit* did it two days ago,' the Dane deadpanned. 'But I haven't, no, because I'm no good on boats.'

Stuart snorted in stunned disbelief and, for want of a better audience, turned to me.

'You believe our fucking luck? Stuck with the only fucking Viking who's scared of boats,' he snarled.

I smiled in a lobotomised way. The Dane said nothing but resumed his doleful looking at his coffee, which was now swirling around in its cup in the palm of his large hand. He was a good head and shoulders taller than Stuart and maybe half his width again. Stuart, like Nasser, was small but his compact body was tightly packed with venomous energy. If there were to be a physical fight, I was unsure who'd win.

Once the strawberry farm plan was agreed, they both retreated to their rooms to get their flaks while Nasser went to queue for petrol. I stayed sat in the lobby, avoiding movement, and smiled benignly at nothing. My phone rang.

'Good morning Neil,' I answered, because who else would it be.

It was, in fact, Jason Argent. The foreign editor to whom I had not spoken since day one of the war.

'Hello Sara, it's Jason. How are you getting along?'

Friendly but clipped Jason. How interesting. Meaning that Neil was either sick, sacked or sulking? I decided not to ask but with as much professional charm as my shivering body could muster told him I was very well thank you and in fact just about to head out the door to visit a strawberry farm.

'Not for strawberries. A bombed one,' I added. 'Not an exclusive either I'm afraid as we're working in groups now owing to a shortage of fixers and a glut of journalists. I'm with a big Danish guy called Jan, and Stuart Finch.'

'Right. Nasser filled me in. Collaborating with Finch should be interesting, good luck with that.'

I hoped very much that something terrible had happened to Neil in Putney as Jason instructed me carefully on how to report a piece from Palestine, which he explained was a business of corroborated facts, a minimum of descriptive colour, and always an official response from Israel to any Palestinian accusation.

I noticed Jane Sawyer next to me, quietly writing notes. She looked up briefly and smiled, which was surprising. I smiled back, marvelling at her shirts still being so clean and crisp. She looked like an advert in a woman's supplement, for espadrilles or really expensive incontinence pants. Incredible. Jason was telling me how important it was that I call the desk the minute I was back from my reporting trip to discuss the angle and confirm my deadline, and I was nodding. Why had he been talking to Nasser, though? What had Nasser told him?

'Speaking of exclusives Jason,' I lowered my voice.

Jane was the only journalist sitting close enough to hear. She seemed trustworthy but she was also taking notes.

'Speaking of exclusives though Jason,' I repeated in a whisper and turned my face towards the rocks in the wall. 'Has Neil filled you in on the longer piece I'm working on? The exclusive with the fighting unit? I'm really happy we're doing this. We hear so much from Doron and his type and nothing all from their opponents in the field here. In terms of reporting at least, it really is such an asymmetric . . . '

'Woah,' Jason interrupted before I could reach the war part of my sentence. 'Hold up Sara. If I heard you correctly, the answer is no. *The Tribune* is not in the business of giving a platform to Hamas terrorists. Let's just focus on getting this strawberry farm piece away and when Anthony arrives we'll all talk again.'

I ploughed on.

'I think they're more Fatah-ish terrorists actually. I mean, *they* don't think they're terrorists.'

Jason, now irritable, told me to please do as I was instructed and file 700 clean words of copy on the bombed strawberry farm. He then hung up very much like a cunt but to his credit having said goodbye. I leaned my forehead which was burning with the effort of having to argue against the cool of the stone wall and said cunt gently to it. Why were they all such cunts?

'Are you okay?'

I had forgotten Jane Sawyer. I prized my head from the wall and saw she had stopped writing notes and was instead holding me with her expressionless attention.

'Me? Yes. All good,' I smiled at her and wiped the sweat beads from my upper lip. 'Just trying to figure out editors. If they're human, that sort of thing.'

I laughed without moving my body, Jane placed her pen down carefully by her notebook and said *ah*. I mimed shooting myself in the temple and my brains blowing out the other side.

'You know, I was a foreign editor myself for 10 years before coming here,' she said. 'It's Sara isn't it?'

Her voice had the cooling effect of a hand fan. It was pleasant when she talked. I nodded.

'Have you ever worked in a news room Sara?' she asked me.

I shook my head no, unless she counted the women's supplement in which case yes but I didn't feel like admitting to the foundations of my reporting career being laid in cellulite creams. She said *ah* again and asked if an older woman could offer her some unsolicited advice, to which I said yes please.

'It may surprise you Sara, but most foreign editors don't travel much outside the UK. They rarely leave the news room. Their world is lived between screens of 24-hour news bulletins, the constant tick of news wires, and meetings. Endless meetings. They see very little of real life anywhere, let alone Gaza. Few know what reporting a story like this entails.'

This did not surprise me. I thought of Neil in his sad Putney living room with a microwave meal for one.

'When I was foreign editor, every story I ran from Gaza received hundreds of complaints from readers outraged by bias I hadn't seen but was responsible for. The editor was frequently furious over lost readership, lost advertising, having to squirm through another humbling meeting with the Israeli ambassador all because of a piece I had run.'

She paused for meaningful breath, allowing me time to digest this insight. She was fascinating. This was probably as close to animated as Jane Sawyer could get but she barely moved a facial muscle or altered the tone of her voice. I nodded and smiled, shifting painfully in my seat, hoping she would stop talking so I could stop having to be attentive. I was very thirsty.

'The best advice I can give any young correspondent is to make the lives of desk editors easy. File clean copy and file it on time. Always say yes. Stick to your word counts. Don't cause trouble, keep your head down, make them look good. These are the reporters who do well and *maybe,* one day, can expect to call a few shots.'

She stopped there and watched me, a mother superior delivering some hard truths to a novice, she searched my face for evidence of her instruction having been received. *Those who aim at faultless regularity will only produce mediocrity*, I thought and was lost for a while trying to remember who had said that. Bright spots of colour obscured my view of Jane's face and I wondered if I was going to faint.

'Wow, thank you,' I said stumped for any other response. 'Don't suppose I could have some of that water?'

Jane frowned and squinted an expression between concern and aversion that reminded me very much of my mother. Pouring me a glass from her glistening bottle, she asked if I was feeling alright.

'Fine! Just so thirsty!' I gulped. 'Thanks.'

'You know, we're all colleagues here Sara. If you need help, you can ask,' she said firmly, picking up her pen.

I smiled weakly in thanks and splashed what was left in the glass on my face and neck in the hopes that might keep me conscious. Jane resumed her note-making.

25
A Big Yellow Eye

The obliterated strawberry farm was in Beit Lahiya, a 30-minute drive from the hotel. The Dane and I sat in the back despite our much larger size and Stuart took the front seat next to Nasser because, as a photographer, he insisted he had to be positioned by the windscreen to shoot at any moment. Jan had to fold his giant legs in two to squeeze next to me and his enormous blond head pressed against the roof of Nasser's car. Stuart hung his uninjured arm out of the open front window. Gripping the side of the car with his palm, he was listing his experiences in much worse wars.

'Gaza is without doubt the safest conflict zone in the world. Compared to Iraq or Afghanistan, it's child's play,' he shouted into the car. 'I'd rather be bombed by the Israeli Air Force than any other army in the world, believe me.'

Stuart guffawed and Nasser stared steadily out the front window.

'It's also pointless because when it comes down to it, we all know the Palestinians haven't got a fucking chance. They know it. We know it. The Israelis know it. They're a lost fucking cause. To all intents and purposes, this war was won in '67!'

The overnight airstrikes had changed the shape of the city and big chunks were missing from its oldest parts. The Beach Camp in particular was pockmarked with smouldering holes and the agonising jolts of the car passing over the new bumps caused me to pour sweat, but I remained stoically silent. I had the window down and the warm air pummelling my face helped. We drove past three large houses in a row that had been reduced to their charred foundations.

'Those were the homes of the minister of interior and his family, but they were empty when they were bombed. The minister is in Jordan,' Nasser told us, in tour guide mode.

Stuart wasn't listening, he was talking about Pakistan.

'I never usually work with fixers, or translators. I work best alone. Even in Swat Valley, I can pass for Pashtun. As long as I don't talk. And no one talks to me.'

We finally pulled up outside a smallish brick building missing half its roof and totally blackened inside. This was the bombed strawberry farm. I was slowly edging off my seat to get out of the car when Paula, *The LA Chronicle* and the magazine mouse came out of an even smaller building next door, led by Ashraf.

'Great! It's a fucking junket!'

Stuart slammed the car door behind him, causing it to jump and me to yelp. The great Dane said nothing. We followed Nasser towards the same front door Paula had just exited, our teams filing past each other with polite nods. It felt more like an open house than a junket, I thought, but that was about all I thought because mostly I was concentrating on walking. Things were looking a bit fuzzy.

Nasser was talking to a short, middle-aged woman in a brown hijab standing in the doorway. The woman had a chubby face and was pushing strands of grey-black hair into her scarf nervously with little plump fingers while she talked a lot and quickly. Nasser told us to leave our shoes at the door. This took me some time to do as the pain of bending over to unlace my desert boots made me drip ice sweat. Finally I managed and followed Stuart, Jan and Nasser in socked feet into the woman's very dark house. As my eyes adjusted, I saw we were in a brown sitting room lined with flat brown cushions, the half-drunk cups of tea from Paula's group still on a tray in the centre of the room.

'Got to be careful with this sort of story. Palestinians love to spin a good fucking yarn. We need to make sure we pin them on facts,' Stuart stage-whispered over his shoulder at me and

Jan as he folded himself nimbly into a yogic, cross-legged pose on one of the floor cushions.

Everything in the small room was brown: the carpet, the low cushions, the walls, the curtains, the women. A teenage girl hurried in to remove group one's dirty glasses and our fidgety hostess indicated for us to sit. Jan fell heavily to his knees. I didn't know how best to lower myself to avoid unbearable pain and after some fussing, slid down against the wall in a sort of side saddle, still managing to catch myself on the seam of my jeans. I yelped and the main woman looked at me with concern.

'Tight jeans!' I simpered.

She looked at me uncomprehendingly. Nasser shot me an admonishing glare and did not translate. Yet another woman in a brown hijab came into the room carrying a tray packed with little glasses of brown tea and a plate piled high with chocolate bars. How did every household in Gaza have such huge reserves of tea and biscuits? They had to have been stockpiling for tragedy and its guests. The Dane was wearing bright pink socks and their colour burst out from their brown surrounds. We were inside a giant Liquorice Allsort.

Stuart started his questioning, inviting the woman to tell us what she remembered of the previous night's events. No one took a chocolate bar. The woman launched into her story with energy, talking animatedly at Nasser with expansive arm gestures and dramatic facial expressions, shoving unseen strands of hair back under her scarf. Nasser translated as she spoke.

'I could hear the children screaming, they were all burning in the house . . . My husband ran outside to try to help them, but the fire was too big. There was no way we could save them . . . It was too big,' Nasser said.

Stuart cut across Nasser's translation with a string of practical questions about how many people were inside, what their names and ages were and whether any of them were members of any militant faction. There were 10 of them, Nasser answered, and none of them were militants.

'Course they weren't,' Stuart snorted. 'What time did this happen?'

The woman answered with wide stunned eyes and Nasser translated.

'Yes, like I said, we heard the planes, they woke us up, it was around three in the morning and . . . '

Stuart interjected.

'When you say you heard planes, what exactly did you hear? And can you recall how many rounds of munitions were fired?'

I was staring at Jan's socks. Jan was staring grimly at Stuart. Even resting against the wall, I couldn't find a comfortable position for my legs because it felt like I was squatting on shards of glass. Droplets of liquid were falling from my face onto my notebook, tears or sweat. I smeared them into the paper. The woman said through Nasser that she heard a sound that sounded how jets sound and then there were bombs.

'Bombs? How many bombs?' Stuart asked.

He was speaking very loudly and quickly. The woman said she couldn't remember, maybe three. She was looking at Nasser with a fretful expression, anxiously pushing at her hair line.

'Stuart, if you've finished, I'd like to ask some questions, please,' Jan said quietly, with a quick smile in the direction of the scared-looking woman.

Stuart dismissed him with a wave of his sling.

'Madam, I'm sure you've seen your neighbour's house. It's right next door. The interiors are blackened but much of the roof is still intact.'

Stuart extended his unbandaged palm in the direction of Jan's red face and the word madam looped in my head. *Madam. Mad-dam. Madman. Madddaaam.*

'Everyone in this room has seen what an airstrike does to a building. I imagine you've seen many a building hit by an Israeli airstrike, yes?'

The woman was crying.

'Yes, okay. So the force of an airstrike causes a building to collapse in on itself like a crater, it does not cause a house fire. It will be clear to anyone who has spent any time in a conflict zone that your neighbour's house was consumed by some sort of internal fire. Do you disagree?'

Stuart pointed at the woman with his biro as he spoke. The woman's eyes had become enormous, and she was pushing streams of tears into her cheeks with her stubby hands.

'Would you not also agree that the likeliest cause of the damage to your neighbour's farm was a falling projectile, such as a Qassam rocket, that came through its roof, exploded on impact and started a blaze? Not an Israeli airstrike.'

Nasser had stopped translating to allow the now sobbing woman to be comforted by one of the other women. Stuart was shrill with impatience, his eyes gleaming.

'Ask her, Nasser! Do your job, man! Ask her why she is insisting her neighbour's home was destroyed by an Israeli airstrike when any idiot can see it was hit by friendly fire? Is that what Hamas told her to say?'

'Stop this!' Jan bellowed, his enormous fair head radiating fury, blue eyes bloodshot. 'We are guests in this woman's home!'

The crying woman, stunned to have two strange men shouting in her brown living room, stopped weeping and stared at them fearfully instead. Nasser was talking softly to her in Arabic. Stuart leant forward until he was staring her directly in the eyes.

'Madam, are you crying because you are lying?'

Then came the sound of clattering glass on metal tray, Jan, Stuart and Nasser suddenly all on their feet in the hot fudge living room. Large flashing neon spots, pink as socks. Jan standing over Stuart who was jabbing him in the centre of his large chest with his index finger.

'Jab at me again, Stuart, go on. Do it.'

'I'll do what I fucking want, mate,' Stuart jabbed.

Then screams. Men shouting and women screaming. Me screaming because a flaming knife has cut deep into my body and is carving up from my legs through my stomach to my heart.

Then black. Sound stops. Two great, greasy wings fold over me. Heavy feathers stinking of oil and musk that block out light and pain. A big yellow eye opens in the blackness, looks at me, blinks and vanishes. Everything is cold and quiet. Soft and dark.

26
MAD OR NOT MAD

I had stopped throwing up but was still clutching the metal rubbish bin to my body, which was naked aside from the hand towel around my waist. The doctor's hand was cool on my calf as the metal on my stomach skin. She took a sharp intake of breath.

'Wow-wow-wow!'

I was lying on my back and she was looking between my legs, using the light on her mobile phone.

'Wow!' she said again, quietly to herself.

Then louder, raising her head above the towel line, 'You have a very bad infection.'

I nodded. Her face was Nasser's face but on a woman. It had the same calm, sage, sallowness. Its fine, pointed, toughness.

'Have you had genital herpes before?'

I shook my head.

'Well, you have a severe outbreak now. The sores are ulcerated.'

I blinked at her slowly and she switched off the light on her phone, putting her small, cool, comforting hand back on my leg. She asked if she could take some of my blood and I told her she could. I closed my eyes because it was easier and listened to the sound of her rummaging through her large bag, pulling out packets, wipes and syringes. She asked me to clench my fist and I felt the needle pierce my arm.

'The first outbreak is often the worst, and it can come anywhere between two weeks and several years after transmission. Stress and fatigue are triggers, so that makes sense. You'll have to take care,' she said, fiddling efficiently with her vials packed with my blood.

'It can't be cured, but it can be treated quite effectively with anti-virals and painkillers. Sara?'

I opened my eyes to see several pills in the palm of her delicate hand.

'Take these, please.'

I propped myself up on my elbows, too weak to care that my enormous breasts were bare and smelled of vomit. I took the pills one at a time with the glass of water the doctor handed me. She was telling me about the drugs, painkillers that would make me sleepy, antibiotics that were very strong, creams she would leave me, ice compresses and instructions she would give to the hotel staff. I would have to use the painkillers sparingly as there was a shortage. I needed to drink a lot of water. I wanted her hand back on my leg.

'You have a high temperature. You must be in a lot of pain,' she said.

I was in a lot of pain. It was nice of her to know that. She watched me swallow the last of the pills, her neat form perched tightly on the edge of my bed, and took the empty glass back from me. I wanted her to stay until I slept and also while I slept.

'So what's this about birds?' she asked. 'Nasser tells me you were talking a lot about birds. You were scared.'

I squinted up at her and found she was looking at me steadily. She was pointy and bird-like, like Nasser, but no, she wasn't an actual bird.

'Was I?' my voice croaked out, harsh and alien.

'Have you ever been prescribed any antipsychotic medications?' she asked.

Her words landed with dull thuds in my fog-brain, but I tried to concentrate and be helpful. I told her there was something for the depression and insomnia that I'd been taking, but that had run out. Then I told her about the fat doctor in Jerusalem and his dirty shirt and his thing for rape, but I couldn't remember what his drugs were called.

'Zzz something.' I couldn't find the name because inside my brain someone was screaming through wet cotton balls. 'Zlatan? Zolotov maybe?'

'Zoloft?'

'Maybe,' I agreed. 'Yes.'

The effort of all that thinking had brought on another wave of nausea and I took to retching in useless spasms over the bin, bringing up a froth of pills and water. This retching went on for some time.

'How long had you been taking the Zoloft?' she asked when the spasming had stopped and I was resting my heavy chin on the rim of the bin.

'Couple of years,' I whispered, spitting out a last bit of puke foam.

The bright white of outside sliced through a crack in the heavy green curtains to hit me in the eyeballs and I winced.

'And you just stopped while you were here?'

I nodded.

'Well, you may be experiencing some withdrawal symptoms: dizziness, irritability, some nausea. These are drugs you should come off slowly, so we'll get you back on those. Lucky we still have plenty in Gaza. No equipment for surgery of course, but lots of anti-depressants.'

I shuddered, suppressing a retch, and closed my eyes. As much as I wanted to, I couldn't talk to the doctor anymore, so I lay on my pillow breathing. Then I was asleep. I dreamt of blackness and when I woke, the room was dark and empty.

The balcony door was open and a breeze coming in from the sea reached me on the bed in stroking wafts. The Israeli boats were back, bombarding the shoreline. They sounded like thunder. I was shivering so I wrapped myself tightly in the sheets and lay listening to the cosy artillery fire until, in a shock of clarity, I remembered Fadi. Grabbing around for my phone, I found it charging on the bedside table next to a neat stack of drug packets. Bringing it close to my face, I peered into the bright screen. It was full of messages, mostly from Nasser.

I spoke with your editors and told them you are unwell. Please rest.

Let me know if you need anything.

A message from Anthony: *Hello Sara, I'm heading into Gaza tomorrow morning as soon as the crossing opens. Can we meet for coffee at The Beach at 8.30?*

There was Fadi: *Can I come meet you? I have news.*

Something from Doron, but the green glare of the phone was making me intensely nauseous and I couldn't read anymore. I fumbled with the packages of drugs, took some of the pills the doctor had left for me and lay back on my pillow. The naval ships rumbled on in the distance and I closed my eyes.

I woke to the sound of gentle rapping on my bedroom door and called out in a sleepy croak for the doctor to please come in. The door opened a crack and I smiled at it.

'Sara? It's me, Mohammed. I have some food for you. May I come in?'

I lay silently with my disappointment that Mohammed wasn't the nice lady doctor for a while before realising that I was in fact aching with hunger.

'Yes!' I croaked. 'Yes please!'

I cleared my throat and Mohammed breezed into the room clean and fresh, his large silver tray held high. He set about delivering its contents to the low coffee table deftly, announcing each dish as he set it down, eyes averted discreetly from my sick bed: 'Omelette, plain *without* yellow cheese, better for the stomach. Labneh, *good* for the stomach. Arabic salad. Fresh pita, still warm. I made you a special tea with herbs and honey and, please, I would like you to drink this while it's hot because it is very good for your strength.'

At this, he allowed himself a stern glance towards the bed. The colour drained from his handsome features and he brought a soft fist to his mouth, dropping his eyes quickly.

'The doctor told us we should bring you ice, often,' he said meekly, indicating a small metal ice bucket he'd placed on the table beside the food. 'She also left you this package.'

He placed a white paper bag onto the crowded table and lowered his empty silver tray to his side. Taking a deep, steadying breath, he turned back to face me.

'We are all so sorry that you are sick, Miss Byrne. Me, Mohammed, Mo. Jihad. We want you to know that we are all here for you. If there is anything we can do to help, anything at all, please call the front desk.'

I smiled and nodded gratefully in reply and Mohammed looked quickly away again.

'Yes,' he said, sliding swiftly towards the door. 'I will leave you now.'

He gently clicked it shut and I lay breathing in the yeasty deliciousness of the fresh bread smell. Freed from the sheet, I swung my legs over the side of the bed. A white hot pain cut through me like a docking saw and I screamed. Stunned, I tried slowly reaching one timid foot towards the ground but the same shock of pain seared down my legs and up into my stomach. I flushed hot with panic. Gripping the side of the bed, I panted in the bread smell that was now pitifully out of reach. I was dying. I was diseased and dying, alone, in agony in Gaza. Clinging to the mattress edge, I started to sob painfully.

'To be 33 years-old and *still* crying over food cannot be normal,' I thought I heard.

I stifled my sobs and listened. There was a muted flurry of matter against fabric and I scrambled to cover my nakedness with the discarded sheet. I stared with alarm at the lowest section of the heavy green curtain, which was flapping and rustling unnaturally.

'*Quod me nutrit, me destruit.*'

There it was again, a strange voice, like bitter wind through bare trees. A dread chill crawled across my skin. Somebody was trying to get in.

'Is someone there?' I croaked out.

I clutched at the sheet, eyes wide and fixed on the drawn curtains. The long, weighted fabric rustled and I quailed.

'Who's there?' I croaked again, louder.

A grey wing broke through a gap in the drapes. A sharp black beak followed, then a single pink talon. Slowly a complete bird entered the room, wings spread wide in a gesture of warning. It locked its shiny yellow eyes on me and cocked its purple head.

'Sara? Do you hear me?'

The notes of that voice were outside the normal human register, but I knew it. I knew that bird. I trembled violently.

'No,' I rasped.

It hopped on the spot and I cried out in terror, covering my face with the bedsheet. When I dared look again, there it undeniably stood, a pigeon blinking its demon eyes at me.

'Yes! You do hear me!'

The bird cocked the smooth cap of its velvet head in triumph and puffed the oil-spill ruff of its mermaid neck. The grimy, grey cloak of feathers on its muscular shoulders rose and fell as it raised a pink foot and let it hover with precise menace, one talon tip on the tile. It directed its yellow laser gaze over the white carbuncles on its beak at me and I felt it in the most hidden parts of my brain. It was inescapable. The bird moved to stalk towards me but slid, skidded and let out a bright white shit before flapping up to perch on the edge of the wooden desk directly opposite my bed.

'Shits!' it screamed.

I roared with fear and buried my hot, wet face in my hands.

'You've gone mad. That's it. You're totally insane,' I told myself.

I peered out to check if it had disappeared and the bird took another hop closer, narrowing its citrine eyes on me. I wailed and it bent its neat head philosophically.

'*Mad*? How reductive.'

Falling back on the bed in distress I delivered a deep stab to my abdomen and howled in pain.

'Mad or not mad, dead or undead, who cares? Histrionics are so embarrassing. You smell of vomit.'

Under the pile of pillows that were failing to block-out the bird's voice, it did smell very much of vomit. I listened to the tight little clips of its talons on the tiles. Where was it going? I peeked out to see the pigeon bounce up to perch unsteadily on the corner of the coffee table. It was hopping towards the breadbasket. I sat up, wiping the snot and tears from my face with the bedsheet, and stared directly at it for the first time.

'Get away from that,' I growled.

It didn't move, so I threw a green bed cushion and it flapped up into the air to land unsteadily in a ripple of oil feathers back on the floor. The bird grunted then looked at me and startled.

'Shits, your face!'

27
To Live Is to Fight

I had stopped crying to eat and ate in a ripping, stabbing frenzy until I had consumed everything edible on the table. The painkillers worked, in that I could move, sort of. I'd lured the bird onto the balcony by throwing it a large chunk of bread and watched through the glass as it threw ragged pieces of crust clumsily up in the air aiming for, but mostly missing, its beak. I sat back on my napkin packed with ice and sipped at Mohammed's herby tea. It was bitter even with all the honey and no longer hot, but still soothing.

There was definitely a pigeon. I watched as it skewered a chunk of crust with its talon and pecked at it. Why was it talking? I shifted on my icepack, finding an unmelted bit to sit on. Was it talking or was I insane? And did that matter? I sipped carefully. The fact was, mad or not mad, I heard it. The fact was that I was sick and my injured body needed to heal before any insanity was likely to improve. Healing had to be the priority.

Wiping my grubby hands on the sheet I'd fashioned into a toga, I inspected the contents of the white bag the doctor had left for me. There were packets and small tubes of ointment with a note in her sweet, neat handwriting, instructing me to apply the cream directly to my sores four times a day. There was half a packet of precious painkillers, one packet of penicillin, two packets marked anti-virals and two full packets with *ZOLOFT - TAKE IMMEDIATELY* written in red capital letters on the side. I took two of each pill immediately.

With the bird safely occupied outside, I proceeded slowly to the bathroom to undertake my gory ablutions. I took care to wash my hair, armpits and legs with frothy soap. I found it too painful to do anything more than splash the warmish water between my legs but splashed as well as I could. Cleaner, I stepped toward the mirror to examine myself. My hair was wet from the shower and combed back like that, it looked dark and sleek. My unglossed lips were pale and cracked. There were my eyes. I leaned in closer towards them. The black of my pupils had dilated into large polka dots and what was left of the irises that were usually blue were, yes, yellow. The whites of my eyes were also yellowish. I blinked. Why were they yellow?

I sat on the side of the enormous bath, the tube of cream open and ready beside me. I had found in the depths of my wash bag a broken powder compact with a partially intact mirror. It took a while to establish the correct angle and see through the clumps of old, congealed bronzer, but then I found it. Flushing ice cold, I dropped the mirror. I was going to faint. Plunging my head between my knees, naked legs thrown wide, I inhaled and exhaled deeply several times before trying again. I refound the angle but unable to understand what I was seeing, slathered cream indiscriminately, yelping and cursing from the stinging and the searing pain.

'Holy fucking shit!' I smeared. 'Fuck, fuck, fuck. FUCK!'

'Histrionics!' that reedy voice called from the bedroom.

I bit down hard on my cracked lip to stop swearing and just moaned. When I was confident I could stand, I emerged from the bathroom wrapped in the filthy old robe and moved carefully towards the bed. The bird was back in the room, finishing the crumbs on my plate. It turned to look at me.

'Shits! Your eyes! *They're yellow!*'

That horrifying grating voice! I could feel my heart beating too hard. I had to try and calm it. Lowering myself gently onto the rumpled sheets and slowly lying myself flat on my back, I breathed deeply as my body worked to normalise its blood pressure. Fresh droplets of distressed sweat sprung onto my upper lip.

'The devil wouldn't throw *those* eyes out onto the street!'

I licked the sweat from my lip and tasted blood. What devil was it talking about? *The* Devil? Neil? Anthony! I hadn't thought about that. Anthony Harper. He was coming to stay in a hotel with no rooms. The bird was on point. He would want *The Tribune*'s room, leaving me where? Fixerless and roomless. Well, Harper was welcome to his fan boy Nasser but he was not having Room 22, no chance in hell. He couldn't take it from me because I was sick! Yes! Horribly, pitifully, immovably sick! And I would remain very, very sick until my exclusive was published. I would fight for my war. *My home in Gaza*!

The bird twitched its head incredulously as it watched me struggle to pull on my jeans, which was causing no small amount of agony, swearing and sweating. It wiped the piece of stringy cucumber dangling from his beak onto its chest feathers and cooed sombrely.

'*Vivere militare est.*'

I brushed the tears from my face and, whimpering, fastened the top button of my jeans. The bird was right, life is war.

A middle-aged man walked into reception, letting in a flash of hot daylight. Pale with fair, thinning hair, firmly built on little legs, he carried a small black holdall. Here was Anthony Harper. I had been re-reading his Wikipedia entry while I waited. Like him, it was short. He was 45, it said, although I remembered him looking at least a decade older. I already knew he lived in Jerusalem, where he was married with two children, but did not know he had been born and raised in Dulwich, the most aggressively mediocre of London's suburbs. If *The Tribune* were a living being, it would be ordering garlic bread at Bella Pasta in Dulwich Village. Reviewers had described Anthony's book on British rule in Jerusalem as *comprehensive* and *a must read*, for which I read very long and dull. I had neither bought nor read this book because even in paperback, it was far too big.

He entered the hotel the way a plumber might approach an

overflowing toilet. Setting down his small overnight bag at reception, he looked around the lobby assessing the war at hand. He opened a worn, brown travel wallet and handed over his passport and credit card to front desk Mohammed, who smiled at him ingratiatingly. Who has a travel wallet? Nasser spotted me and a look of concern or relief or something empathetic registered on his tight face and he raised a hand in greeting. I smiled weakly in response because I was very, very sick and he moved across the lobby towards me.

'How are you feeling? Should you be out of bed?'

He knelt down next to me, weighed down at the knees by sincerity.

'Anthony asked to meet me,' I said softly, raising my gaze to meet his. 'I hope he doesn't mind, but I still need a few minutes to pack my things.'

'Sara! Your eyes! What happened?' Nasser gasped.

I looked about meekly and shrugged, rolling my yellow eyes slowly in their sockets for full yolky affect. I actually had no idea what had happened to them.

'Were they like that when Mariam saw you? She didn't say anything?'

'Who?'

'There was a doctor in your room. Do you remember?'

He was talking slowly and staring at me as you might a person with a serious brain injury.

'Yes. A woman. She was very kind,' I said weakly.

'That's right. Mariam, my cousin. She's a doctor. Did she tell you why your eyes are yellow? I don't think you should be out of bed, Sara. You don't look well.'

The painkillers had started to wear off, so my blanching and sweating was actually quite authentic. Nasser's face was even more pinched than usual. He really did look a lot like a raisin. Approaching briskly over his left shoulder was Anthony Harper.

'Hullo there, Sara! How's Gaza been treating you?' he said chummily, stretching out his palm towards me.

He smiled his disengaged, awkward to have to be talking to anyone but particularly a woman smile, and I rose slowly to my feet, feeling suddenly very unsteady.

'You're feeling a bit peaky I hear. Been tucking into those prawns in a clay pot have we? I never trust the seafood here myself.'

I answered by vomiting omelette and a surprisingly abundant volume of bitter herbal tea onto the floor in front of him, splattering his neat hiking boots.

'Oh!' Anthony said, taking a large step backwards. 'Oh right.'

Nasser moved quickly towards me, stopping me from falling with a firm hand under my sodden armpit. Desk Mohammed also rushed towards the commotion. Bent over but still standing, I continued to heave like a cat birthing a fur ball.

'You're burning hot, Sara! Let's get you back to your room,' Nasser said.

'Please, Miss Byrne, let us help you get back to your bed,' Mohammed strained from underneath my other arm.

I nodded my consent and wiping my mouth with my sleeve, allowed the two men to half-carry me up the wide, stone stairs from the lobby, leaving Anthony to consider his vomit-splattered shoes. Once safely back and alone in my secured room, I took more pills and called Fadi. I spoke quietly but distinctly from underneath my pillow as you could never be sure how far sound carried out of my room and down those echoey tiled corridors.

'Sara?' Fadi's voice was loud and surrounded by traffic noise.

'Yes it's me. I've not been able to call but I'm free now. Can you come to the hotel?' I whispered precisely into the handset.

'What? Sara?'

'Can. You. Come. To the hotel?' I whispered again, more hoarsely.

'I can't really hear you well. You want me to come to the hotel?'

'Yesss!' I hissed.

'Okay. When?' he asked.

'In one hour! But Fadi! Don't come in through the hotel reception. Yes? That's very important. Come in the back, from the beach through the broken window into the empty restaurant.'

There was a loud beep of a horn on Fadi's end of the line and a child laughing.

'Why are you whispering? When you whisper, I can't hear you!' he shouted.

His not hearing properly was filling me with rage but after a moment of reminding myself how much I needed him, I took the pillow off my head and raised my voice to a slightly louder than normal volume.

'I want you to meet me in one hour in the big dining room facing the sea. The one that's closed off. But don't come in through the main entrance of the hotel. Come in from the beach through the broken window,' I said so loudly so that anyone who happened to be passing would have heard every word.

'That's better. I can hear you now. Are you sick? What's wrong with your voice? It's all scratchy.'

With extraordinary calmness, I asked Fadi to repeat our plan back to me. Then I hung up and set about applying all the ointments that would make our meeting possible. The ice helped. I considered fashioning myself an ice nappy but then thought it might melt before I could get back to my room, leaving a messy watery trail, like an enormous, dripping snail, and then everyone would know where I was and where I had been and that was exactly what we were trying to avoid.

28
Hunting Birds

There was a narrow staircase at the back of the first floor that only one-eyed Jihad used. It was so unimportant the concrete steps weren't even tiled and it smelled of cleaning trolley and laundered linen. The door leading to it was tucked behind the pillar next to Room 17 and I had no idea it was even there until Jihad's huge beige body emerged from it one morning mop in hand. I had screamed and Jihad had laughed for much too long.

The stairs led down to a small courtyard, which was for hotel staff only. It was lined with buckets and strung up with drying beige uniforms. This courtyard led onto the closed-off restaurant. I was only able to make slow progress but by taking small steps and moving in gentle inches, I got there without being spotted and arrived in the restaurant sweaty but with wits sharp as cats' claws. The splintered glass had all been swept up and tidied away by Jihad's large meticulous sweeping strokes, but the huge blown-out windows had not been replaced and the flapping sheets of plastic taped over them blew loose in the wind and did nothing at all to keep anything out. The birds could come and go as they pleased.

I scanned anxiously for the pigeon but found just one lone gull standing in a blasted-out window frame looking placidly out to sea. Several metres away, perched on the edge of a shit-covered chair, was little Jihad's tom cat, white fur matted with dirt. It pretended not to see me when I entered the room but continued glaring with fierce, concentrated hostility at the gull, the congealed mud tip of its tail twitching furiously.

The glassless windows let a cool, salty breeze in to wash the room and I sucked the fresh air in greedily as I waited for Fadi. Israeli observation drones hummed busily in the sky outside and their floating fortress of naval ships bobbed on the horizon. The gull flew off to investigate something on the beach, leaving the cat alone to glare at the room. It flashed its hard green eyes at me. Was it about to speak?

'You're not at your usual table.'

I started painfully and turned to see Fadi climbing through an empty window frame.

'My usual table has become a bird toilet,' I said.

'It wasn't so easy getting in this way,' he complained, fussily dusting off his jeans. 'There's so much glass and trash and shits out here.'

I appreciated then for the first time how carefully assembled Fadi was. His tight, clean jeans, his gelled hair and ironic t-shirts, because he didn't really heart Brooklyn at all. He flicked rogue flecks of chipped paintwork off his sleeve with prissy irritation and sat down next to me.

'Want one?'

He offered me a cigarette, but the thought of smoking made me recoil in disgust. Fadi looked at me, surprised at this refusal, and took a sharp intake of breath.

'*Al'ama*! What the fuck?'

A cigarette drooped hopeless and unlit from the corner of his mouth.

'Your eyes! What happened?'

These reactions were becoming tiresome. The colour had drained completely from his smooth face. What a big pussy, I didn't look that bad.

'Yes, my eyes are yellow,' I said, rolling them. 'I've been going through something the past few days. They're a side-effect. It's passing.'

He dragged his gaze away to study the horizon and after a long, uncomfortable pause, cleared his throat.

'So, guess who they asked to take over as leader?'

This was an irritating game. How was I meant to guess the new leader of Fadi's terror gang when the only people I knew in it were him and fat Sami. Was *he* the new leader? Fadi huffed with annoyance. Well, no. Obviously, no. They had asked his uncle.

'He told them no at first, he has a family, but then he realised there was really no one else. We have this one other cousin who wanted it but he's weird in the head, been killing cats since he was a kid.'

The manky cat, who had crossed the room unnoticed on silent paws leapt at this moment onto the table and settled itself within a claw's swipe of Fadi's face. Fadi eyed it with alarm and it stared back doing nothing cat like: no purring, no grooming, no cute eye squinting, just staring.

'That's a weird fucking cat,' Fadi said.

His left leg started to spasm furiously. All of a sudden being alone in a much too large, blown-up restaurant with a yellow-eyed English woman, his uncle the head of a terror cell, his cousin a life-long torturer of animals and now this manky cat eyeballing him, had become a bit much for Fadi. The drones buzzed in the sky outside. I brushed the cat off the table and it yowled with displeasure, rubbing itself sulkily against a nearby table leg. It really was not a natural feline.

'Look,' I made my new cracked voice as soothing as I could. 'I want to apologise for the other day. I was tired and disappointed when the other commander blew himself up and I lost my story. I wasn't feeling well. Of course I'm going to pay you.'

Fadi scoffed quietly then continued his smoking with quiet magnanimity. After a long, shifty pause he said, 'No problem.'

He finished his cigarette and stubbed it out with his heel on the shit-encrusted tiles. We sat in silence and stared at the charred, ground tobacco leaves of his crushed cigarette butt.

'How's Abu Yasser doing?' I asked, shifting the mood. 'Poor guy. It doesn't matter how many brothers you've killed, it can't be easy to lose a son.'

Fadi petrified and I covered my mouth with my hand. I had

forgotten he didn't know that I knew. Or had I? It was quite fun fucking with Fadi. I laughed.

'That handsome man with the tea and the dates, he's *the* Abu Yasser, right?'

Fadi gave me his dumbstruck face again. Over by the table leg, the cat shimmied its bony shoulder bones and growled a self-satisfied purr. Fadi's left eye had started to go.

'I fucking told them you're a Jew! What, you're Shabak?'

A new cigarette trembled in his hand. I told Fadi to relax and that, for the last time, yes, the first Sara was probably Jewish, but so was pretty much everyone at that point. And no, I wasn't Shabak or anything other than a journalist doing some basic journalism. The cat twitched his ears and stared up at Fadi with unblinking eyes. Also, why does everyone think Israeli intelligence are the only ones who know anything? They're not *that* good!

'It's not rocket science!' I told him, sharing a laugh with the cat as I realised what I'd said.

I needed to wrap this meeting up. It wouldn't be long before someone saw us, or noticed I was missing, or this stabbing pain in my groin rendered me unable to move. Fadi was still sitting frozen and wide-eyed.

'Listen, if Abu Yasser is smart, which he is, he will agree to give me a good, honest, history-making interview. Think 1980s Gerry Adams talks to the BBC.'

Fadi was gawping at me with a fearful blankness.

'Jesus Fadi. YouTube! We need him to be the intelligent, open, reasonable terrorist to change the narrative. I won't go too hard on all the stabbing, but he'll have to tell me a bit about how the group's funded, its tunnels and the rockets of course. Then it can be all *oi defend our roight to resist and oi'll debate that with anyone* sort of a thing. We'll take a nice picture, you guys get your hearts and minds changing front page, I get my career changing front page. *Ching ching*, everyone's a winner!'

The gull pack was back, chattering and picking lice out

of their wings. The cat caterwauled at them, raising the dirt-clogged hairs along his spine into matted spikes. Fadi nodded uneasily.

'Yes? You'll tell him?'

'Okay.'

'Good, thank you. Now off you pop.'

I shooed at Fadi who was still dragging unhappily on a cigarette.

'Quickly Fadi! I need to get back to my room!'

With a long, last shifty look towards the cat, who was yowling lowly at the gulls, Fadi got up and sauntered off on his stick legs, smoke rings rising into the air above him like a sulky steam engine. The weird cat trotted off after him, tail held high and twitching, out through the broken window and into the sand and rubbish. I had been sitting still for too long and my skin had stuck to the fabric of my cheap Ramallah market underwear. As I gently tried to stand, a top layer ripped clean off.

'FUCK!' I screamed, so loudly that the gulls screeched and flew off in a terrified flock.

I could feel blood running hot and thick down the inside of my jeans. Bent over and breathing through my teeth, waiting for the pain to ease off, I caught sight of two white sneaker tops sticking out from the side of a stack of folded chairs.

'Who's there?' I called.

The sneakers retracted but didn't answer.

'Hey! I saw your shoes! I just saw you move them!'

There was a shuffling and clattering of limbs on folded plastic, then a pair of green eyes, steely and expressionless, revealed themselves defiant above the chair pile.

'Jihad! What the fuck are you doing in here?' I asked, straining to talk through my pain-gritted teeth.

His gravelly voice called back at me across the room.

'I'm hunting birds.'

He stepped slowly out into the room, clutching a pointy stick and smoothing his thick, gelled hair with his free, dirty hand.

'I was already here hiding and waiting to spear one when you came in. I wasn't spying.'

'Only a spy would say they weren't spying,' I croaked at him. 'What did you hear?'

'I wasn't spying!' he shouted, hard eyes flashing furiously.

I told him to keep his voice down otherwise we'd both get caught and gently sat back down, unsure how to deal with my captive.

'You're the one screaming,' he said, lowering his voice. 'Why were you screaming anyway? You look strange. Are your eyes *yellow*?'

'Yes, they're yellow and you're a midget with the face of a 100 year-old,' I snapped.

His parched face flushed pink with hurt feelings.

'They're yellow because I've been sick. But I'm getting better,' I softened.

'That's not what Mohammed says. He says you're dying, and no one knows what to do about it.'

'Which Mohammed?'

'All the Mohammeds.'

His small face was so hard and serious I wanted to laugh but when I started laughing my whole body hurt down to its bones, so I just asked him if I looked like a person who was dying. He studied me.

'Maybe.'

He was still standing a good distance across the huge room and our voices calling across at each other were definitely going to get us caught, but I couldn't move any closer, owing to the blood still dripping down my legs.

'Come and sit next to me,' I said, patting the seat beside me where Fadi had been sitting.

'No.'

He stayed where he was by the chairs, regarding me cautiously.

'Okay. So, Jihad,' I started confidingly. 'If you tell your dad or your uncle Mohammed that I was in here with Fadi, I'll tell them that I saw you from my bedroom window playing with the bully boys on the beach. And they will tell your mum and that will upset her a great deal. And then she will have no choice but to keep you safe at home watching *The Bold and the Beautiful* every single day. There will be no playing outside. No birds. No spying. Just *The Bold and the Beautiful* for days and days with your angry mother.'

His little eyes narrowed into thinking slits and glinted furiously.

'Well, if you tell them that, I'll tell them that you and Fadi are working for Abu Yasser.'

'That's a stupid threat. I'm an English woman who writes for a big newspaper. Who would believe you?'

'You're a mad English woman that no one likes.'

'Whom. *Whom* no one likes.'

I leaned heavily on the back of my chair and looked at Jihad, who was standing rigidly upright with his stick.

'Why do those football thugs beat you up?'

'My cousins?' his cheeks flushed scarlet.

'The ones that punch you and laugh at you. They're your *cousins?*'

'Cousins, neighbours, whatever. They live in my building. They don't laugh *at* me! It's just a joke.'

'Funny joke.'

The boy shrugged and involuntarily rubbed his punched cheekbone until it was a deep furious red. We were at an impasse.

'Okay Jihad. So I guess the deal is that neither of us says anything about this to anyone?'

Little Jihad glared at me, then nodded. Short of killing him, I couldn't do much else but trust he would keep his word. Very slowly and carefully, I straightened myself and readied my body for the painful return to my room feeling a surge of affection or respect for the kid. He was certainly smart.

'You should go for the pigeons,' I told him, lowering my voice again in case the bird was listening. 'They need culling. And be careful of the glass.'

I started to inch slowly towards the small back staircase, feeling little Jihad's hard stare on my back.

'Careful your eyes don't get any yellower and you die!' he called after me.

He had intended to be cruel but what came out sounded like genuine concern and I smiled to myself. He wasn't wrong though. The nice doctor probably should take a look at my eyes.

29
The Truce

I lay on my bed with my eyes closed trying to see Abu Yasser at home with his wife in an expensive apartment building on the Beach Road from the perspective of a bird perched on his balcony. Abu Yasser in his neat red sports shirt. His family are rich and his wife is old but her long, plaited hair is still black. She wears gold, which is very attractive to birds. Fadi is there giving younger, ginger relatives dead arms. Their balcony houses a large collection of cacti.

'Slattern! This is a very bad war! You are very bad at this!'

My skin crawled with goosebumps. I was not better. There was that weedy voice back, and in a terrible sour mood. I opened my eyes and saw the bird was indeed on my balcony, for some reason covered in filth and seaweed. It was dragging its wet, soiled wings up and down the balcony wall, smearing the white concrete with brine and shit. It did this angrily for quite some time.

'Humiliating!' it muttered. 'Totally humiliated! Here she is napping in cold blood. Just look at all that blood!'

Blood? What blood?

'Look at the blood!' it screeched again.

Panicked, I searched and researched the sheets around me for signs of gore but found only crumbs and sweet wrappers. I had washed the blood from my jeans and they were drying outside in the sun. The bird must be talking metaphorically. Or prophetically? I flushed cold and turned on the television hoping to drown out the bird's unnatural bitching.

The Arab channels were showing a considerable amount of bombing going on in the neighbourhoods near the border. Shejaiya in particular was being pounded with jet and tank fire. Was the bird talking about Palestinian blood in general? Outside, predator drones were circling the city like ugly robot eagles. The news had counted at least 30 Hamas rockets whistling towards Israel, and not just the usual homemade stuff, the proper Iranian ones. Something was up. This war is either ending or about to get a lot worse, I said out loud.

'*It's either war or peace, I understanden!*' the voice mocked. 'Awash with blood, she'll see!'

Blood again? Mine? I looked in horror at the furious, damp pigeon as it stalked the balcony. It saw something coming, something awful.

'What blood?' I asked, my voice irritatingly tremulous.

But the bird had decided to stop talking. It cooed vituperously then flapped off in a fury leaving me alone to ponder my terror. I looked desperately again about the bed sheets but there wasn't any blood. I was fine. Was I breathing? I formed my mouth into a tight *o* and breathed in and out of it. I was. I was fine. I would list all the ways in which I was fine:

I was no longer vomiting.

Now that Anthony Harper was handling all the Neil calls and the Doron calls and the chaotic UN schools and the child hordes, I finally had time to think.

Thanks to the doctor's drugs, the pain was easing and my brain was clear.

There was no blood.

Now the bird was gone too! I should make the most of it. After a cleansing douche, I settled down on an icepack to read my competitors' work methodically for the first time all war. I started, of course, with Steve Sweeney. He had covered the region longer than anyone and as the only one of us to speak both Arabic and Hebrew fluently, having married one of each, he had the advantage. Eccentrically, his coverage turned out to be an obsessive, episodic exposition on the Al Muzaner family airstrike delivered in long, dense, agonised pieces crammed with esoteric detail, times, and dates.

He had started with an extensive profile of the man Israel had been targeting, Yasser Al Muzaner. The 33 year-old traffic policeman had survived the initial strike on his family home but succumbed to his injuries in Shifa Hospital several days later. He had five children and according to everyone, no interest in politics whatsoever. He had been terrified his children would be drawn into anything violent. Sweeney could find no evidence that he was affiliated with Hamas or any other militant faction.

His next very long report benefited from some Israeli military leaking of data and images apparently proving there had been no terrorist rocket fire from the area around the Al Muzaner house in the hours and even days before the strike. And so it went on, occasionally erupting in lines of lyrical sentiment—*a blood line wiped out in a careless case of mistaken identity that the Israeli authorities will not admit and likely will never be held accountable for*—quickly reined in by some meticulous argument or corroborative fact or figure. Demonstrating their fanatic loyalty, his editors had not only run but promoted every one of these Al Muzaner articles on their front page.

Apparently buckling under this unusual editorial pressure, the UN had announced that very morning there would be an enquiry into *the Al Muzaner Incident* and all the other correspondents had already written versions of this UN inquiry story. Anthony's was his first dispatch from Gaza. Even Paula Miranda's website was leading with it, a piece written by Ashraf using phrases like *war crime*. Israeli media outlets with English language websites were running comments from Israeli government officials discrediting the results of this UN inquiry which had not yet begun. News cannibals! All of them! Where was the *new* news?

Paula Miranda's biggest piece of original reporting all war had been about Hamas recruitment. She seemed to have spent some time hanging about at Hamas funerals talking to young men about why they had joined the movement and her conclusion was that Hamas was a death cult, brainwashing young Palestinian men into becoming terrorists. Her writing style was as repellent as her gum chewing. *Mohammed's goal was to terrorize and obliterate Israel and his dearest wish was to die in pursuit of that goal. On Saturday morning, aged just 17, his wish was granted.*

That was quite enough, Paula Miranda. Jane Sawyer had written a lot about Egypt, which was odd because who gave a fuck about Egypt? She'd done a bit about why some militant groups were using Russian rockets rather than Iranian, like everyone thought, which was a bit interesting. Stuart Finch had written some ranting comment pieces about Hamas being a proxy for Iran and this war being a proxy US Iran war, which read like someone shouting spittily at you in a bar.

It took me four hours and three icepacks, but finally I had read every article I could find written in English by any reporter staying at The Beach over the course of the war. Not a single one of them had been anywhere near the head of a Palestinian militant faction. None of them had stepped foot near a terror tunnel or glimpsed a rocket arsenal. Were they all stupid or just monumental pussies? Either worked for me. The war was still mine for the taking.

The sea breeze blowing in from the balcony had whipped up into a wind that hit me in the face, lifting the lank hair from my forehead. I hummed with energy and a divine impulse struck me. I would call Michael and tell him about my story. This was a defining moment in my career, he would want to be part of it. We had done months and months of this not talking, it was stupid to pretend we would keep that up. He was missing me I could feel it, feel him wanting me.

I beamed with the clarity of just knowing and called his number hurriedly, pressing the phone to my cheek, which was chubby with grinning. The line crackled and my heart leapt. I waited hotly for it to ring, but it didn't. Instead of Michael's dark syrup voice, a distant automated woman told me I had dialled an incorrect number, which was impossible. I knew those numbers better than my birthday. I called again. The same woman. Could you not dial English phones from Gaza now? I dialled 10 more times and met the same clueless voice. I punched the bed with frustration. The line must be down. I would send a text message.

You know, I can feel you thinking about me.

I pictured him reading it, how his deep sea eyes would crinkle. He'd make his sexy grumble noise. There was another gentle rap at the door.

'Yes!' I trilled, before remembering to speak weakly because I was still very, very sick.

'Yes?' I said more meekly.

The door swung open gently and there again was gay Mohammed, slim in his beige uniform with yet another huge silver tray stacked with food.

'Mohammed!' I beamed.

'I thought you might be ready for something to eat. And more ice. May I come in?'

'Yes please,' I said sweetly.

By now, I reasoned, we were both used to my nakedness. I did my thing of wrapping myself in the sheet and Mohammed was queer as a nine-bob note anyhow.

'So, finally we have some good news!' he began chattily, happily organising his plates on the table.

'Oh?' I smiled. 'And what's that?'

What could it be? A special treat from the kitchen perhaps? Had Paula Miranda left?

'The truce!'

He glanced up briefly, surprised I didn't seem to know what he was talking about, and returned to his fussy table-arranging, removing a linen napkin from the tray and placing it precisely next to the hummus.

'Truce?'

I swung my legs over the side of the bed, clutching the sheets tightly to my chest, and screamed a blood-curdling cry owing to the rip this action had inflicted on my healing wounds. Mohammed jumped and dropped his silver tray with a loud clatter. The basket of bread landed catastrophically, slices of toasted pita scattering across the tiled floor. We looked at each other wild with shock.

'Are you okay?' Mohammed asked.

'What truce?' I replied, hoarse and urgent.

Mohammed was on his hands and knees apologising for the clattering, picking up bread.

'What truce, Mohammed?' I repeated gravely.

'You didn't hear?'

He was hunting for a piece of toast underneath the coffee table.

'They're saying the Egyptians got them to agree a ceasefire in Cairo, all the big news channels. They just don't know when it starts.'

He stood up straight, his basket once again full of pita, fixed his perfect hair and beamed.

'It's good news, yes? The fighting stops, the border opens, you get to go home!'

Mohammed gestured towards an imaginary home somewhere out the window with a sweep of his breadbasket, cheerful at the idea of me having somewhere to return to. I looked at him in horror, my mind racing, and his smile faded.

'I'm sorry about the bread, I'll get more.'

'No!'

Mohammed jumped again. I heard the violence in my croaked shout and attempted a gentler tone.

'I mean to say don't worry, Mohammed. This bread is fine. Please don't trouble yourself.'

But he wasn't moving.

'You can go!' I prompted.

'Of course,' Mohammed said, tartly, placing the breadbasket on the table. 'Oh. I have a note for you, from your Italian *friend*. I'll leave it here.'

He pronounced the word friend as if he were spitting out bad wine. Removing a folded piece of paper from his breast pocket, he tucked it carefully under the breadbasket before moving gracefully out of the room, empty tray taut by his thigh.

'Thank you, Mohammed!' I called towards the slamming door.

I was still sitting bolt upright on the side of the bed, sheets bunched tightly around my nakedness when the bird hopped back through in from the balcony wanting to know what all that clatter and screeching histrionics had been about. I stared at its tiny, shiny, purple head, thinking about what I was going to do about this truce and whether that was blood I could feel trickling down my thigh.

'Slattern!'

The bird spread its dirty wings to their full width and bellowed. My legs were trembling violently.

'*Coo roo-c'too-coo! Tempora Heroica! Tempora Heroica!*'

It was right. Now was the time. Now or never.

Coo roo-c'too-coocoo!

If they had already agreed the truce, if they had announced it, it would have to come into effect by the following day, wouldn't it? I asked the bird but it said nothing. I reached to call the front desk and ask them but as the phone rang, I realised that was a ridiculous idea and hung up.

Fadi's ringtone had changed. It was now one of the militant anthems I'd heard playing on loop on the radio in Nasser's car. He wasn't answering but I kept calling with the phone on loudspeaker. The bird was doing an odd dance on the balcony with a piece of Mohammed's floor bread, hopping from one foot to the other and lifting his wings up and down. It danced on as the phone rang until finally the room filled with the sound of car horns.

'Fadi!' I yelled so he could hear me.

I was mid-way through trying to dress and my jeans were still around my ankles.

'Sara?' he answered.

'Fadi! We need to push the plan forward. Everything needs to happen today! Is he ready?'

Fadi was again struggling to hear and shouted irritably at me to pick up the phone and speak into it properly because he couldn't hear a word I was saying. I closed the balcony doors, sat carefully on the side of the bed and took the phone off speaker. This annoyed the bird, which flapped in protest at the glass.

'Sara,' Fadi said, loud and distinct against my ear. 'The plan has changed.'

I told him that was exactly what I had been telling him, the plan had changed. How had his plan changed?

'My uncle will meet you today. Come to the cemetery in an hour.'

'Your uncle? No, I wanted Abu Yasser!'

'My uncle or no one.'

I froze in momentary panic. The uncle would do. But in my injured state, I could barely walk to the bathroom let alone the cemetery. The bird's head cocked in confusion and it blinked furiously at me through the window. It hopped up and down in frustration.

'It's too dangerous to meet in the cemetery,' I said.

The bird cooed at me urgently, small head jerking, and I nodded.

'Tell your uncle to come to the hotel. We'll meet in the same room I met you in earlier. He should come in the exact same way.'

'Bring him to the hotel? Are you crazy?'

A volley of horns echoed his shouts. It was an excellent idea.

'Fadi, can you think of a single place in the whole of the Gaza Strip safer than The Beach Hotel?'

There was a pause on his end. It was settled, Fadi would bring the commander in exactly one hour's time while everyone else would be out covering the truce. I planted my large flat fleet squarely on the cold tiles and made my way with brave, bold steps towards the food Mohammed had delivered. I did not feel the searing pain in my abdomen. I would eat and I would feel strong. I was not bleeding.

'Mind over matter!' I said aloud.

'*Solvitur ambulando!*' the pigeon encouraged.

I sat on the low sofa and began to shovel oily hummus into my mouth with the floor bread, cold sweat dripping gently from my forehead. I took one of each of my pills. On the Egyptian news channel, the waxwork anchor had talons like the shopping network women. She sat in front of a blue screen broadcasting live footage from Gaza City, which was illuminated with explosions of light and apocalyptic flame. The ceasefire had been announced for 9pm. We had a little under five hours to interview the commander and have our piece written before deadline in London.

Outside the open windows of Room 22, the Israelis were also working to a deadline. Jets and naval ships were listlessly blowing up as many things as they could before the ceasefire took hold, their last chance to *mow the lawn*. That's what the Israeli general had called it on day two, off the record, retired and chatty over the phone from his Tel Aviv garden. Every few years we need a war, he said, to trim Hamas back a bit. From what I could see on the cartoony graphic behind the waxwork Egyptian, they had already blown up the headquarters of the National Islamic Bank and the homes of a few important ministers. Hamas rockets squealed through the sky outside in the opposite direction, but the news channels weren't taking much notice because they had so far failed to hit anything. This didn't stop the hopeful shouts of *Allahu Akbar* ringing out on the street every time one was launched, wafting into our room on Gaza's perfume of sea salt, bomb smoke and diesel fumes.

The alarm on my phone chirped. It was time for the meeting.

30
THE CRADLE OF CIVILISATION

'You've *really* never heard of Diane Segal?'

Dad had arrived late and drunk at the restaurant with his tie loose and his breath smelling of acid white wine and onions because he had been at a book launch at the Frontline Club. The book was a war memoir by Diane Segal, a foreign correspondent represented by Dad's literary agent, Michael Frazer. I had not heard of Diane Segal. Steve Sweeney and Jane Sawyer had also been at the party. I had heard of Steve Sweeney.

Diane Segal's book sat imperiously with its blood-drenched cover on the red gingham table cloth next to my half-eaten roast chicken and mashed potatoes. I had ordered with greedy impatience while waiting for Dad but when he finally arrived he was unexpectedly followed by Michael, his very favourite person, my chicken looked like nursery food and I lost my appetite. Michael ordered a steak, rare, with buttered spinach and fries from the pretty blond waitress. Dad wasn't hungry, he was drinking. The book was called *Where the Tigris Runs Red.*

'Do you *read*, Sara? Books? Newspapers?'

Dad, mortified at the offense my not having heard of his agent's most famous client might have caused his agent, was taking me to task. I opened my mouth and shut it again but there was no retracting my not knowing. I swallowed and the high neck of my frilly collar dug into my gullet.

'It seems she's been very busy reading, *Wilhelm*. Congratulations by the way! Oxford, was it?'

'LSE.'

'Ah, so chic.'

Michael raised his glass and clinked it against mine. I blushed, and we sipped at our wine. Dad was occupied glaring through the slats of the venetian blinds out into Soho.

'She's attractive isn't she, Diane? An attractive, older woman.'

My father's face hardened as he mused into the dusty lines of dusk light streaking our table. Michael hummed in polite agreement. The burble of the pub crowd on the street outside reached up through the open window making me, for some reason, woozy. Michael's suited knee grazed my bare one under the table as Dad talked on in half-thoughts about Diane Segal.

'But the very definition of a vulture, no? Choosing to work *exclusively* in the world's most fucked up places, that's some sort of disorder, surely. What? Narcissism? *Psychopathy?*'

'A vulture?' I blushed at having to confess more ignorance.

'People who make a living from death and disaster,' Michael explained.

'Misery merchants. Conflict cowboys. What is it she said *Michel*, about a *journalist's responsibility?*'

'A foreign correspondent's. *A correspondent's function is to give voice to the voiceless.*'

Michael performed the quote for my benefit and I raised an eyebrow. Can you *give voice* to something, I thought? Give *a* voice maybe?

'Well, she can write. Or someone can, that conflict really does come alive on her pages. The cradle of civilisation lost to barbarity and bloodshed. It's a pretty extraordinary book *Michel*, congratulations.'

Dad fell silent and stared glumly into the fading sunlight in Dean Street, perhaps considering how well he could have written about a lost cradle of civilisation had he ever left his study. He was either in love with Diane Segal or despised her. Michael turned to face me.

'So what next, Brains Byrne? You must have big plans.'

'Not really. I need to make some money so I can move out.

Ma knows someone on a Sunday supplement. There's something going there researching diets or something,' I blushed again, infuriated to be blushing so much.

'Isn't your degree in international relations?'

Dad issued a yelping bark at some new memory causing us both to jump in our seats.

'I asked her how she gained such a profound understanding of the place, Iraq I mean—she's from Surrey, right?—and she asked *me* if I knew where the word understanding comes from. It's Old English, of course, from the word *understanden*. To stand in the middle of something. "That's really all I do," she said. "I just stand in the middle of it all and listen."'

He popped his grey eyes out of their triangle sockets and thumped a heavy hand on his *Where the Tigris Ran Red* causing the small room of diners to also jump in their seats. Dad had decided to loathe Diane Segal and this had raised his spirits dramatically. He beamed at us. Michael treated him to a charming smile and I smirked back.

'I didn't know you spoke Old English, *Wilhelm*.'

Dad began to thump the table rhythmically, drawing more glares from the other diners.

'The wile wench she broughteth bad mead, so off I charged at a godly speed! I composed that just then,' he grinned.

'Beautiful. Is there more?'

'Off I charged on my goodly stead, actually. Scans better. Right Bob? She's the scansion queen. Fine writer my daughter. At least she drinks like one. More wine garcon! *Garconess?*'

Dad had emptied the last of a bottle of wine between our glasses and was searching the room for our waitress.

'Oh, where is our wine wenche?' he complained. 'Do you see her Bob?'

'I like it *Wilhelm*! A memoir in Chaucerian stanzas! *Where the Thames Runneth Rouge!*'

'June?'

Dad had taken off his jacket and was waving his arms in

seated jumping jacks at the pretty blond waitress, revealing large sweat patches that had turned the thin fabric of his underarms completely see-through. The waitress, who was about my age with skin as pale as mine, also flushed bright red as she stood over our table.

'Thank God you're here, June! We've run out of Meursault!'

Dad turned the empty wine bottle demonstrably upside down into the melted bucket of ice, splashing himself and adding yet another transparent patch to the shirt already struggling to conceal his thin man's paunch.

'I'm Melissa. I think you're confusing me with the month, Bill. Would you like another bottle?'

'Melissa! I'm so sorry. But you look so much like a June,' Dad accused. 'It's my favourite month.'

He was being winning.

'Thank you Melissa,' Michael smiled sweetly. 'We would love another Meursault if you have one please and a fresh bucket of ice. Bill's been bathing in this one.'

'It is awash with *understanden*,' Dad agreed remorsefully, peering into the bucket liquid.

Melissa returned with fresh ice and a sweating bottle of chilled white wine, which she opened, delivering a small amount into Dad's glass to try.

'Pour June, pour!' he instructed, gesturing elaborately for her to fill my empty glass.

Melissa filled all of our glasses practically to the brim before removing herself with evident relief. Michael raised his towards me.

'To academic triumph!' he announced.

I laughed, embarrassed. Michael glinted at me as he sipped, which Dad watched before pivoting in his seat to look at me in a pantomime of surprise. His eyes had clouded with that familiar amused cruelty. He had just given in to being very, very drunk.

'Triumph?' he queried conspiratorially.

Dad and I were meant to be having a celebratory dinner. We were there because, as I overheard Ma tell him behind the closed door of their bedroom, it's the sort of thing fathers do with their daughters. He had objected. In his day, the only degrees anyone celebrated were firsts or thirds. *Those who aim at faultless regularity will only produce mediocrity*, he had quoted unconvincingly. Ma slammed their bathroom door and the argument was ended.

A table for two was booked at The Garter on Dean Street, a favourite of thespians and my father. Ma took me to one of her middle-aged women's boutiques on the Kings Road to buy a celebration outfit and picked out a high-necked, pink, lace dress in a size smaller than mine. I complained from the changing room that the button was too tight against my neck but the sales assistant agreed with my mother that it didn't look too tight at all. Watching the dress as it was folded and wrapped, Ma added in a sisterly whisper that it might not be such a bad thing if I swallowed a little less anyway.

'Oh *Michel*, you are very kind, but we don't reward mediocrity in our household, do we Bob?'

My father eyed me savagely across the table and the much too tight too pink dress colluded by choking me, flushing my cheeks an ugly, clashing puce. I blinked hard.

'I got a 2:1,' I admitted.

'But that's wonderful!' Michael insisted.

Dad snorted and our table languished in awkward silence as Melissa delivered Michael's steak and his many condiments. She withdrew but Michael didn't touch his cutlery or say another word, resting a look of undisguised disapproval on my father.

'Don't you make that judgy face at me *Michel*!' Dad, chuckled unconvincingly, slapping his hand over mine with brittle affection. 'I will not patronise my daughter! She's been conjugating Latin verbs since she was five for Christ's sake. She knows very well she *should* have stuck to Classics. International relations? Pah! I'm yet to see her pick up a newspaper without chips in it! Speaking of which, is that béarnaise?'

Slowly sensing his overstep, my father retreated into a sheepish grin and reached a pale, long-fingered hand deep into Michael's bowl of french fries.

'No, but we're still very proud, of course. Her mother thinks she'll do well in the Civil Service. Isn't that the thinking now Bob? Civil serving?'

Dad squinted his eyes into a weak smile at me and dipped his clutch of fried potatoes into one of Michael's multiple sauces.

'Excuse me,' I said, pushing myself back from the table.

Michael looked up at me with concern.

'Here we go,' Dad chewed exhaustedly.

'What? I can't pee?' I snarled at him.

My father's fine, booze-flushed features contracted with disgust before opening into a broad exasperated smile at Michael.

'Clearly we need to work on the civil bit.'

He issued a loud exhale.

'And the service bit. But at least she doesn't want to act! Has June told you? *She* wants to act,' Dad hoarse whispered as I turned to navigate my way through the tight maze of tables away from him. '*Why* is it that all pretty girls think they can act, *Michel*? Is it the same rogue gene? Like red heads and freckles?'

Michael's reluctant laugh and Dad's much louder one followed me up the narrow wooden stairs. The toilets had been squeezed into such a small space that I had to breathe in to squeeze through the door and then flatten myself against the wall to close it. Fucking midget thespians. Hooking my finger underneath the fabric digging into my neck, I tugged roughly. The button flew off and released tears of black mascara streaks down my mottled cheeks. I inspected my pale neck in the mirror above the sink and found it ringed with a dark red groove. A fat mediocre neck. Fat-necked civil servant in a child's party dress. My larynx spasmed.

Footsteps thundered up the staircase chased by shrieks of

laughter from the bar downstairs. There was an urgent rap on the toilet door. I smeared at the black tear stains on my cheeks, running cold water into the basin at full speed. The door pushed opened forcing me up against the sink.

'Give me a minute!' I yelled, rubbing the mascara streaks into my cheekbones.

Michael's head popped in through the crack grinning clownishly at me, which made me laugh and then start crying again.

'Oh no! Are you okay?'

I tried to say that I was fine but issued a loud sob instead, then tried to laugh.

'Of course you're not! May I come in?'

I nodded, leaning back over the toilet bowl to make room. Michael made a performance of squeezing in through the sliver of open door, bending his body like a suited snake, until we were both in the tiny room, pushed up against one another. He turned the tap off and tilted his head back so he could look at my blotchy mascara face.

'Actual tears!' he wrapped his arms around me. 'I'm sorry girly.'

It felt weird hugging Michael. He smelled of the cloak room at an expensive restaurant. I let myself be hugged and noticed that we were almost exactly the same size.

'You know, when you're not around, all he does is boast about you. It gets boring actually. He's just a mean tit when he's drunk. *In vino tittus.*'

I laughed. I liked how Michael felt, how his stylish suit arms were holding me and I let myself relax into them, crying now mostly because he was being so nice. He squeezed me tightly and rested his chin on my head, looking about the tiny room.

'Why is this toilet so ridiculously small?'

I raised my head from his shoulder, noticing that we were exactly the same height.

'Because all actors are midgets. Midgets with huge heads,' I told him.

'That's true!' he laughed.

'Huge heads are photogenic. I don't know why they're all so short.'

Our faces were aligned feature to feature. He had deep lines down his cheeks, scars from sun tans, cigarettes and twinkling. His navy blue eyes looked Irish, even though they weren't. They were sexy when he crinkled them like that. His mouth twitched and he made a grumbling noise. I could feel he wanted to kiss me but wouldn't so I pressed my body tighter to his and kissed him.

'Oh no, girly. No. That's not a good idea.'

He tried gently to push me away but owing to the tininess of the room, and how little he wanted to, couldn't. I kissed him again and this time he kissed me back, pressing his grey-stubbled mouth onto mine. Grabbing me by the waist with one hand and pushing the door shut with the other. He slid the lock.

'This really, really is not a good idea,' he breathed heavily onto my bruised neck, his mouth hot and stubbly.

This would kill my father.

'It feels like a good idea to me,' I told him.

He didn't argue again.

31
Blood

I expected Fadi's uncle to be a young Abu Yasser. I'd heard of him so often, so admiringly, I expected a charismatic leader. But the man who followed Fadi through the windowless window with footsteps crunching noisily on the broken glass was just bones and shadow in baggy jeans. No fatigues, just a black t-shirt draping from his clavicles and a walkie-talkie clutched in his hand.

Fadi led the new commander through the darkening, abandoned air-hanger of a restaurant to the chair facing me and he wafted into it, cigarette pinched in his right hand, walkie-talkie in his left. The radio was hissing and murmuring but the commander wasn't paying it any attention. In his animated skull, black hole eyes scanned me briefly but without much interest. Fadi took a seat behind him grinning with pride, delighted to see the two of us sat together at last, all thanks to him. The bird was nowhere in sight. No sign of the cat either. No movement from the stacks of chairs where little Jihad usually spied. I gave the commander a formal hello, opened my notebook and began the interview.

'What is your name?'

The commander smirked at this. Fadi continued to grin idiotically.

'You can use Abu Mohammed.'

'And what is your position?'

'I am commander of the military wing of the PLB. The Al-Yasser Salah al-Deen Front.'

He paused.

'We were the ones who fired the rocket at the Zionist tank. And kidnapped their soldier.'

I nodded, indicating that I was familiar with the faction's work, which seemed to please him.

'Why are you fighting Israel?'

The commander spoke English well enough but on the topic of ideology, switched to Arabic. His leg began to jiggle energetically, bouncing the bleating walkie-talkie up and down on his knee. Fadi listened attentively, his leg also jiggling. An awkward trait for a family working so closely with explosives, I thought. The commander indicated for Fadi to translate.

'All of the land from the Jordan River to the sea is ours. Palestine, not Israel. We are fighting for what is ours and we will keep fighting.'

The militant drew tightly on his cigarette, staring at me through the smoke with his sunken, black, eyeholes as I wrote down what Fadi said: 'We never agreed to a ceasefire. Until Israel agrees to end its siege on Gaza, until it stops its attacks, we will never agree.'

A loud hum of drones had struck up overhead and the evening's heavy artillery fire began to pound the black coast nearby. The militant's eyes darted along the inky horizon. His walkie-talkie crackled. They may want to fight, I told him, but how could they win? They didn't have Israel's naval ships, jets, predator drones or tanks. They barely had rockets. The skinny commander shifted his bones in his seat.

'Our equipment like the resistance doesn't end. We have a lot,' he said.

'You have a lot of what?'

The commander sighed and looked weary.

'We get money, lots of money from all over to spend how we like. From the USA, from Europe, Syria, Arabs. But not from Iran!' he added emphatically.

'Not Iran?'

'No, it's Israel who says we get money from Iran but really, we have nothing to do with Iran.'

His eyes flickered fiercely before dulling again. He started to list the missiles in his arsenal, bored.

'We have the Fajr 5. M75, thousands. Katyusha. Qassam of course, thousands and thousands. Anti-tank missiles, Yasi RPL, al Bana RP.'

'And where do you get these from, if not Iran?' I asked.

He lifted his bony shoulders and looked around through the cloud of his cigarette smoke as if to say, where do you think they come from? I made an expression that said I had no idea where they come from. He looked towards Fadi as if to ask was I an idiot, and Fadi raised his shoulders in confirmation that I must be. The commander clicked his tongue in disdain.

'From *here*! We make them in Gaza, mostly. It's not hard,' he said.

'It's not hard? How many actually work?'

'You saw what happened to the tank?'

I had seen the pictures of the blown-up Israeli tank, I told him. But then I'd also seen a Palestinian strawberry farm that looked much the same. I also pointed out that they hadn't worked so well for the last commander. His face darkened. Suddenly the commander was on his spindly legs and moving with surprising speed towards the glassless windows. He stared intently into the horizon, walkie-talkie to his ear. Without prompting, he started talking again in Arabic and Fadi translated, speaking quickly to keep up.

'Since this all started, the Zionists didn't kill one person from the fighters other than Al Jabari, they just kill normal people, children.'

'You kill normal Israeli people too, children. Why do you do that?'

The commander's expression lurched suddenly from blank to fury, his bottomless eyes urgent and terrifying.

'We fight because we are occupied! Because we have to. You see anyone coming to help us? All of Gaza, all the West Bank is a prison. Our children see their mothers killed. We starve but America fights for Israel, the British fight for Israel, and we are alone! We fight because we have to,' he repeated, his bones shaking with fury.

I focused on writing down steadily what he said.

'Israel says they attack the resistance and teach us lessons. But was the Al Muzaner family resistance? No! They were old women and children. We are the resistance, and we are strong, why doesn't Israel hit us? Since the Zionist assault began, Gaza has 80 martyrs, 20 are children, 30 are women and old men.'

He slapped a bony hand to his chest, his face dark as the grave.

'I am a fighter! Why don't they fire at me?'

Blood! I didn't feel good. I needed to get back to my room. The commander went on talking, spit flying from his dry lips, jabbing the air in front of him with his cigarette so that ash rained over his empty trousers.

'In the last war, Israel started the attack. Now again the same. In two years? It will be the same. Worse and worse. Why must we always lie and wait for them to attack us? Why can't we be the attackers?'

'It's not our truce, it's Hamas' truce,' Fadi parroted, arbitrarily.

The commander jabbed at me with his smoking hand and I noticed the wedding ring, loose on his bone finger. Abu Yasser's son-in-law. Did he have any choice? A heavy drone sound filled the room and he jumped to his feet, striding towards the sea, a purposeful shade. He glared at the silent radio in his hand, snapped his head upwards in a listening gesture, then clicked his finger bones at Fadi.

'We're going,' Fadi said, jumping nervously to his feet.

The commander stalked back towards me and leant over my notebook, eyes burning like coals.

'We don't attack from the area near the Al Muzaner family, no one does. Write that!'

He stabbed at my notebook with his long, knobbled index

finger until I started to write. Why was *everyone* so obsessed with this *one* bombed family?

'Israel has a video of the attack on the house. You saw it, Fadi?'

The commander gestured impatiently for Fadi to speak.

'Yeah, I saw it, crazy,' Fadi replied dutifully.

The commander continued his story in rapid Arabic, letting Fadi translate.

'Find the video, you can see a satellite of the whole area, you can see where the rockets are fired from, where the Israelis strike. You can see, no rockets come from anywhere near the Muzaner house. They wouldn't accept the resistance to attack from their streets, and still they were massacred.'

Satisfied he had delivered this message, the commander turned to leave.

'Aren't you afraid to die?'

My voice was thick and raspy and the stupid question slipped out before I could stop it, but the already-dead commander answered quickly.

'Why would I be afraid to die? There is no living here.'

He walked swiftly in the opposite direction from the broken window toward the lobby, Fadi jogging to catch up. I called out to them that they were walking the wrong way, but it was already too late.

First came the unearthly whine then time stopped, suspended, rocking in its abyss, before finally the explosion. This one so loud it flashed white. My thoughts turned white. I don't know how long it was before I noticed that my shoulder was throbbing underneath me with a dull ache and I was on the ground, the air blown clear from my lungs. I lay still, waiting to be able to breathe, and listened to the screaming. It wasn't normal screaming but a high unnatural wail that could shrivel souls like salted slugs.

There was blood all over my hands, hot, black red and sticky, but it didn't hurt too much. It wasn't bad. When I was finally able to breathe again, I raised myself onto all fours and then pulled myself to my feet. It was painful to walk, but I moved slowly through the dust-filled restaurant towards the screaming and found Fadi gripping a wall with a filthy, bloody hand, his face bleached white with dust, ossified in horror. He was staring out into the courtyard.

The potted palms were upended in new jagged mounds of dust and rocks. Through a veil of thick smoke I saw that the lobby was missing a wall and through the fresh gap in the brickwork, a mortified tableau. Paula Miranda, front desk Mohammed, Stuart Finch and Anthony Harper stood in a line, staring out into the courtyard, the air between us powdered with concrete and sulphur. Paula's hand was raised to her mouth.

The noise was coming from a woman in a dark headscarf who was on her knees screaming like her heart was on fire. Beside her, Steve Sweeney's arms were rigid in front of him, pumping down hard. He was shouting instructions back into the hotel, but I couldn't make out what he was saying over the woman's screaming and the ringing in my ears.

Beyond the courtyard, the long black form of the commander splayed out over the pavement. His skinny body missing its head. A growing slick of dark gore spilled from his neck over the kerb towards the smouldering frame of a car where a bloodied, plump arm dangled out of the charred driver-seat window.

Jihad's huge frame charged into the smoke and fell heavily to the ground next to Steve. When he rose, he was cradling a body. A very small person. I couldn't see the hard little face, it was covered in stone dust and bent at an unnatural angle against Jihad's chest, but I recognised the sinewy limbs hanging limp. Russian gymnast limbs. Little Jihad's limbs.

Steve's face was now in his hands and sobbing. I couldn't stand the woman's wailing anymore so I turned and walked away back into the windowless restaurant, dripping a trail of blood from my hands into the bomb dust, up the staff stairs to my room.

32
SAD PSYCHOPATH

I picked out the large pieces of glass and brick sticking out of my palms one at a time. As each shard wiggled free it released a fresh spring of bright red blood and I let the tap water run over the open flesh holes creating a pink whirlpool that swirled around the bowl and down the drain. I ran the water until there was no more blood, then I wrapped my hands in two hand towels and went to sit on the bed. I studied my white mittens as red slowly seeped up into their fibres. Dark brown blood lined my nail beds.

The bird blinked its reptilian eyelids and curled its pink toenails around the edge of the television making a small scratching sound. My brain rang with white noise and my hands throbbed in their towel-mittens in my lap. On the television, the Egyptian waxwork woman was sitting with her talons folded, footage of an exploded white bus and an Israeli police cordon playing behind her. I jabbed at the control until it flicked onto the American reporter who was standing in front of the same smoking bus shell.

'So far, Anne, 15 people have been reported injured, four of them critically in this terror attack in the heart of Tel Aviv's busy business district,' he said.

The reporter's feet were thrown wide in an action stance and he leaned into the camera as Israeli police moved behind him. On her side of the split screen, Anne tried to frown.

'Police here are working on the assumption that this was not a suicide attack, Anne, so that's not a suicide attack but most likely an explosive device of some sort left on the bus to detonate, probably activated by a timer or remote control.'

'Oh my,' said Anne, pointlessly.

'This is the first terror attack on this scale the city has suffered since 2006 and let me tell you it has blown apart more than this bus. That ceasefire that was due to come into effect this evening in the Hamas-run Gaza Strip? Well, Anne that's also been blown sky high, and so too any hopes of peace.'

'Such senseless brutality in Tel Aviv today, Josh,' Anne said.

'And Anne, it will be answered, believe you me. My sources in the Israeli military have already told me they will answer this attack swiftly. They will take an eye for an eye. And you can be sure the Israeli prime minister will be asking the secretary of state, who landed in Tel Aviv just a few hours ago, as he has asked time and time again, how can he be expected to make peace with a people who put such little value on human . . . '

I turned the television off. The bird stalked towards me, pecking at the tiles by my bedside table. The impossible angle of little Jihad's head when his father scooped him up.

'Slattern!'

He was 11 and his dad could still pick him up like a pile of towels.

'Bloody slattern!'

I looked at the bird, at its bird heart beating visibly underneath its feathered ribs, its metallic purple face. It blinked at me and its tiny head spasmed in a series of jerks. Narrowing its yellow eyes over its sharp crustaceous beak it cooed.

'You do know you're *awash* with blood?'

Little Jihad was dead. He was dead because of me. The bird turned away in disgust and strutted bossily to study the tiles at the end of the bed where it issued another spasm of coos.

'And that fat one! Exploded like a watermelon! Except the arm.'

I winced. It saw everything. The bird hopped up onto the coffee table and pecked absent-mindedly at some withered slices of cucumber. My heart was being strangled by my oesophagus.

'I'm just a little vulture! I don't understanden!'

A lump that had been gathering mass in my throat began to bubble and surge. I covered my ears with my towel mittens but the voice grated on.

'I don't understanden! I'm awash with blood!'

The mass was growing quickly, pushing against my larynx, then passed it, until suddenly it flew out of my mouth: an immense noise. I was wailing, a huge alien wail. I launched myself at the bird. I wanted to feel its rib cage crack and its wings tear off. I had it between my towel mitts! I felt my fingertips gripping it's soft gritty body. It flapped its wings violently but I gripped harder with my bloody nails, closing my eyes tightly against its flapping battery.

I bellowed again but this time in surprise. The bird's oily feathers had slid free of my padded grip and it was stabbing me in the neck with its crusted razor beak. I swiped with my bloodied towels to get it off me but its sharp talons were in my hair.

'Get the fuck off me!' I screamed.

It clawed at my scalp, then pecked at me hard just beneath my ear.

'Get the fuck off me, you sick fucking fuck!'

Peck. Claw. Hiss.

I shook my shoulders furiously, swiping at it until it released its talons and flapped furiously to perch on the curtain rail above the balcony door far out of the reach of my swinging fists.

'Come on then you fuck! Come back here and I'll fucking kill you!' I screeched up at it, eyes burning with hateful rage, hair wild from the fight.

But I heard it, my threat was pathetic. The bird was unkillable. It ruffled its shoulder feathers into a hateful balloon, its swollen purple chest pumping, and issued a series of sharp grunts. I fell onto the bed to weep and it watched me sob until I choked, then as I just lay there breathing and crying.

'Sad psychopath,' it concluded.

'Psychopaths don't get sad,' I protested weakly.

The bird ruffled its wings and cooed.

'Get up now please. You're embarrassing yourself.'

I breathed a bit more and considered what the bird was saying. What use is a crying journalist to anyone? Slowly, I got up. In the bathroom I washed my neck, head, hand and arm wounds carefully with soapy water, took my pills, rebound my hands. Then I sat down in front of my laptop with my notebook. The bird watched from its corner perch, yellow bead eyes scanning the pages of my dusty, bloody notepad. It was hard to type with mummy hands and it craned its neck to follow the cursor across the screen. But in a little over an hour, I had written a piece.

'There. It's done,' I said.

I hit send, launching my story at London, and slumped back in the chair, feeling myself pulsate with injuries. I had started to cry again but silent tears this time. The bird shook its feathers with a dramatic peacock flourish and jumped down from its high vantage point onto the floor. It stalked with dignity through the open doors of the balcony and out into what was left of the war.

33
Something Light

When I woke, the bird was still gone. I peered about for it from my bed but saw only the violent green curtains flapping noisily. My bed was filthy with blood and feathers, chocolate wrappers and breadcrumbs. The sky outside was grey and the room desolate. I shuffled slowly towards the desk and opened my laptop, which was also blood-smeared, and clicked towards *The Tribune*'s website. The top story on the site was that the manager of a football club had been sacked. The second top story was that another newspaper had published pictures of a prince in a helicopter in Afghanistan and *The Tribune* asked if this was treason. Underneath these two stories was a picture of the blown up bus in Tel Aviv and my story.

EXCLUSIVE: *'We will fight until there is no Israel'*
Palestinian terrorist vows to destroy the Jewish state minutes before his assassination

I clicked on the piece and above my name, there was my face as a digital postage stamp. My passport picture. I glared out of the blood-smeared laptop screen square-jawed, intense blue gaze thundering from under a crooked fringe. They had kept the bit about the woman on her knees wailing and Steve Sweeney trying to save little Jihad, every detail of the dead commander's death and everything he'd told me about his group's infinite supply of rockets made in Gaza. They had pulled in bold the paragraph about the English and American funding. They had taken out the bits about why they fought, Iran and little Jihad's fluent English. There were two other Gaza stories below mine.

Fragile ceasefire holds in Gaza despite bus bomb and fatal airstrike on journalist hotel

Israel blames Hamas for death of child in hotel strike

The first had Nasser's by-line, the second Anthony Harper's. The final paragraphs of Anthony's story ran: *The child and the leader of a lesser-known terrorist cell, the Al-Yasser Salahadin Group, were thought to have been killed instantly when a car parked outside The Beach Hotel was hit by a missile fired from an Israeli predator drone. The terrorist had been meeting a freelance journalist reporting for this newspaper at the hotel, which has served as a base for international media throughout the eight-day conflict.*

No longer our contracted stringer?

IDF spokesperson Captain Doron Weiss told The Tribune that Israel deeply regrets any civilian loss of life, but that such casualties are inevitable in asymmetric wars such as the one it is fighting in Gaza.

'Responsibility for the tragic death of a child lies first with the cowardly leadership of Hamas, who conceal their most dangerous terrorists among women and children, but also with any journalist or journalists who would meet a terrorist, responsible for countless Israeli deaths, in a civilian environment,' Weiss said.

The Tribune will be conducting an internal investigation into the incident.

I crawled back under the filthy sheets and closed my eyes. When Michael read the newspaper in bed, I made him read aloud. He used different accents for different types of stories.

'Madame Rodhaam Clinton yesterrrday launched a vigorous counterattack on behalf of her husband's beleaguerrred presidency, declaring ze president a victiiim of a vast right-wing conspiracy!'

He used a French accent when he was reading about sex. He looked at me severely over his glasses.

'*C'est énorme* the conspiracy. *Énorme*, Sara. *Comme ma bite.*'

I laughed and he moved my hand that had been stroking his smooth belly onto his cock to prove the point, holding it there.

'She knew him betterrr than anyone in the worrrld! She still loved him! And believed his denial of allegations that he had entered into a sexual relationship with a White House intern. Wow.'

He dropped the accent mid paragraph and stopped reading to whistle.

'What?' I asked.

'That's insane,' he laughed.

'What is?'

'The world's most powerful woman has gone to war in defence of her husband's intern-fucking. That's insane!'

'It's not insane. It's smart,' I stared up at him earnestly, still holding his cock.

Michael peered back at me, amused over his reading glasses.

'She owns him now. She's won.'

'Jesus Christ,' he laughed lowly, pressing my body to his with his big hot hand.

I kissed his neck where the grey stubble ran out and his smoothest skin began.

'You're terrifying,' he said.

Had he seen it yet? My picture by-line staring up at him from his newsagent's counter. Or his doormat. He would be shocked at first, then proud. He would also worry. I should call. I could do it quickly while the bird was away, put his mind at ease. From the room phone this time. I smoothed my hair and licked my cracked lips. His number rang and my heart pounded in my palms. It kept ringing. Was he not going to answer? I should have washed first.

'Hello?'

Was that his voice?

'Hello,' I echoed.

'Hello?'

He sounded remote and out of breath and not at all like himself. Had he run to pick up the call?

'Michael, it's me.'

'Who is this?'

I felt the strong curling grip of his fingers around mine and laughed into the receiver.

'Sara?' he lowered his voice.

'Hello Michael,' I said and laughed again.

'Where are you calling from? What's this number?'

His words were coming out tight and whispered. He did not sound good.

'I'm still in Gaza.'

'You know you're not meant to call me. What do you want?'

There was a delay on the stupid war-battered line. I sat bolt upright in bed, hugging my knees to my chest and pressed the phone close to my dry mouth.

'I wanted to let you know I was alright. I didn't want you to see the paper and worry.'

'We agreed. I blocked your number, for Christ's sake! What did you think that meant? I wanted you to keep calling, just from different phones?'

He was stressed. I hated it when he sounded like that.

'What's that? It's a terrible line,' he growled.

He hadn't seen the paper. I supposed it was still early in Gaza, so even earlier in London. He was walking, I could hear the effort in his voice, the sound of his footsteps striding up some stairs. They had stairs. A door closed behind him.

'This is really not a good time. The little one's finally sleeping and Cathy's arriving at some insane hour to drop the boys.'

He was breathing heavily.

'Did you say you're in Gaza?'

The little one. Those weird tennis boys. His sad life without me.

'Are you okay? Are you in some sort of trouble?' he asked, softer.

He coughed to clear his throat and I laughed.

'Trouble? I'm calling to tell you I'm okay. I have a big story in the paper today and I didn't want you to worry. It's been rough, I lost a friend actually, but I'm fine. I didn't think my messages were getting through. Blocked me, eh?'

She would have done that. The line clicked like it was going to break and I pushed the receiver more tightly to my ear, hoping the pressure would hold our connection in place.

'Are *you* okay? It sounds like *you're* in trouble?' I laughed again.

'Ah,' he said lowly. 'I haven't seen the papers yet. That sounds bad. You sure you're alright?'

He was talking like himself now, his warm butter voice. I wanted to drink it.

'Yes, I'm alright,' I said.

'Okay, that's good. Congratulations on the piece. Bill would be proud.'

'You think so?' I asked, smiling.

I waited.

'I saw Steve Sweeney's been in Gaza. Those stories he's been doing on that poor family wiped out by the Israelis, just horrific. Have you met him yet? An amazing man, you must be learning so much.'

'Steve? Yeah, of course. We're staying in the same hotel.'

There was a shriek of gulls outside and a violent crash on the balcony. Was that the bird back? There was a clatter of claws on glass and I buried the phone receiver in the sheets bunched in my lap. Had I left the balcony door open?

'Bird?' I hissed.

'Sara? Are you there?' Michael's muffled voice came from under the covers.

I craned to look for feathers poking through the curtain but couldn't see any. I raised the phone back to my face.

'I'm here Michael,' I whispered.

'Listen, I'm actually glad you called. I've been thinking for a while that we should talk, but of course this isn't the time. When you're back next, maybe we can get a coffee.'

He missed me. Of course he did. He regretted it all, poor man. I could feel it, his wanting me spreading like a warm glow through my chest.

'I can talk for a bit now,' I said and smiled.

'Really?' he took a long breath and cleared his throat again. 'Alright. I just wanted to say sorry, finally. I know I should have told you about me and Mimi. At the time, I mean, and I feel badly about it. I should have been honest with you.'

'Oh? Okay.'

He sighed deeply.

'The thing is, I suppose that after everything, after Cathy, all the years of guilt, all the heaviness, our thing was always so difficult. I just wanted, I don't know, some fun. Something light.'

He took another breath, easing himself into honesty like it was cold water. Our *thing?*

'I was a bit lonely, I suppose, and I know it will probably annoy you to hear it, but we always had a good time, Mimi and me. She didn't expect anything from me, and that turned out to be exactly what I needed. I didn't plan for any of this to happen but when it did, it just felt right. You know? I'm happy.'

Michael issued a light laugh of surprise and blood throbbed heavily into my brain. *Something light?*

'Something *light?*'

'Don't do that, Sara. You know it wasn't easy for me either. And Cathy's been a total nightmare since the baby.'

She didn't *expect* anything from him? She had everything!

'I wasn't *light?*'

'You left! We both moved on. I didn't do anything wrong.'

He was angry, whisper-shouting. That was definitely an animal bang on the glass.

'I have to go,' I whispered back.

'Sara, wait.'

'No it's the bird, it's back, I have to go.'

'What?'

'I need to go now but we'll speak again soon. It'll be okay Michael, I love you.'

34
MICHAEL

I was angry because my legs had been maimed by goosebumps. Legs I had scorched in the sun until they blistered and peeled and then finally tanned as close to golden as they were ever going to get weren't golden anymore. They were blue and bumpy because it was fucking freezing and everything was fucking ruined.

I was under the crab apple tree at the furthest end of our garden, clutching a sticky champagne flute and barbecuing my bare blue legs on a flaming garden taper hoping they might actually catch light. I'd turned 17 in the spring and after a summer of metamorphosis, my childhood fat had stretched and reformed into freakish height and huge new tits. I'd forced my legs to tan in unbearably hot Algarve sun so that I could wear my ass skimming Kookai miniskirt for James, the son of Ma's tennis coach Brian, who was always the waiter at our parties. But he had been avoiding me all night owing to the revolting sight of my bare, blue, legs on that unseasonably cold and damp late August night. He wouldn't even meet my sexy eye contact, so what was the fucking point of any of it?

I watched my parents' guests from inside the crab apple branches and slugged down their discarded glasses of Buck's Fizz. The same women who came every year in their pearls and crushed velvet dresses. Women like Ma's fragile friend Cathy threw their blow-dried heads back and gripped the arms of men who were making them laugh. The men wore shirts and suit jackets and shouted over each other and the too-loud band. I saw my mother in her backless dress talking bossily to James, telling him no doubt to go easy on the champagne top-ups, determined to see me die of humiliation.

A tiny marquee extended our dining room about five feet beyond its French doors into the garden. The three-piece band Ma had hired led by James' tennis coach father Brian played an earnest set of Doors, Neil Diamond and cringey falsetto Beach Boys songs. Brian wore an earring and tight jeans and looked too young to be James' father. I watched James as he walked from the kitchen bar with a freshly popped bottle of champagne towards a clutch of laughing women.

'Oh no, girly! You're freezing!'

A man's voice spoke in my ear and I stiffened with shock, unsure if it was talking to me as no one had spoken to me all night.

'I've never seen goosebumps *bump* like that before. You want my jacket?'

I turned to find a face lit eerily by taper light, Celtic features booze-moulded into a satiric grin. It was my father's agent Michael Frazer and he had a dinner jacket hooked on the end of his index finger which was pointed at my face. I shook my head and shivered.

'No thanks, I'm fine.'

'Hello Fine, I'm Michael,' Michael grinned, struggling to force his arms back into his jacket while gripping the cuffs of his shirt-sleeves like a toddler.

He was very drunk.

'I know,' I said.

'And you're Fine.'

'I'm Sara.'

'Hello Sara. I think you need a slammer.'

'*What?*'

I screwed my face uncomprehendingly. Michael Frazer had clearly failed to recognise me from all the dinner parties he'd come to at our house. The countless times I'd taken his coat, offered him Bombay Mix, brought him a whiskey and

Cathy her gin and tonic then been sent upstairs to bed as Dad made jokes he thought I couldn't hear about the miracle of his having sired Augustus Gloop's and Veruca Salt's love child.

'I said you need a Tequila Slammer! It'd warm you right up!'

I shivered again and shrugged to indicate I had no idea what he was talking about, scanning the party for James.

'You never had one? It's this magic made from champagne and tequila. And it just so happens that I have here with me a bottle of tequila gifted from one of the finest tequila purveyors in all the salty lands of Mexico. It's even got a worm in it!'

Michael opened his jacket to reveal a glass bottle poking out of his breast pocket and wiggled his index finger through a button hole at my face. I laughed despite myself. He was ridiculous.

'I've had four and look at me! Toastie as a tostada! You want one?'

He looked at me hopeful and solicitous from the corner of his drooping eye and I shrugged sure.

'*Si? Si! Vamos!*' Michael exclaimed, grinning unsteadily. 'No! Wait!'

Brian wailed from our conservatory and Michael punched a fist high into the crab apple branches, face contorted with emotion as he sang along.

'*I ammmmm, I said, to nooo one theeerrre. And - no one - heard - at - all - not EVEN THE CHAIR!* How genius is that lyric? I think it's my all-time favourite lyric. Follow me!'

He swayed his suited frame through the bodies in the garden like a water snake and I followed close behind, sniggering at his drunkenness. He wiggled his suited arse at me. We passed my father and Michael gave him a smooth wink, snaking on towards the champagne bar in the kitchen.

'*Michel*!'

My father had grabbed Michael forcefully by the elbow.

'Hold your horses kiddo! Why won't you join us?'

He was pleading.

'But *Wilhelm*! I'm helping this very cold girl get a Tequila Slammer! It's urgent. Look!'

Michael pointed at me and I froze, ready to plead ignorance, but my father boomed with laughter. He always found Michael hilarious. The two women Dad was standing with did not.

'You can't do that *Michel*! We're socialists, not bandits!' my father wagged a playful index finger at him.

The women, who were Laurel the Californian essayist and a shorter woman in a black velvet pant suit, winced.

'Can't we be both?' Michael grinned.

I gripped the sticky champagne flute behind my back and cast my eyes hopelessly at my man-sized, grass-covered Doc Martin boots hoping to avoid interacting with any of them.

'Hello Sara darling, how are you? Are you having a nice time?' Laurel asked me in her low, serious voice.

'Yes thanks,' I smiled politely.

'Have you met Lizzy?'

'Hello Lizzy, nice to meet you.'

Lizzy, who had very short hair, large blue eyes and peach cobbler cheeks, smiled at me with deep concern and I wanted to die. Dad had caught Michael's eye and was executing obvious eye-rolling in the direction of the lesbians, who either didn't notice or didn't care. They were friends of my mother.

'It's been years since I last saw you. You're so grown! I love your skirt. It must be almost A-level time for you, is it?'

Laurel spoke with unnatural care at an unnervingly slow speed, pulling a grey sheet of hair carefully from her face with a heavily ringed hand.

'Yep. Next year,' I nodded.

'Awful. Can you imagine having to go through all that again, Liz? School is absolutely the worst time of your life Sara. Really, it's abuse. I promise you it all gets so much better!'

Laurel smiled at me with pitying reassurance and her girlfriend shuddered in agreement.

'Fucking ridiculous,' my father erupted, allowing a conversation's worth of irritation to erupt on the topic of my schooling.

'Sara's doing brilliantly! Aren't you Bob? A born Classist, like her dear old Dad. Top of the class in Latin!'

'Are you Sara?' Laurel judged. 'That's very impressive.'

I tugged at my miniskirt and stared desperately at the ground.

'I'm the *only* one doing Latin A-level, actually,' I confessed, then shivered.

'Amazing!' Michael gawped, finally placing me as Bill Byrne's overweight only child.

'Was that your choice or your father's?' Laurel drawled with a smirk. '*Non scholae sed vitae discimus,* wouldn't you say sweetie?'

I laughed uncomfortably and nodded. Drunk Michael furrowed his brow in confusion. My father's eyes were ablaze.

'I think we'd say *disce aut discede,* wouldn't we Bob?' he growled, looking very much like he wanted to throw his champagne in the essayist's face.

I muttered something about needing a coat and stalked off in search of James. I found him in the kitchen, busily loading a tray with half-full flutes of champagne. His long, perfectly formed limbs exercised effortless balance, the tray poised happily on his muscular forearm. Even his acne was sexy. Athletic, hormonal.

'Hey, mind if I take one of those?' I said, reaching a long arm out awkwardly for one of his bubbling glasses.

'You allowed?' he said coldly, frowning with concentration.

'There you are girly!'

Michael emerged from behind me to swipe two glasses of champagne from James' tray and two empty high balls from the table. The bitter mortification that had been churning in my stomach hardened. I turned away from a miffed James to smile at my old, drunk friend.

'Here I am!' I smirked at Michael.

'Quick!' he hissed over his shoulder. 'Lead us to a secret slammers spot?'

Michael swayed up the stairs after me like a crooked Fred Astaire. Our laundry room was tiny and warm and smelled like tumble dryer fluff. My school sports kit hung from the Lazy Susan, a hollow scarecrow next to Dad's white work shirts.

'Make wayyy for the worrrm!'

Michael sent piles of our dryer-tangled bras and unmatched socks tumbling to the floor with a grand sweep of his arm, clearing a patch of countertop. He drew a small, yellow, glass bottle from his inside jacket pocket and placed it with deliberate care next to the champagne and the high balls.

'Now you watch closely, girly, because you're making the next round. First you put the tequila in, the prettiest bird gets the worm.'

He winked.

'Then in goes the champagne. You get your hand and you put it on top of the glass like this. Then bang! Whoop! Knock it back all at once! Go!'

He pushed the highball frothing like a liquor cauldron into my hand and I gulped its contents down until champagne foam spat out of my nose. I covered my face with my hand, cold with terror that I might be sick like a child in front of this man who was treating me like an adult woman. Michael hooted with delight.

'What a gal!'

I giggled, wiping the champagne foam from my nostrils with the back of my hand.

'You like it?' he asked, grinning.

I did not like it. It was revolting but I nodded and smiled.

'Didn't I tell you? Magic!' he cried.

The frothing drink leapt wildly about in my stomach like a goldfish out of water, up my throat until I couldn't stop it any longer. I leaned further into the sink that smelled of hand washing liquid and vomited fizzy tequila orange juice. Michael groaned behind me.

'Oh no. Girly!' he said, patting my back understandingly. 'What a waste!'

I grabbed a drying hockey sock from the rack to wipe my mouth and he rubbed the small of my back.

'Are you okay? Let's stay here a minute. Maybe drink some water?'

I nodded into the long red sock. He smacked his mouth, which seemed to feel very dry to his tongue, and leaned back against the tumble-dryer to watch me better. I ran the tap and leaned in to drink the running water, feeling his eyes run over my bent body.

'You know, you're a pretty cool chick,' he slurred. 'Even when you puke.'

The way he was looking at me chilled me deeper the cold water running down my gullet. He smacked his mouth again and I gulped on at the water longer than I needed to, adjusting to this new feeling of his eyes on me. I kept gulping, thinking that he was going to look away but he didn't. This man wanted to drink me. When my stomach couldn't hold any more water, I turned off the tap and wiped my mouth with the back of my hand, letting the last drips of water run off my chin onto my chest. I let out a long satisfied exhale and he watched my tits as they rose and fell. I felt good. So good in fact that I laughed out loud.

'Did you say *chick*?'

35
Do Not Enter!

The media was checking out and Mohammed's reception was filled with journalists, cameras and luggage. I teetered on the edge of the staircase and scanned the room. I hadn't been down since the strike. They would all have read my piece, the other pieces with the Israelis blaming me, but waiter Mohammed had never arrived with my breakfast. Whatever they thought, I was still a guest at the hotel and I still had to eat. I spotted an empty table at the edge of the lobby and moved self-consciously to claim it.

The missing wall had been covered with a white curtain, and it rose and fell with a hymeneal flicker. A handwritten sign with the words *Danger! Do Not Enter* had been tacked to it. As the sheet billowed, it teased glimpses of earth, broken concrete and upended palm trees. No one paid me any attention. There was no gay Mohammed with his quick step and big tray. Only the small, sweaty waiter weaving through the pit of bodies and bags with harassed, heavy steps.

'Yes, Madam!'

The sweaty waiter had been scuttling back and forth past my table without stopping so I was forced to grab him by the arm to order my usual plain omelette, fresh watermelon juice and black coffee, and when he stalked off again, it was not to the kitchen but towards reception. I followed him closely, my stomach roaring with hunger, wondering where he could be beetling off to with my breakfast order. He had gone to engage front desk Mohammed in agitated gossip. The waiter was animated, with much raising and lowering of arms revealing large dark sweat stains on his overly snug beige uniform. Desk

Mohammed, ashen-faced and nodding, picked up his phone, a gesture that seemed to mark an end to their exchange, and I watched with relief as the waiter disappeared at last into the kitchen.

I had woken to an email from Jason Argent telling me that as I had defied his instruction and interviewed the terrorist commander with such tragic consequences, *The Tribune* would no longer work with me. As I waited, I busied myself drafting a respectful but challenging response until I felt a presence standing over me. I looked up expecting a neat, apologetic Mohammed holding my food but instead, there was Nasser.

'Sara, may I speak with you privately for a moment, please?' he said in a low voice.

'Nasser!' I called up to him.

'I'm actually just waiting for my breakfast,' I began, but he made a face so severe that I stood up and followed him silently in the direction of the closed, bombed-out restaurant.

We met on the edge of the platform overlooking the large, rubble-strewn dining room. The stage was usually used for weddings. The bride and groom would sit here on their big, white nylon-covered thrones, looking down over their guests as they danced and ate. I smiled affectionately at Nasser, thinking that we were a husband and wife of sorts, professionally speaking. Alessandro was right, you see enough death with someone.

'I have to be quick because I'm on my way to the office of Hamas internal security,' he said. 'They gave me an hour to get there. I came because Mohammed at reception insisted.'

Was Nasser in trouble? I felt another rush of warmth. Proud Nasser had come to ask me for help and of course I would help him, as far as I was able. I asked him what the problem was.

'Did you forget? I told you many times the arrangement with Hamas. I vouch for you, they let you in. I am responsible for you while you're in Gaza. They think I arranged that interview.'

I breathed with relief and smiled knowingly at him. He was angry that I had cheated on him with Fadi.

'I'm sorry I didn't tell you Nasser. But you were busy with Anthony,' I reminded him.

He blinked at me.

'You know Mohammed, the waiter?'

'*Gay* Mohammed?' I smiled. 'Sure.'

Nasser's conquistador face contorted in confusion.

'I mean the tall waiter who's been taking care of you.'

I nodded and smiled to indicate that we were indeed talking about the same person. He flinched, shook his head and continued.

'He was taken from his home last night. Hamas has just issued a statement saying he is a collaborator and that he called in the strike on the hotel. He will be executed.'

Bright white sunlight was flooding into the dining room, making my eyes water. I struggled to understand what Nasser was saying.

'I don't understand. Mohammed is a collaborator?'

Nasser's small foot stamped in a spasm of fury.

'Sara, they're going to kill him! Mohammed! He is going to be dragged out in public and shot in the head. His wife will see it, his children will see him shot!'

His thin frame was shaking, searching my face for a reaction.

'Mohammed has children? And a *wife?*' I asked, amazed.

Nasser's ashen face flushed pink at the cheekbones. Shaking his head, he moved to walk away.

'Wait! Wait a minute Nasser,' I called after him. 'I want to help!'

He stopped and his hunched shoulders began to shake with low, disturbing laughter. Burying his face in his hands, he let out a strange, strangled squeal.

'Stop it! Will you listen to me, please?' I insisted.

Turning to look at me with his familiar, exhausted features, I felt an exhilarating surge of confidence. If anyone was going to understand, it would be Nasser. He was the most spiritual person I knew, practically a shaman. Still, I spoke slowly in an effort to sound as reasonable as possible.

'Nasser, I think my father is here. In Gaza.'

My shoulders dropped heavily and I sighed with the relief of having said it out loud.

'You told me your father is dead.'

'Exactly.'

Nasser stared at me irritably and I gave him a significant look, lowering my voice confidingly.

'I think he's back, as a pigeon. You remember the bird? That lives on my balcony? I think it's Dad. Or at least he talks through it. I've no idea *how*, its beak doesn't even move most of the time. But if it *is* Dad, and if he can make a bird talk, then he should be able to do something to help Mohammed. Don't you think?'

I smiled hopefully and raised my hands to grab Nasser's and celebrate our new cosmic secret together, but remembering how uncomfortable he was with physical contact, retracted them. Nasser studied the horizon behind me with his hands on his skinny hips.

'So you think your father is here.'

He paused again.

'As a bird. How has he helped you so far?'

He folded his skinny genie arms while I thought. It was a good question. How had the bird helped me?

'Well, you might not like this, but he helped me with that story about the commander. Encouraged me.'

Nasser's eyes popped wide in his bony head and turned heavenward. He started again with his new, deranged laughing.

'Wow! So you think that your father, back from the dead, wouldn't try to *stop* you from getting a little boy killed? From causing all this horror. You're saying he crossed over from the spirit world, defying all laws of nature, to help *make* that happen.'

The mention of little Jihad made my throat tighten.

'I don't know, Nasser! I told you, I don't know how it works. Maybe if *you* could talk to him?'

I turned on my heels looking around for a pigeon, but the only birds in the room were a pair of gulls sat on the broken window frame staring out to sea with dead shark eyes. When I turned back to look at Nasser, he was shaking his head. I sighed.

'You think I'm insane.'

'You shouldn't be here Sara.'

Nasser exhaled a deep sorrowful weariness.

'The reason I came is that the hotel wants you to leave. They can't have people staying here who endanger the lives of their guests and staff, obviously. And they're afraid you won't go freely.'

I nodded, not having really listened. I was thinking.

'Did you hear that, Sara? You need to check out and leave this morning. You need to go home.'

I nodded again more emphatically and he wrung his hands behind his back. I knew that tight-lipped face. He was deciding whether to say something or not. His temple vein throbbed.

'Just promise me you won't try to help Mohammed,' he said finally. 'You can only make things worse. Do you understand?'

I nodded, then he nodded and said okay. He turned around, walked a few quick steps, then stopped again.

'My cousin Mariam asked me to tell you that she's sorry but you have hepatitis. It's why your eyes are yellow. You'll need to get medical treatment in England.'

'Oh,' I said. 'Thank you.'

This time he walked away without stopping and I followed the back of his quick, small head into the bustling lobby until it was lost in the pit of journalists jostling for front desk Mohammed's attention.

36
CHECKING OUT

There was zero point in sentiment. I was not going to get mawkish about the bed I'd had injurious Italian sex in. Or the coffee table still littered with scraps of food that kind Mohammed had brought me. Or the balcony the bird haunted, covered in its crap. Packed and dressed, I took a last look at myself in the marled bathroom mirror. My eyes were still an arresting shade of yolk but they didn't *feel* like anything. Physically, I was almost normal. I could walk, more or less.

On a last scan of the room, I found Alessandro's unopened note, tucked carefully where Mohammed had left it under the breadbasket. I dusted the hardened crumbs off their grease stains and opened it. It was written entirely in backwards slanting shouty caps.

CARA SARA, I GO TO ROME. MAX IS THERE AND HIS MOTHER WANTS ME THERE TOO. I AM SORRY I DID NOT DO YOUR STORY WITH YOU. I THINK IT IS INTERESTING TOPIC BUT ALSO YOU MUST BE CAREFUL. I DON'T LIKE THE LOOK OF THIS BOY YOU WORK WITH. DANGEROUS EYES! CAREFUL CRAZY WOMAN!

YOU DON'T FIND ME ON SOCIAL MEDIA. I HAVE PROBLEMS IN THE PAST, TOO MUCH WOMAN ATTENTION [WINKY FACE]. BUT I SEE YOU SOON ON ANOTHER FRONTLINE PAZZA SEXY!

UN BACIONE!
SANDRO X

[MOHAMMED AT THE RECEPTION SAID YOU ARE SICK. I HOPE YOU ARE BETTER SOON! I THINK ALSO MAYBE I HAVE SOMETHING? I'M NOT FEELING GOOD DOWNSTAIRS [DOWNTURNED SMILEY FACE]!]

Front desk Mohammed was absorbed with the stacking and re-stacking of his piles of paper. The Beach was fastidious about paperwork. Mohammed had my stack of bills ready and pushed it towards me as I approached his counter. *The Tribune* had paid my tab, he explained without looking up, but each individual bill still needed to be signed, stamped and countersigned.

I began to work my way through the long log of hummus and mini-bar chocolate in obliging silence. I noticed that waiter Mohammed hadn't charged me for any of his special herbal teas or unsolicited coffees and prickly tears stung my eyes. I blinked them back fiercely. I would not cry, for desk Mohammed's sake. He wouldn't survive the scene.

'I. Can. Not. Wait. To. Get. Out. Of. HERE! I'd sell my kidney for a decent coffee! Scratch that, I'd sell my son's kidney!' Paula Miranda rolled up to the front desk, yapping at the man from *The LA Chronicle*.

'Right,' the LA man monotoned. 'That's funny.'

'Oh look, John! If it's not Miss Hamas!'

There was no way I could escape, so I raised my gaze to meet Paula's with an expression that I hoped conveyed solemn dignity.

'Holy shit!' Paula screeched, raising a stumpy hand to her mouth, and lurched backwards. 'What's wrong with your eyes?'

I didn't answer but averted my yellow gaze back towards my paperwork. When she had recovered, Paula directed her verbal assault at the floor around my feet.

'I've been looking for you, Missy, but no one seemed to know where you were. I wanted to tell you, as a journalistic courtesy, that I interviewed the mother of that kid you got killed.'

Paula turned towards her side-kick whose name apparently was John.

'The kid's dad is a cleaner here. You knew that, right? You'll have seen him. The big one with the one eye?'

The LA Chronicle scanned its brain bank for a cycloptic member of hotel staff but seemed to come up short. Paula shrugged and retrained her shrewish focus on me.

'Anyway, so I thought you should know the kid's mother told me she blames you for his death and that's the story we're running tomorrow. Like I said, I couldn't find you to get a comment, which I would have included in my piece as a right of reply, so I spoke to your boss Anthony, who apologised to the family on behalf of the paper.'

'You know Anthony Harper? Nice man, solid journalist,' Paula told LA.

'Horrified, he is *horrified*,' she stage-whispered at Mohammed.

Mohammed shuffled desperately behind his counter. The LA man registered no response but watched me closely.

'Okay,' I said. 'Thank you.'

'Thank you? She thanks me!' Paula exclaimed in disbelief, looking towards LA to share her outrage but finding it blank.

'Un-believable. Okay Mohammed, you done checking out Miss Hamas here? I've got a border crossing to get to so quick sticks, rob me blind!'

She flapped a huge leather wallet stuffed with dollars open on Mohammed's counter and he treated her to a deferential laugh.

'I'll be with you momentarily Ms Miranda,' he bowed slightly.

With a flurry of precise stamps and signatures, Mohammed dispatched my pile of paperwork neatly into an envelope and sealed my history at The Beach Hotel like a contagion.

'Please, here are your documents Miss Byrne.'

His big pale face gleamed at the forehead as he pushed the thick manilla envelope towards me with a soft, manicured hand.

I wanted to tell him that I was sorry about little Jihad, and the waiter Mohammed. For the ruined courtyard and the bird shit in my room and the scratch marks on the TV. For his life having turned out to be working as a receptionist in a war-zone resort. But he had already focused his broadest beam on Paula Miranda, so grasping my envelope tightly, I turned and wheeled my bag silently through the swing doors.

Outside the daylight was bright and the street was thick with dust and diesel smoke. I pulled my bag, haemorrhaging dirty clothes, through the heavy sand for about 50 metres until I reached the entrance of the Al Mansour Hotel. I squinted up at the large modern building. It was very ugly.

37
LITTLE JIHAD'S MOTHER

The new room had a weird feeling. The bed had crinkly sheets that irritated my skin and the door to the bathroom didn't close properly and banged unpredictably. I had left some bread for the bird on the sill but locked the window. When it finally found me, I was getting ready for bed and it stalked the ledge, head jerking in spasms of fury. It lost several oil spill feathers in the violence of its apoplexy, and they swirled about it like violet demonic confetti as it fumed on its narrow new perch.

I tried to ignore it, turned out the light and crawled into bed but the sheets scratched and the bird kept cooing and clip-clawing up and down the narrow ledge on its tiny angry feet. When it finally fell silent, its menacing outrage kept me awake.

Paula Miranda's stupid face. Her piece would be out by now, with little Jihad's mother blaming me for his dying. *The unnatural angle of his neck.* The first call to prayer crackled loudly into the room and I hadn't slept a wink.

'I haven't slept a wink,' I said out loud.

There was a pause before it spoke. I let my eyes pop open and the bird's shadow appeared in a dark corner of the room, a feathery shadow octopus emerging from black rocks.

'*Si vis pacem, para bellum*' it said, its tone unusually sensitive.

'I was thinking about little Jihad's mother,' I told it.

It was still dark but I stared with sleepless eyes at the listening shadow.

'About how she thinks I killed her son.'

I lay considering how I might find her and explain my side of things but then considered how all my recent interactions with Palestinians had resulted in their arrest or death. She was very unlikely to want to see me. Also, what was my side of things? I blinked my sore eyes. Somewhere, there was a baby. Another boy, like the sad tennis boys. Mine would have looked like Michael. His skin, my height. Why hadn't he made her take the pills? I must have fallen asleep again because I dreamt of blood in a green toilet bowl and the coo of wood pigeons and was jarred awake by loud screams in a room flooded with light.

'She's waiting!'

The bird flapped its greasy wings excitedly against the window pane and I strained to focus on its frantic grey form.

'Get up! Slattern! She's waiting!'

I sat on the sand in front of the new hotel making and destroying little castles, pretending to be considering the waves, as little Jihad's bullies played. At some point his wild cat joined me, watching from a predator's distance the little thugs boot their ball at each other. We exchanged a discreet glance of greeting. When the gang finally moved to leave the beach, the cat and I moved too.

We walked together passed The Beach Hotel. I cast a lingering look towards Mohammed's reception but the front doors were closed. The cat's paws stalked through the soft ground, bloody tail stub twitching. It had somehow lost its tail. I looked down at its filthy muzzle keeping pace with me.

'So you're coming too?' I asked it.

It said nothing but glared back at me self-importantly. I quickened my pace as the boys turned off the beach road and the cat turned too. I stopped in my tracks to look at it and it stopped to look back, tilting it's head, indignant either at the delay or being scrutinised. The outrage on its filthy cat face was so funny I doubled over laughing. It was so like Jihad. I reached out to give it a consoling stroke but it hissed viciously.

Making an awkward leap into the air, it howled and took off at a rocking-horse gallop down the sandy backstreet back towards the hotel and out of sight.

I had never really walked in Gaza before. Foreigners generally didn't. UN staff were forbidden from stepping foot on Gazan pavement without a chaperone lest they got kidnapped and were ferried the hundred metres from office door to apartment building entrance by drivers in dark tinted cars. It felt good to stretch my legs in the outdoors.

Gaza's parents had released their children charged with 10 days of fear and restlessness. The football boys moved among them, kicking their ball between each other and occasionally other kids. They stopped to yell and pass their ball around a blackened pile of masonry that had until recently been the front wall of someone's home until they were beeped out of the way by a taxi driver. After shouting what sounded like pretty foul insults at the taxi driver, they loped off into the city like a pack of hyenas.

At the corner where the side street met the main boulevard, a body shop spilled the innards of dismembered cars out onto the pavement. The oil-smeared men stopped their work to stare. I raised a hand in greeting and they raised theirs in return, gaping with confusion at my face. I needed to buy sunglasses.

Every grocer, mobile phone shop and kebab stand was open, frying meat and selling bejewelled phone covers as though no war had ever happened. The air hummed with generators and choked on their petrol fumes, but the kebabs smelt delicious and I realised I hadn't eaten anything but hummus for as long as I could remember. I very much wanted a kebab.

'Slattern!'

The bird screamed down at me from a telegraph pole and I jumped in alarm. The mechanics gawped. I walked on, stopping again outside the patisserie shop with the lurid orange knafeh in the window. Nasser and I had driven past it a hundred times but we'd never been in. I didn't want to arrive at Jihad's mother's empty-handed, I said out loud.

'*Fat neck*,' the bird sneered back.

I blushed because it was right. The slimming effect of my illness was being quickly undone by hummus bread and mini-bar chocolate, and the fabric of my jeans strained as I bent over to inspect the knafeh cabinet. I watched the man fill a large box with gooey, sweet, phosphorescent cheese trying not to wear the expression of a greedy woman.

We resumed our slow progress through the busy backstreets, the bird flapping in circles overhead, the football boys too busy jostling each other to notice they were being tailed, the box of hot goop banging against my legs. Finally, the gang stopped at a tall concrete residential block and scattered. Its balconies were draped with bedsheets and carpets and it broadcast children's shouts like a minaret. Crying birds circled its peak. This is where little Jihad lived.

An old woman on the second floor with one eye pointing up and another pointing sideways was baffled by my appearance at her door and outraged by my offer of knafeh. The deaf man on the third floor looked appalled when I yelled Jihad's name at him, and no one answered on the fourth. The woman who opened the door on the fifth floor was tiny. She had a hard, pale face and angular cheekbones brushed with freckles. Her hair was completely hidden by a neat black scarf that emphasised very large, very quick green eyes set within deep, black circles.

'*Marhaba! Ana Sara Byrne. Ana Sahafiya.* I am looking for the mother of Jihad. *Um Jihad?*'

The woman was more or less my age but when she frowned, as she was doing, deep lines appeared around her eyes that looked ancient. She didn't seem to speak a word of English.

'*Ana Sahafiya Inglese. Ana Sara Byrne.* Did you know Jihad? He lived in this building. The son of Jihad, from The Beach Hotel?'

'*Al-iinjilizia*,' the woman said, abruptly.

This was a disaster. How was I ever going to communicate what I had come to say when my only Arabic was *journalist, how are you, Jew, delicious*. It was hopeless, but for Jihad's sake I had to try. I wiped away the balls of sweat that had burst onto my upper lip with my sleeve cuff.

'I'm sorry, I don't speak Arabic. *Fish Arabia*.'

I gesticulated my linguistic deficiency with outstretched empty hands.

'*Inglese* isn't a word in Arabic. You were trying to say English? It's *al-iinjilizia*,' the woman said, opening the door wide. 'I know who you are.'

I stepped into her large, empty living room. It was blindingly white and dominated by an enormous television and an even larger poster of little Jihad. His portrait was about five times the size he had been in real life and festooned with Palestinian flags. It was a school photo and someone had forced him to smile, his hair swept to the side and gelled like a groomed animal. He looked both irritated and embarrassed, as if already aware of the outlandishness of his size on the wall. I wandered up to him, smiling.

'You're his mother.'

'Yes,' little Jihad's mother said.

'I'm sorry, I don't know your name.'

'It's Nour. And his name is *Ji-had*. Not *Geee-haaad* like you say it.'

There was no one else in the apartment. No sign of cleaner Jihad or any other children. Her white tiled floor gleamed like a freshly scrubbed temple.

'Your husband is out?' I offered.

'He's at the hotel. They don't pay you to grieve here. No one would ever work.'

She indicated curtly for me to sit on a large cream leatherette sofa, which I did, sweating heavily. Nour perched lightly on the chair opposite me, her head directly underneath Jihad's. Their matching faces regarded me with cold intensity.

'What do you want?' she asked.

So there would be no tea. I placed the plastic bag of knafeh awkwardly at my feet as I groped about in my brain for the script I had rehearsed on our walk.

'Thanks for inviting me in, Nour,' I stalled.

'I didn't.'

'No, sorry. Well, thank you for letting me in. I've come because I wanted to tell you in person how sorry I am for your son's death because I hold myself at least partly responsible for it. I invited a dangerous man to the hotel where Jihad should have been safe but instead he died. Was killed.'

Nour regarded me, and I pushed on.

'I can't do anything now to correct that awful mistake but I want you to know that I accept responsibility for my role in his death and I would like to help you in any way I can. He was a very unusual kid. He was smart. An unusually smart boy. I liked him and I'm very sorry for your loss.'

That was it, more or less. Jihad looked down at me from the wall, unblinking, his fixed grin stern. I rubbed my sweaty palms together and Nour raised her eyebrows.

'Okay,' she said, and stood up.

But I wasn't ready to leave. I stayed in my seat.

'You know, we would chat sometimes. Quite a bit actually. I think we were similar, in some ways,' I said and laughed.

Her glass eyes flashed.

'You are nothing like him.'

'No,' I agreed, and clasped my knees.

Nour resumed her perch on the arm of the chair opposite me and tilted her head to look at me the way little Jihad did when he was trying to see into my soul better. Her eyes glinted dangerously, like broken bottles.

'Sara Byrne, isn't it?'

I nodded.

'So Sara, you know that my son, my only child, died two days ago. Yesterday I watched as they put him in the ground.

His dirty clothes are sitting unwashed in my laundry and still, here you are.'

She folded her pale hands neatly in her lap.

'You invited yourself into my home saying you want to *help* me. How will you help me?'

I threw my eyes in earnest contemplation towards the knafeh bag at my feet but found no adequate answer there.

'Please, tell me,' she insisted. 'Do you plan to stop the next war? Save the rest of my family from getting bombed? Next time, if it's me who's killed, if it's my home that's destroyed, will you write a story about the time you came and visited me here? Will that help?'

Nour leaned her slight, furious frame forward.

'Listen to me now because I want you to tell all the other journalists at that hotel. I have watched you all for years. You come, you watch us die, watch us grieve, take our stories, go home. You wait for another war, you come back, you watch, you take our stories, you go home. Do you help? No. My husband cleans your sheets, you kill his family.'

Her voice was low and urgent. I stared past her to little Jihad's enormous face.

'I'm sorry,' I said.

Nour's eyes sharpened into shards and she cocked her tiny head back to examine me.

'The war is over. Why haven't you left? You've no home to go to? No family?'

'I have a mother,' I said quietly. 'Do you think I could see his room please, before I go?'

Little Jihad's bedroom was bare and neat like the rest of the apartment. A small bookshelf by his bed was stacked tidily with books. It looked like he had swiped the D shelf from a library: Dahl, Defoe, Dickens. There was a poster on the wall of Newcastle United Football Club, glossy-haired players captured in frozen heroic action. I didn't recognise any of them. His bed was neatly made with a black and white striped Newcastle

United pillowcase and a folded felt blanket. A rolled-up prayer mat leant against the bookshelf.

'Why did he support Newcastle?' I asked.

'He just liked castles, stories about castles,' Nour told me from the doorway, her slim arms folded tightly, lips thin with misery. 'He wanted to be a writer.'

A little desk by a small window had a huge English dictionary on it, a pile of school textbooks and notebooks covered with doodles of weird, distorted faces and winged figures. Next to the desk was a mirror hung at what must have been Jihad height. It had a fan of feathers stuck to it with sticky tape, four huge white and grey sea gull feathers and a clutch of smaller white feathers. One black glossy one stuck out at the top and I ran my index finger along it.

'Do you think I could take one?' I asked.

'No,' she said.

Nour refused my bag of knafeh and closed the door quickly behind me. Two pairs of little Jihad's trainers sat in a neat row outside the front door alongside his father's. He had small feet, even for a child. He would probably have been a short man, which was weird given his father was practically a giant.

I threw the bag of knafeh into an overflowing dumpster. I walked quickly passed the smouldering wreck of the old police station, through the shreds of police paperwork still swirling around on the street. I passed the Gaza tourist shop now re-opened, green Hamas baseball caps out on display, and a chain gang of donkeys pulling carts piled high with the rubble of destroyed buildings. Old rubble to make new buildings to get bombed again.

Rounding a corner at speed, I slammed hard into the flank of an animal, releasing a cloud of dust and sand into my mouth and eyes. The animal let out a groan of surprise. It was a donkey. Its owner, unseated, screamed and struck it hard with his stick, drawing another deep moan of pain from the animal. The donkey looked towards me with its huge dark eyes, doleful and resigned, but said nothing.

The jarring force of our collision, the donkey dust in my mouth, the hopelessness of the animal and the pointless fury of its owner drained me completely. I wanted to leave Gaza. There was no story here, not one anyone wanted to hear. I walked past the checkpoint at the roundabout manned by the tired bearded men in their fur-lined bomber jackets and flip-flops, past The Beach Hotel, past my new hotel's empty reception, into my egg coloured room and began to collect my things. I gathered my medication and my very dirty clothes and inspected the black feather I'd taken from little Jihad's mirror when Nour's back was turned. It was glossy, probably from a crow. I wrapped it carefully in toilet paper and packed it.

The bird was hopping about on the window-ledge, pecking at the last of its breakfast crumbs.

'They're coming!' it taunted.

If someone was coming for me, they'd have to be quick I told it. I tied the handles of my plastic bag of medication in a tight double knot onto my suitcase handle and it beat its wings powerfully against the window.

'Slattern! They're coming for you!'

The zipper on my cheap East Jerusalem market bag had split and clothes were spilling out through yawning gaps in its rusted teeth. I shoved them back in as best as I could but succeeded only in creating more zip holes. The bird bellowed, flapping its wings in a wild frenzy against the glass.

'You're embarrassing yourself. *Virtus tentamine gaudet!*'

That was it. I dropped my battle with the fucked-up zip and walked towards the window to confront the possessed pigeon. If I stood at my full height, we were more or less eye to eye. Its bird eyes bright through the sand-splattered glass, mine tired as the yolk-yellow walls. It blinked at me and narrowed its awful gaze.

'*Virtus?* Look at me! Do you see *virtus?* Look at my eyes! I have no money, no work and the only person here still talking to me is a fucking bird!'

I was shouting, because I no longer cared who heard. The bird did look at me through the grease prints of its own oily wings and after a few blinks, lowered its threatening wings to a droop by its side. The puff drained from its chest feathers. It cooed and I went back to shoving things into my bag.

'Call your mother!' it ordered after some reflection.

'Jesus Christ! What the hell has she got to do with anything?' I yelled again, because I was enjoying the yelling.

But it was true that I didn't have enough money left to settle my hotel bill. It tilted its head to one side.

'I'll think about it,' I muttered.

38
Pigeons

On Sundays, Dad took me to feed the ducks at the pond in Battersea Park. I didn't mind them. They stank of mud and pond weed and were stupid but they weren't frightening. I didn't like the swans that were taller than me and hissed with wide beaks and razor teeth, but it was the pigeons I hated. There were way too many of them, swarming the pond in their red-eyed demon hordes. Flapping, clawing and swooping for the bread in my fists. Jurassic, dirty, winged psychopaths. What I liked most was walking with my father. It felt solemn and adult. Our visits to the duck pond had become the most important event in my five-year old week and so I made sure to love the ducks and be brave about the pigeons because this is what the occasion required.

That Sunday was grey and cold. Ma dressed me in the too tight woollen jumper she had knitted for me and I had immediately outgrown. She forced me into it even though I argued that it choked my neck and scratched my skin because she had spent eight months knitting it. I chose to wear my favourite pink and cream scarf and matching woolly hat, a red plastic raincoat and yellow wellington boots because it had started to drizzle as we left the house.

In the park, the rain fell steadily. Puddles gathered muddy mass on the footpaths and I tried to walk, as I always did when wearing wellingtons, directly through the middle of each of them. The crisp autumn leaves had softened in the dirty water and become adhesive, sticking to the side of my boots. I stopped in each deepening pool to gather as many as I could. The dark rain fell heavier and I pulled up my hood.

'I thought you loved the ducks,' my father complained.

'I *dooo* love the ducks,' I replied without looking up because I had managed to get one brilliant red and yellow leaf to stick to my left ankle entirely intact.

'Then we'd better hurry! They're probably dying of hunger, poor things. Who else would come to feed them in a monsoon?'

I didn't answer because I didn't know what a monsoon was. My most exceptional red and yellow leaf had peeled off and was sliding back into the puddle. It was only through extraordinarily concentrated ankle manoeuvring that I managed to re-attach it to the plastic. Satisfied, I looked up to find my father's dark, Barbour-clad figure walking towards a rubbish bin, the mouldy bag of Hovis outstretched in front of him. He moved steadily against a stream of other families flooding out of the park. A fast-moving boy on a tricycle forced him to pause and contort his body into an arch to avoid collision.

'Wait!' I called out to him, but he didn't hear me.

I ran to catch him up, tripping on my long scarf, but he wasn't looking, he was focused on the bin. Finding myself not badly hurt, I picked myself up and ran until I could pull down hard on the hem of his oily coat.

'Don't throw it! I'm here,' I panted.

'Oh!' he looked down at me, feigning surprise. 'You still want to go? Okay then.'

We walked on together towards the pond, my too long scarf trailing on the wet ground behind me. My father's grey, squinting, triangle eyes fixed on the path ahead, watering against the cold rain. He had not yet started to wear hats and his thinning, wolf-coloured hair clung to his scalp in limp, damp strands. His already wrinkled neck retracted into its upturned collar like a tortoise, his shoulders high and hunched against the weather. He held my small clammy hand warmly in his large dry one, thrusting them together deep inside the tartan-lined oilskin of his coat pocket.

'*Amo, amas . . .*' he started.

'*Amat*,' I answered.

'*Amamus, amatis* . . .'

'An ant.'

'Not bad,' he laughed and I giggled, warm with the success of my joke.

'Come on Bob, keep up.'

I had stopped again because my scarf was now wet and heavy from the puddles it had been dragging through and it was becoming difficult to walk with the extra scarf weight. Also, I wanted to check on the progress of my boot leafing.

'What does *amo* mean?' I asked, stalling, peering down to check my big red and yellow leaf marvel was still in place, which it was, looking very much like the label on our maple syrup bottle.

'It means love, as well you know because I have told you many, many, *many* times.'

Dad frowned at me and his mouth disappeared in comic impatience as I gathered up the dripping scarf, now studded with twigs and blackened leaves, into my gloved hands.

'I *amo* you Dad,' I smiled up at him charmingly, wringing a stream of wet puddle water from the sodden wool.

He grimaced down his fine hawk nose, which had large rain drops rolling down and dripping off it.

'*Te amo Pater*. Look at what you're doing Bob! You're ruining your scarf!'

When we reached the duck pond, it was all but abandoned owing to the now driving sheets of bitter, frosty rain. The ducks did indeed seem to be starving and had flocked in a thick quacking pack around the only two other children in yellow anoraks who were cautiously distributing bread crusts. They were with a woman, whose long dark hair was uncovered and drenched, blinking into the rain. A wet Snow White, pale-faced with flushed rosy cheeks, surrounded by birds.

'Lovely day!' she called out, laughing the tinkling bell laugh of a Disney cartoon.

'Glorious!' my father bellowed and returned a low, strange laugh.

'Come on darling,' he said to me because I had stopped to gawp at the woman.

I stared up at him in confusion. He never called me darling, always Bob. He nudged the bread bag at me, smiling weirdly. The bag had mould growing on its insides, and I rooted about for the few slices of crusted bread at the bottom. I tossed it onto the wet ground in crumbs, hoping there would be enough to go around. The ducks hurried urgently towards me in a waddling, quacking, flat-footed surge, and Dad wandered over to chat to the woman about the weather. Her yellow plastic children stared up at him, not returning his smiles. The smaller blond one had a stream of snot running interrupted from his nose into his mouth.

The swans were missing, presumably sheltering on the island, cloaked in rain mist, but the pigeons were undeterred by the weather. Their circling number soon grew thick against the black sky, eying us with hungry eyes. I could hear the flapping before the flock swooped and my heart quickened with dread. I threw the last of the bread chunks at the ducks and the pigeon pack dove. Brined, oily wings flapped against my yellow coat and I screamed. They had got me. I closed my eyes tightly, dropped the bread bag and screamed again louder.

The bird swarm descended in a dense cloud onto the duck's crusts behind me as I ran blindly away from them towards my father but I tripped again on the long, sodden scarf and fell into a deep puddle of pondy rainwater. Shocked to find myself suddenly submerged in the silty, freezing, filthy wet, I screamed again, clear, high and piercing into the cold wet air.

'Bob! What is that awful noise?' Dad called out to me, his voice still laughing from a joke he'd shared with Snow White.

But I lay still in the puddle, bracing for another assault of feathers and talons. The taste of silt grains from the puddle water was bitter and made me wail even louder.

'Sweetheart, are you okay? Did you hurt yourself?' the woman yelled over to me too despite not knowing me. She had a funny accent.

'What is it, Sara? Are you hurt?'

My father's voice followed, closer, with a steeliness that I knew signalled a death of fondness. I curled up in a tight ball in the dirty puddle and sobbed. Dad's boots edged into sight.

'Get up now please. You're not hurt.'

I raised my dripping arms towards him, inviting him to pick me up.

'Oh come on, you're far too big for that. And look at you!'

I looked down and saw I was entirely coated in mud. My father's hand reached down and clutched me by the bicep, a well-practiced grip that could pierce through plastic and sodden scratchy wool to separate sinew from bone. He pulled me to my feet and I squealed in outrage and pain. The wet foreign woman gasped at the noise and raised a gloved hand to her blueish pink lips. My father laughed again. The silent snot children looked at me, rain water dribbling into their open-mouths, oblivious to the pigeons pecking and flapping around them.

'Stop it! You're hurting me!' I squealed.

'Come on Bob, let's get you home,' my father laughed lowly.

'You're too mean! NO!' I screamed into a screech and stamped my boot powerfully into the puddle, splashing my father's brown brogue boots.

The pigeon flock raised and fled in one cooing cloud. Dad released my arm and grabbed my hood tightly in his fist, bending his rain dripping head low to my ear.

'Stop these histrionics immediately. You are embarrassing yourself,' he hissed in my ear with a fixed, grim smile.

'Amazing little performer isn't she?' he called over to the still gaping woman. 'Big talent, we're very excited. Come on now darling, show's over.'

The foreigner giggled and Dad raised his hand in brief

farewell before driving me in a quick march through the abandoned park into horizontal sheets of rain towards home.

'Wait! My scarf!' I wailed because my best scarf had been lost in the pigeon frenzy.

But my father drove us on with diabolical purpose, pulling me along in a half-run half-scarper across streams of footpath, the wet wool of my jumper digging into my neck.

Ma was furious at the state I was returned in, which was sodden, filthy and sobbing. As she ran me a bath with bubbles from the pink lady Bubble Mate, I told her about the pigeons, about my lost scarf and meeting Snow White, who was foreign and giggled a lot.

Ma called out through the bathroom door, down the stairs to Dad that he would never again be taking me to the duck pond. All that bread was bad for their stomachs, she told me. She and I would spend Sundays at the adventure playground in future. I sunk down into the warm water and allowed my dirt-matted hair to be washed, crying gently. Ma asked me what I could possibly be crying about now and I started to sob again, not because of the suds in my eyes but because I understood. I had lost access to my father and it was all my fault.

39
INTO THE FIRMAMENT

The taxi driver couldn't get his head around it.
'You are sure you want Rafah crossing?' he asked, cracking seeds between his teeth and looking perplexed. 'Going through Israel is better. Much, much better.'

Our shared language wasn't sufficient for me to explain my situation. That having been very publicly consorting with terrorists, I would not get the usual English woman treatment at Erez Crossing. I would most likely be kept in an underground interrogation cell until the Israelis saw fit to deport me and while that may be fair enough, I really was in no physical state for detention and deportation. I told the taxi man I had business in Egypt.

'But it's not a good crossing. Erez is better,' he tried one last time, shaking his head ruefully as he eased himself into the driver's seat.

We set off agreeing to disagree. As the car pulled off down the beach road, I noticed I was crying again behind my Gaza Old City sunglasses. I cried all the time now but would usually only find out when I tasted salt or happened to touch my cheek and find it wet. I wasn't yet sure whether it was a symptom of my condition or some emotional problem. I probed myself for feelings.

I would never be able to come back to Gaza through Israel once I had left through Egypt. Was that upsetting?

The Beach Hotel would never let me stay again. Sad?

'This is probably the last time you will ever drive down this sewage-smell road,' I told myself out loud.

The taxi driver glanced at me in the rear-view mirror.

'You will never again see that roundabout checkpoint.'

'Eh?' the driver asked quizzically.

I waited for the surge of grief but it didn't come, just more numbness and tears. It was all likely to be bombed into non-existence before I had the chance to come back anyway, I thought, and continued to stare out the window, crying freely.

'Are you married?'

The taxi driver was making conversation.

'You have children?'

'No.'

The driver made a whistling noise followed by a pitying exhalation and examined me closely in the rear-view mirror. He was not overly concerned with what was happening ahead of us on the road.

'You don't want children? Children are a blessing!' he said, admonishingly.

I told him that my husband was dead and I couldn't have children because of cancer. His eyes widened in the rear-view mirror and he looked very sad about this lie. Then he raised his eyes and a finger towards the car roof to indicate that God must have a plan with that sort of tragedy and we spent the rest of the journey in companionable silence, me crying noiselessly and him eating his seeds and humming. He swerved to avoid a crater in the road as we passed a row of blown up homes and I looked at my phone to reread the email from Michael. I knew it by heart but liked re-reading it.

Sara, you didn't sound well when we spoke. Dr. Paul Mitchell is a friend and a fine psychiatrist at the Maudsley: paul.mitchell@kcl.ac.uk. He is expecting to hear from you. I think it's better that we don't speak again but wish you the very best. Michael.

It was raining and the enormous line of Palestinians queued at the entrance to Rafah crossing glowered at the muddy puddle splashes jetted towards them by passing cars. The queue stared with glum curiosity at the unusually tall, white woman arriving late and joining the end of their line with an erupting bag.

'Erez crossing is much better,' the taxi driver called out cheerfully one last time, raising a large hand in farewell out of his window as he drove off.

He splashed through a large, deep, sandy puddle, propelling a gutsy spray of filth towards the queue, which directed resentful scowls at me. There were lots of pigeons and some giant crows, but none approached me. Standing in the rain and hostile chaos of the border crossing it seemed impossible that the bird would find me.

In the day since I had left little Jihad's home, I had resolved my many insurmountable problems with underwhelming ease. Ma had agreed to wire me money quite literally without question. Only asking how much I needed, she sent enough for me to pay Fadi and settle my hotel bill with quite a bit to spare and I collected it from the Western Union an hour later. Ma, I learned, had freed up a substantial amount of money with the sale of our family home. In our brief call, she concluded that for the time being, I would move back home with her where I would have time to give my future some proper thought. I didn't tell her that was the last thing I would be doing. Nor did I tell her about the bird or my new eyes. That could all wait.

I was being pulled without explanation to the top of the line by an arm-grabby Palestinian Authority official when the bird swooped down, damp and mud-splattered, landing just outside the bullet scarred terminal building into a particularly large puddle. As we were surrounded by a dense crowd of tutting travellers already looking at me with suspicion, I pretended not to know it. It stalked the ground next to me, shaking off the wet from its feathers, pecking at bits of dry bread dropped by the messy, shouty children who were now being yelled at by their parents. But it was too late. It couldn't stop me crossing the border now and once I was safely across and in an Egyptian taxi, there was no way it could beat me to Cairo. The border guard inspected my British passport and frowned. The angry crowd shouted behind me, outraged I was being seen ahead of them.

'Why are you crossing here? You entered through Erez,' the guard barked officiously.

By the time I had convinced the short-tempered official that I had no other way of leaving Gaza, explained that I had absolutely no intention of returning and he had reluctantly stamped my various tattered documents, the border was closing. Pushing and desperate shouts erupted in the packed yard behind me. The irritated sick and injured wanted to get to a hospital that had electricity and medicine, but they would have to wait now until the next day or whenever it was the Egyptians next felt like opening their border because the guards were closing the gates behind me.

I turned and saw that the bird had hopped onto a eucalyptus branch to escape the yelling mob. The rain had begun to fall more heavily. Raising my hand in defiant farewell, I called out to it.

'*Per angusta ad augusta!*'

The bird raised its wet inky wing, either in theatrical salute or threatening retribution. Then it pushed down hard on his pink reptile legs and sprang off the branch up into the wet. It didn't seem to be flying in any particular direction but it was making an exit, so I stood and followed the rain sleek, feathered body as it rose. I waited and watched until it had disappeared into the firmament, then I turned and rolled my rupturing suitcase across the border into Egypt.

40
Back to Work

I'm watching the video of Mohammed's execution on my laptop at the desk-table in the kitchen drinking the last of a bottle of red wine. It's freezing because it's December and Ma turns the central heating off at night in the interests of health and economy, and my frozen nose is running. I wipe it on my pyjama cuff. A big, cold, white moon has risen over the tall leafless trees in the park to hit me full in the face.

He was shot in the big concrete yard behind the new police headquarters. I don't know when exactly, but it must have been a few weeks ago at least because Hamas has had enough time to produce this surprisingly high-quality promotional video of the execution with both English and Hebrew subtitles. It opens with drone footage of Gaza in ruins and orientalised Hollywood music.

'Gaza has suffered another brutal Zionist assault,' a silky-voiced narrator tells us. 'Occupation forces have again attacked innocent civilians, killing and injuring hundreds of women and children.'

There is Shejaiya as rubble. There is The Beach Hotel, voluptuous and cracked at sunset. There is Al Jabari, alive and hugging a child. There is the Israeli satellite footage of the drone strike on the Al Muzaner building, broken down into frames. The footage is proof the voice tells us that Israel deliberately targeted innocent Palestinian families.

'But even worse than the Zionist enemy are the traitors who attack Gaza from within. The collaborators who have betrayed their own country, killed our people and destroyed our homes.

They have committed the ultimate crime and will pay the ultimate price. Revolutionary justice will be delivered.'

The faces of four men flash onto the screen, Mohammed's last. Three of them have been interviewed, shot closely in dramatic shadow, and their interviews are intercut with Hamas-gathered evidence proving their guilt: photographs, emails, grainy security camera footage. Fast moving, red-washed graphics map out each man's journey from weakness, to betrayal, treason and death.

Some of the men cry in their confession videos. One man with thinning hair and a snub nose says he was a security guard at the Al Jabari compound. He tells the camera through teary sighs that he had big gambling debts that an Israeli agent cleared in exchange for information. He had been the one who had told the Israelis what time Al Jabari would be driving home and along what route. He wanted God and his country to forgive him.

Then there is young Mohammed in his neat waiter's uniform in the restaurant at The Beach. With his pretty wife and two young kids looking at emaciated monkeys in the sad Gaza City Zoo. Snaps of him happy and handsome, smoking in a bar that the voice tells us is somewhere in Tel Aviv. He is the only one who has refused to confess, so the smooth-voiced voice man does the confessing for him over the montage of his guilt.

Mohammed was a sodomite, the voice tells us sadly. The Zionists recruited him during an interrogation at Erez crossing and threatened to tell his wife and family about his secret sinful life unless he gave them information. Mohammed used his position at The Beach to feed intelligence to the enemy about the comings and goings of senior Hamas fighters and officials, the voice said. He told his Israeli handlers when the commander Abu Mohammed arrived at the hotel. He called in the strike that martyred a commander, a soldier and an 11-year-old Palestinian boy.

'But the people of Gaza are strong, not defeated. The blood of our martyrs is always avenged.'

A group of burly men in army fatigues lead Mohammed out into sunlight and he squints into the brightness. His face is shadowed with grey stubble and his yellow skin clings tightly to his cheekbones. In the oversized shirt and flip-flops they have dressed him in, surrounded by all those giant men in green caps and green berets, he looks frail but very calm. How can he be that calm? Is he drugged? What is he thinking about? His family? His lover? Is he praying? They stand him in front of a big concrete block.

In the next shot he's tied and blindfolded. The firing squad fires at him and the three other men and their tied bodies slump. It's only on my third watch that I notice a bird perched on the high fence behind him. It's small. It doesn't startle at the gunshots, it just watches.

I've come back to that bit again and am pausing to get a closer look at the bird, when Ma walks into the kitchen and screams. She has her thick flannel pyjamas on and as usual one enormous breast is straining to break loose. Her thinning, grey hair is vertical with sleep and static.

'Sara!'

On my smeared computer screen, paused, blindfolded Mohammed is bracing for the first shot.

'What the hell are you doing out here in the middle of the night?'

It has only just passed 10pm. She peers into the screen, more or less blind without her glasses.

'Good Lord, what is it that you're watching?'

Her voice is thick with sleep. She clutches at her pyjama top in horror, gasping at the execution scene.

'That man there is Mohammed, he's a friend of mine. Do you see that bird?'

I point towards the bird on the wall behind blindfolded Mohammed. I'm about to explain about the tea Mohammed made when I was sick, but she isn't looking or listening. She is staring at my face with that now familiar look of desperate, uncomprehending concern.

'Bob! Sweetheart! Didn't we agree with Dr Mitchell? No more war, no more birds!'

Ma spies my glass of red wine shimmering like a small blood lake in the moonlight, and wails.

'And certainly no booze! Sara! What are you thinking? Just when we've got your eyes back to normal! Your poor liver!'

I look with remorse at the partially spilled red wine and at the frozen image of Mohammed's blindfolded face.

'It was only one, for my friend,' I say, raising the half-drunk glass towards the screen.

She walks towards me and draws my large, heavy head towards her vast, soft breasts. I don't pull back as I usually would but put my glass down on the table and let myself be clamped to her huge papery bosom, my cold nose running onto her pyjamas. I listen to her heartbeat, which is flighty like a sparrow's, and her shallow breathing. She smells of night cream and laundry powder. Exhaling her stale night breath on me, she leans forward and closes my laptop shut. Clasping my face between her cool, enormous hands, she peers into my eyes.

'Can we agree to call it quits on the horror at least for tonight?'

I nod in mute consent, feeling drowsy from the red wine anyhow, which has mixed quite deliciously with my meds. I allow myself to be led by the hand by my giant, elderly mother, along her narrow, carpeted hallway. She opens the door to my small office bedroom, stands in the doorway and watches me climb between the cold sheets. I pull the blankets up to my neck and fill the single bed entirely.

'Do you need anything?' she asks.

I want a glass of water because my tongue feels like carpet, but her voice sounds tired and dry and she is looking at me with her new fragile look. Her wispy eyebrows draw together with worry and form lines in her old face deep as parched canyons. I shake my head and she closes the door. I hear her pad back to her own bed and I smack my carpet mouth. I listen to the loud tick of Dad's sticky watch on my wrist. The bird only comes at night here. *In nocte consilium.* It tells me I need to get out of bed and back to work and I'm beginning to think it's right. Syria. Or Iraq maybe. But I'm sleepy.

The full moon has found me again. It streams into the small room through a crack in the broken blinds and onto little Jihad's black feather, which I've tied to a string and sticky taped to the mirror. It gleams and sparkles in the bright reflected moonlight and I watch it twist and glisten until my eyelids droop.

ABOUT THE AUTHOR

Phoebe Greenwood is a writer and journalist living in London. Between 2010 and 2013 she was a freelance correspondent in Jerusalem covering the Middle East for the *Guardian*, *Daily Telegraph* and *Sunday Times*. From 2013 to 2021, she was an editor and correspondent at the *Guardian* specialising in foreign affairs.